QUEEN OF HAWTHORNE PREP

JENNIFER SUCEVIC

ALSO BY JENNIFER SUCEVIC

Campus Flirt (novella)

Campus God

Campus Heartthrob

Campus Hottie

Campus Player

Claiming What's Mine

Confessions of a Heartbreaker

Crazy for You (80s short story)

Don't Leave

Friend Zoned

Hate to Love You

Heartless

If You Were Mine

Just Friends

King of Campus

King of Hawthorne Prep

Love to Hate You

One Night Stand

Protecting What's Mine

Stay

The Boy Next Door

The Breakup Plan

The Girl Next Door

"**Mmm.**"

A contented sigh falls from my lips as I stretch against the boy in my bed. His muscular body is in perfect alignment with mine as he feathers seductive little kisses along the curve of my neck. "That feels so good." When he nips the flesh between his teeth, a punch of arousal hits me straight in the core.

Let's just say that if I were wearing panties, they would be drenched.

Is it any wonder I'm addicted to Kingsley Rothchild?

He jogged into my life a couple of months ago, and I haven't been able to evict him from my head since. Not that I want to. He's mine, and I'm his. And that's exactly the way I like it.

Does that mean I'm ready to get hitched tomorrow?

Hell, no.

Thanks to some archaic agreement between our parents to end eighty years of bad blood, my hand has been promised to him. The expectation is that we'll get married sometime during college.

Have I totally come to terms with the new direction my life has swerved in?

Not really.

I'm an eighteen-year-old girl who just started her senior year in high school. I haven't even been accepted to college yet. I don't like the idea of being forced into anything, let alone something as permanent as marriage.

Then I stare at the dark-haired boy with his sexy eyes and a mouth that was meant for all kinds of sin, and I know without a shadow of a doubt that he's the one for me. It's only been a month, but I feel it deep in my bones that Kingsley and I should be together. He completes me in ways I never imagined. And I'm a twin, so I know exactly what that feels like. To experience the same intimate connection with someone other than my brother is mind-blowing.

That being said, there is something unsettling about having my entire life mapped out at such a young age. All the major decisions have been wrestled out of my hands. It all seems preordained.

College.

Marriage.

Where I'll eventually settle down.

And probably where I end up working.

I won't lie, it's that knowledge that continues to claw at me. It's an itch beneath my skin that I can't quite quell. I keep telling myself to let it go and be happy. There are times when Kingsley and I are together, and it sits perched on the tip of my tongue, waiting to explode from my lips. Unsure of his reaction, I haven't mentioned anything to him. He's not aware of how much it bothers me. I've convinced myself it's better that way. If I confide in him, it'll only stir up problems between our families and between us. It's just going to take time to wrap my head around the hand fate has dealt me.

"Know what would feel even better?" he rumbles against my ear, calloused fingers scraping over my rib cage to cup my breast before tweaking the nipple. Shivers dance along my flesh in their wake.

Actually, I do. Desire thrums through me, pounding a steady beat until everything that crowds my mind falls away. As my whimper of need echoes off the walls, there's a soft rap of knuckles against the bedroom door. I freeze, a sharp inhalation lodging in my throat as my eyes pop wide.

"Summer, are you awake?"

Shit.

Mom.

The untimely disruption doesn't stop Kingsley from nipping at my bare shoulder. He doesn't give a damn if one of my parents is standing on the other side of a two-inch plank of wood. What I've learned about Kingsley is that he does what he pleases, when he pleases, and the consequences can be damned.

While I find that sexy as hell, it's not how I live my life.

My mother doesn't know that Kingsley has been sneaking into my room every night to sleep in my bed. Since returning from the beach house a month ago, we haven't spent one night apart, and I love it. I love being wrapped up in his arms. I love when he's on top of me, driving into my body, making me fall apart beneath his fingertips.

There's no better feeling in the world.

A heavy wave of anxiety crashes over me as I claw at his arms, fighting my way out of his embrace. The possibility of Mom finding me in bed with a boy is enough to send me into cardiac arrest.

This is definitely *not* how I imagined starting my Sunday morning.

Instead of relinquishing his hold, Kingsley tugs me closer, locking me in place as his teeth sink into the delicate flesh of my neck. His fingers toy with the erect tip of my breast before grazing the contour of my belly and thrusting deep inside my pussy.

A strangled groan breaks free. *"Stop."*

He teases my heat with sharp, forceful strokes that leave me panting.

"Is that what you really want?" he growls.

Yes.

No.

With the next knock comes another punch of concern.

"Summer?" Mom says, louder this time.

"Please," I whimper, squirming against him. I have no idea if I'm trying to escape or burrow closer. This is exactly what he does to me. Scrambles my brain until coherent thought becomes impossible.

"What are you begging for, baby girl?" He tweaks my tightened bud, a little harder this time. It's enough to send a flash of pain streaking through me before dissolving into pleasure.

Baby girl.

Another shiver of need dances down my spine. I could almost get off on the deep scrape of his voice when he calls me that.

"Hmm?" He continues to toy with me, purposely fanning the flames of my desire.

I'm not sure. And that's part of the problem. He's the only boy I've ever known capable of making me lose my ever-loving mind. How else do you explain my current predicament?

"Should I keep going or..." His fingers drift over my clit before homing in on it like a heat-seeking missile. "Stop?"

In a matter of weeks, he's learned how to touch me to elicit the most amount of pleasure. It's almost as if he takes pride in it. And what he's doing right now is my kryptonite.

My mind spins as my core throbs to life.

When I fail to respond, his hand splays wide over my pussy before giving it a possessive squeeze. "Guess I'll stop. Your loss."

It takes a moment for the sexual haze clouding my brain to clear as air leaks from my lungs.

Mom is waiting.

On the other side of the door.

That's all it takes for my brain to click back on, and then I'm elbowing him in the ribs.

He grunts as a chuckle slips free. "What was that for?"

"You know what!" I hiss before flipping over to face him and shoving my palms against his chest. I'm not sure if I'm angry with him for leaving me hanging or working me up in the first place. Although I won't be admitting that to him because it would only stoke his over-inflated ego. *"Now go!"*

"Why?" He smirks, falling onto his back and lounging on my bed as if he doesn't have a care in the world.

I bite back the sigh that wants to fall from my lips. His dark hair is in sexy disarray. I'm tempted to sift my fingers through the thick silky strands. It takes effort to shake the impulse loose and focus on the moment at hand.

"What do you mean *why?*" I jerk my hand toward the bedroom door as if the answer isn't obvious. "Um, hello? My mother is standing outside the door! She'll flip out if she finds you here." When he doesn't blink, I tack on, *"With me!"* Another beat passes by. *"Naked!"*

My mini tirade only makes the grin on his face stretch wider.

Ugh. So annoying!

I love the guy—wait a minute. No, I don't. Not yet. But my feelings are definitely migrating in that direction. Our relationship has been rocky from the onset. We met at the beach in June and spent one magical day together on his boat before I disappeared, only to resurface a few months later at Hawthorne Prep, where he made my life miserable in an attempt to push me away.

"What the hell does it matter?" Instead of rolling out of bed, he hauls me closer. "We're practically engaged. Who cares if she finds me here?"

Umm, I care. The convo I'd be forced to endure would be seriously horrific. I don't even want to contemplate it.

"Summer?" The knock becomes more insistent. *"Hon?"*

That's it! This boy needs to exit stage left!

"Get!" I grunt, using my hands and feet to eject him from the bed. Kingsley is six foot three and a solid two hundred pounds. He's all steely strength and conditioned muscle. Normally, I love that about him, but not so much at the moment. It takes every ounce of my power to shove him to the edge of the mattress. A moment later, he hits the floor with a loud thump. *"Out!"*

He laughs, staggering a step or two before regaining his balance. "You need to calm down, woman." Kingsley straightens to his full height and scratches his head. "Your reaction is a little excessive, don't you think?"

His sheer masculine beauty is enough to have me losing focus. Even with my mother hovering in the hallway, I can't help but eat him up with hungry eyes. Hands down, he's the most gorgeous guy I've ever seen.

Tall.

Muscular.

Mahogany-colored eyes that match his hair.

And a thick...

Let's just say he makes quite the striking picture in all his erect glory.

I give my head a quick shake to loosen those dangerous thoughts.

"Nope, not one bit." I point at the closet at the far end of the room. "Hurry and hide in there!"

I'm almost afraid he'll brush my concerns aside and jump back into bed. Instead, Kingsley gives me an exaggerated eye roll before taking a step toward the small room when the door handle turns.

The nightmare unfolds in slow motion and there's not a damn thing I can do about it. Before I can screech at the top of my lungs for her to stop, the door is flung open, and in walks Mom with a pink and brown floral basket full of folded laundry. For one sliver of a moment, she's blissfully unaware of the naked boy standing in the middle of the room.

"So, I was thinking—" Her voice abruptly falls off as her gaze crashes with Kingsley who, instead of making a mad dash to the closet, doesn't move a damn muscle.

Shock washes over her features as her feet grind to a halt. Her impression of a deer caught in headlights is spot-on.

Mortification sears my insides, making it impossible to breathe.

I'm not sure who I feel most sorry for.

Her.

Or me.

Want to guess who doesn't seem the least bit bothered by the circumstances?

Kingsley.

He stands buck naked, his erection out there for everyone to see. And trust me when I say that my mother *definitely* sees it. It would be impossible not to. It's long, thick, and...

Yeah.

Twin flags of color stain her cheeks as she hastily averts her eyes.

Even so, I'm pretty sure she got an eyeful of what our next-door neighbor is packing. My guess is that if it ever became necessary, she could give an accurate description to a sketch artist.

I'm tempted to throw the comforter over my head and pretend this isn't happening.

"Umm..." Her gaze skitters around the room to avoid settling on Kingsley as she presses her lips together until they turn bloodless. With halting steps, she moves toward the antique armchair in the corner before gingerly setting down the pile of clean laundry. Everything about her movements look awkward and rusty. Like she's the Tinman and her joints are in desperate need of lubrication.

How will I ever look my mother in the eye again?

And you know damn well she'll blab this to my dad. A tortured groan escapes from my lips. And then Austin will find out and I'll never hear the end of it.

Ugh.

With a great deal of deliberateness, she straightens and turns, her attention fastening on to mine like I'm a life preserver in a turbulent ocean. Only then do I remember that I'm also naked. Thankfully, the sheet is still crumpled around the lower half of my body. With shaking fingers, I grab the cotton material and yank it over my breasts, shielding them from view. Although, we can all agree it's a little late for modesty at this point.

I wince at the shock and disappointment that echoes throughout her expression. Heat singes my face as my teeth sink into my lower lip. Kingsley has yet to budge from the center of the room.

Oh my God, why is he still standing there, naked as the day he was born?

The least he could do is grab his boxers and cover up! His hard-on is only making the situation worse. I'm embarrassed to note that his erection has not deflated in the slightest.

"So..." Mom clears her throat before stabbing a finger toward the hallway. "I'm going to, umm, go."

"Yeah." What else am I supposed to say? I want to scrub this moment from our collective memories.

Her feet pad softly across the floor. Hours tick by torturously before she reaches the threshold. Instead of crossing into the hall, she hovers awkwardly in the doorway. "Summer?"

Even though her voice barely rises above a strangled whisper, it breaks the silence of the room like a gunshot, and I cringe. Any hope of coming to an unspoken agreement that the past five minutes never occurred is about to be shattered.

My fingers bite into the sheet as I clutch it to my chest. "Yeah?"

"After you get dressed, I'd like to speak with you downstairs."

"All right," I mumble. "I'll be down in a few minutes."

"Thank you."

As she closes the door behind her, I collapse against the mattress before dragging a pillow over my face and pressing down on it. If only it were possible to smother myself. This episode ranks as a top contender for title of most mortifying moments ever. And just to be clear, the past month has been filled with a shit ton of humiliation.

Light filters through my eyelids when the pillow is removed and chucked to the side of the bed as Kingsley slides beneath the sheets.

"Problem solved." His body shakes with silent laughter. "Now we don't have to hide."

My mouth tumbles open. I'm on the verge of blasting him into next week when he lifts a finger and rims the edges of my lips. "Open your mouth that wide and it's going to get stuffed full."

Oh!

My teeth snap together. "How can you joke around at a time like this?"

"Who says I'm teasing?" He smirks, heat filling his eyes. When he shrugs his broad shoulders, it's almost enough to distract me.

Almost.

A growl rumbles up from deep in my chest.

"Oh, come on, it's not that bad." He laughs. "So your mom got an eyeful of cock. Big deal."

Hearing him say mom and cock in the same sentence has me on the cusp of hyperventilating. "Are you kidding? It's a huge deal!"

He peels back the covers and points at his hard dick. "No, *this* is a huge deal."

Oh my God, I'm seriously going to kill him!

"Do you realize the can of worms you've opened?" When he remains silent, I hiss, "Now I'll have to endure yet another sex talk!"

"Guess you'll have a lot more to contribute to the conversation this time."

Argh! He's impossible!

My lips flatten. "Yeah, I don't think so." I cradle my head in my hands as if it's moments away from rolling off my body. "Given the fact that we'll both have fresh visuals, it'll be significantly worse."

Before I can whine about the situation any further, he pulls me into his arms and presses a kiss against the top of my head. "Want me to come with you?" There's a pause. "'Cause I'll do it. You know I will. It's doubtful Eloise will appreciate my presence, but that's too damn bad."

"No," I grumble, some of my anger melting away as he continues to pepper me with soft caresses. "You'll only make it worse."

"How is that possible when I make everything better?" As he snuggles against me, his boner pokes my thigh. "We probably got a few minutes—"

"Are you serious right now?" What am I asking? Of course he is! "Hell no, we're not having sex!"

"Aw, come on, babe," he wheedles like a petulant child, pouty face and all. "Thanks to her untimely disruption, the cat is already out of the bag." He gyrates his hips, stroking the hard length of his cock against my leg. "Your mom can wait. I won't take long."

Not giving him the chance to convince me otherwise, I shove my way out of his arms before sliding from the side of the bed and stalking to my dresser.

Kingsley sits up and the sheet falls down his sculpted body. "Looking good, baby girl."

He chuckles when I give him a one-fingered salute.

I grab a pair of panties and bra before yanking them on. "You need to go."

"Fine." With an exaggerated huff of breath, he throws off the covers and rises from the bed before sauntering toward me. When he's within striking distance, his hand snakes out, yanking me into his arms. As I land against his chest with a soft grunt, his lips descend. "See you tonight?"

His sharp teeth nip at the plump flesh of my bottom lip.

A sigh escapes from me. "Yeah."

"Same place, same time?"

Those words melt all of my resistance.

Most nights, we lay on the thick carpet of grass at the back of the yard. Tall pines delineate our property from the golf course. With my head pillowed against his chest, we stare at the dark canvas of night sky as it stretches over our heads. I point out constellations, and we talk for hours.

"Yeah," I sigh.

He grins and smacks another kiss against my lips. "Good."

"Now go," I repeat, still aggravated at the situation I'll have to contend with in a few short minutes.

"You gonna let me get dressed first?"

My gaze drops to his cock. It's still impressively hard.

"Don't worry," he whispers roughly, "you'll get that tonight."

Yeah, I better.

2

It takes five more minutes before I'm finally able to shove Kingsley out the private entrance off my deck. I pull on black leggings, a gray Hawthorne Prep hoodie, and throw my hair up into a messy bun before reluctantly heading down the staircase to the first floor in search of Mom. Dread pools in the pit of my belly with every step I take.

In a way, I suppose Kingsley is right about the situation.

Is it really that big of a deal if we're sleeping together?

What did my parents expect to happen when they forced me into an arranged marriage?

Once in the double-story foyer, I peek in the study, only to find it empty. Dad is nowhere in sight. If he's not in his lair, knee-deep in paperwork, then he's at Hawthorne Industries. I suppose one positive to Dad spending more time at the office is that I'll only have to deal with Mom.

For the time being.

As I step into the sun-drenched kitchen, I find her sitting at the long stretch of island with a cup of tea in her hands. Her gaze collides with mine as I hover in the entrance. When she remains silent, I force myself to the cherry cabinet and grab a mug before filling it to the brim with java. It looks like I'll need a massive dose of caffeine to get through this.

After a few uncomfortable moments tick by, it becomes apparent that neither of us are willing to delve headfirst into this conversation. The tension rachets up until it becomes almost unbearable.

"Mom—" I blurt.

"Summer—"

Abruptly, our voices fall off.

Her expression lightens as she shakes her head, expelling a lengthy puff of air from her lips. "I wasn't expecting to walk in on *that* this morning."

None of us were.

Unsure how to respond, I remain silent.

When I don't immediately launch into an explanation, she continues. "I didn't realize you two were having sex."

I shift on bare feet beneath the heaviness of her stare. "Umm, yeah."

"When did this start?" She rearranges herself on the chair before fidgeting with the ceramic handle of her mug.

"Does it really matter?" I mumble, my gaze touching on her briefly before bouncing around the kitchen. I would give anything to escape this conversation.

"Yeah, it does. I wish you would have said something." She sighs when I remain tight-lipped.

"Why?" Needing to occupy my hands, I lift the mug to my lips and take a deep drink, scalding my tongue in the process. I wince and hiss out a breath.

"Physical intimacy is a big step in any relationship, and I would have like to know what was going on. We could have talked about it."

Oh, God.

More talking.

Hard pass.

Her fingers drift from the cup to the sides of her head to massage her temples. "I can't believe this is happening," she mutters under her breath.

Ugh.

Kingsley had the nerve to accuse me of overreacting, but that's exactly what this feels like. An overreaction. "Mom, I'm eighteen years old. Weren't you expecting this to happen at some point?"

Instead of answering, she sinks her teeth into her lower lip as she glances out the window that overlooks the greenery of the backyard.

When the silence continues to stretch, I add, "You know, Austin has been sleeping with girls for the past two years." I'm not trying to throw my twin under the bus, but come on...

A little perspective would be nice. We don't need to turn this into some big deal.

Her cheeks pinken as her voice drops. "Trust me, I'm more than aware of your brother's...*activities.*"

All right then. Apparently, there's a double standard going on at the Hawthorne house.

Lovely.

Frustration rushes in, drowning out my humiliation. I snap to attention and frown. "So Austin can sleep around with random girls, but I have sex with the guy you're forcing me to marry, and for some strange reason, that's frowned upon?"

She winces. "That's not it."

"Then what's the problem?" I ask, needing her to admit the truth. Maybe then, Mom will see how hypocritical she's acting.

She shakes her head and jerks her shoulders. "I don't know...In the past, you never seemed very interested in boys or relationships. You've always been so focused on your classes, astronomy, and getting into a good college. I assumed it would stay that way for a little longer..."

Well, she's right about that. Boys have never been much of a distraction. I've dated a few here and there, but the relationships never amounted to much. No one's ever captured my attention the way Kingsley has. Where he's concerned, I'm like a moth to a flickering flame.

"The only way I can explain it, is that it's different when you have a daughter. I worry that he'll hurt you, or God forbid, you'll get pregnant."

"I won't get pregnant," I mumble. The only thing that could make this discussion any worse is if Dad were here, chiming in with his thoughts.

"I hope not." She pauses for a beat before pelting me with another question. "You *are* using protection, right?"

This is *exactly* the conversation I was hoping to avoid.

"Yes," I groan, cheeks flooding with heat, "we're being responsible and using condoms."

"Condoms aren't good enough." She presses her lips together until they are nothing more than a thin slash across her face. "If this relationship is going to continue, then you need to see a doctor so you can protect yourself with the pill or a shot." There's a pause as her attention sharpens on me. "Can I assume it will continue?"

I jerk my head into a nod. Now that we're having sex, there's no going backward. Kingsley and I have had conversations about me going on the pill, but I've yet to find a doctor and schedule an appointment. We moved to Hawthorne in August. I haven't even found a hairstylist, let alone a physician.

"Is he," she pauses as her voice dips, becoming barely audible, "*forcing* you into this?"

Just kill me now.

No, seriously.

There is no way in hell I'm going to own up to enjoying the kind of force Kingsley doles out. Spontaneous combustion would be preferable. And then we wouldn't have to worry about having convos about contraceptives and consent because I'd be dead.

"He's not forcing me to do anything," I ground out, wishing she would drop this particular line of questioning.

Mom shakes her head, appearing as out of her depth as I am. "I don't know, Summer," she finally mutters. "You might want to put the brakes on where this boy is concerned. I realize we pushed you into this arrangement—"

Pushed me into it?

Is that what we're going to call being emotionally blackmailed into an arranged marriage when you're still in high school?

Keaton Rothchild may have been the architect of this particular agreement, but my parents went along with it. I was given a—*we'll be ruined if you don't agree to this* speech.

For all intents and purposes, my parents sold me to the Rothchild family to maintain ownership of the family company. They should thank their lucky stars I'm still talking to them. I was furious when they sprang the news on me, but over the past few weeks, I've made my peace with it. So, in the grand scheme of things, what does it matter if Kingsley and I are sleeping together?

"You're right, I was forced into it." Irritation fills my voice. "And now I'm doing the only thing I can and trying to make the best of the situation."

"I know." Remorse flashes across her face. "At the time, it didn't seem like we had any other choice but to accept Keaton's proposal. The man was threatening to ruin us."

Wait a minute...

At the time?

What does that mean?

"Has something changed?" A flutter of unease fills my belly.

Even though Mom averts her gaze, it's not quick enough for me to miss her guarded expression. "We weren't going to mention anything until there was more information."

"What are you talking about?" When I drop my mug to the counter with more force than necessary, coffee sloshes over the ceramic rim and dark droplets splatter across the granite.

"Your father and I had assumed there was time to get everything sorted out. We didn't expect..."

"What?" My nerves ratchet up a couple of hundred notches. At any moment, I'm going to claw my way out of my skin. *"What didn't you expect?"*

"That you would sleep with him," she mumbles, growing red in the cheeks.

I shake my head, unable to make sense of what's coming out of her mouth. It all feels like a jumble.

"What does it matter?" I pause for a beat before adding, "In a couple of years, we'll be married."

Her silence has the discomfort at the bottom of my belly morphing into a tight knot. I don't know what she's keeping from me, but there's definitely something. It sits between us like a living, breathing entity.

When her attention stays locked on the yard beyond the window, I snap, *"Mom?"* Reluctantly, her gaze slides to mine. "You need to be honest with me. I'm tired of you and Dad manipulating my life to fit your needs."

"That's not what we're doing, Summer," she whispers in a strangled voice. "Your father is working on a way out of this mess. We're trying to help you."

Help me out of this mess the same way they helped me into it?

I wince at the harsh thought as it flashes through my head. "Exactly how are you trying to help?"

"Your father thinks he might have found a way to break the contract." She expels a measured breath as if afraid to release the words into the atmosphere. "If that's the case, we can end this farce without any financial ramifications affecting us or the business."

My eyes widen as shock jolts through me. My tongue darts out to moisten my parched lips. Out of everything she could have said, this is the last thing I was expecting. Maybe I've mentally groused about it, struggling to accept my future, but I never dared to imagine there might be a way out.

Now that it's a distinct possibility...I'm not sure how to feel.

"Let me get this straight—after you forced me into agreeing to an arranged marriage," my gaze hardens, "you're now telling me that I might *not* have to go through with it?"

Un-fucking-believable.

"Nothing is for certain," she mutters hastily, lowering her voice as if someone might overhear our conversation. "There might not be a way out, but your father and I...*we* feel terrible about putting you through this. It shouldn't have happened, and we're doing our best to rectify the situation." There's a pause. "Better late than never, right?"

Is that a joke?

I feel like I've been put through an emotional wringer.

Thoughts swirl through my head as I draw my lower lip between my teeth and chew on it.

"That *is* what you want, right?" Mom probes. "To find a way out of this contract?"

Yes.

No.

I don't know anymore.

Why does everything have to be so damn complicated?

Who wants to have all their decisions taken away? Especially regarding how their future unfolds? But the issue isn't a simple one. I care about Kingsley. Does that mean I want to be forced into an archaic agreement to solve a decades-old grudge?

Hell, no.

Sidestepping the question, I ask one of my own. "When will Dad know more?"

"It could take a couple of days." She shrugs. "Possibly a week. He hired another lawyer, a guy from New York who came highly recommended. Dad is hoping a fresh set of eyes with more experience in these kinds of legal matters will be helpful."

Are there lawyers who deal with contracts surrounding blackmail and brokering a bride?

Interesting.

I want to laugh, but the sound refuses to be summoned. It hits a little too close to home for comfort.

Mom clears her throat, recapturing my attention. "Until we have an answer regarding the situation, you should pull back."

I release the pent-up breath held captive in my lungs.

Pull back from Kingsley?

I'm not even sure something like that is possible. Nor would he allow it. When we're together, he demands everything from me.

Everything.

"You can't tell him about this, Summer," she warns.

Fuck.

"I know." The thing is, we promised to be honest with one another, and lying doesn't sit well with me. It never has. But what other choice is there?

It's almost difficult to believe that one short hour ago, I was wrapped up in Kingsley's arms and my future with him seemed certain. So secure.

And now...

Now I have no idea what will happen.

3

As I grab my lit book from inside my locker, arms snake around from behind, pulling me close until a hard body is aligned with my softer one. Before yesterday's conversation with Mom has a chance to crash through my head, a smile springs to my lips.

Kingsley buries his face against the curve of my neck. "Missed sleeping in your bed."

Even though it's only been a month, it's like I've spent my entire life wrapped up in his arms. Without him beside me, I tossed and turned for most of the night.

"Feel better?" he asks.

The bomb Mom dropped yesterday churned through my head for the rest of the day. Even though I felt bad about lying, I told Kingsley I wasn't feeling well, and we would stargaze tomorrow. What I needed was time to sort through my feelings. That's not possible when Kingsley is near. He's too much of a distraction.

"Yes," I groan when his teeth scrape against the bared column of my neck, sending a million shockwaves skittering across my skin. He knows exactly what to do to drive me crazy.

"Don't expect me to stay away again," he growls.

After last night, I don't think I could deal with being apart from him either. "Come after ten."

"Oh," he says, voice brimming with arrogance, "I plan on it. Probably more than once."

I swear this guy has sex on the brain all the time. Not that I'm complaining since I enjoy it, too.

A lot.

When I drive my elbow into his ribs, he chuckles, his hands sliding beneath the wool of my blazer before migrating upward and brushing over the tips of my breasts.

"Kingsley," I gasp, glancing around the crowded corridor. Thankfully, no one is paying us any attention.

"You love it," he whispers, tweaking the tight peaks.

He's not wrong. I do love the way he touches me.

"I slept for shit last night," he adds, continuing to toy with my body. It's like he's trying to punish me for keeping him away.

"Me, too."

"Don't kick me out again."

I twist in his arms until I'm able to loop mine loosely around his neck before dragging his face close. My body strains toward him like a magnet as his mouth ghosts over mine. "I didn't kick you out." The lie trips off my tongue as guilt flickers inside me. "I wasn't feeling good."

"I know what would have made you feel better." His lips curve as a devilish glint enters his dark depths. "Lucky for you, I've got the cure."

I roll my eyes.

Carefully, he maneuvers me against the neighboring locker until I'm flattened to the metal, and the solid strength of his body covers mine. I crane my neck to hold his gaze.

"You're mine, and I don't like being away from you," he murmurs.

Your father is working on a way out of this mess. We're trying to help you.

My heart skips a beat as Mom's words echo throughout my head.

Is that what I want?

To break off this engagement?

After sifting through my thoughts and feelings last night, I'm not any closer to an answer. My attention stays pinned to Kingsley as questions swirl through my brain. The temptation to come clean is so strong that I have to stop myself from blurting it out.

How can I confess that my family is searching for ways to betray his? Kingsley is bound to the same sense of loyalty as I am. It's a no-win situation. I'm damned if I do and damned if I don't.

His hand slides into my ponytail before wrapping the thick length of hair around his palm until there is no slack. His mahogany-colored gaze sifts through mine as if he can decipher my innermost thoughts. It's a disconcerting sensation. When I divert my attention, his grip tightens, and my lips open on a gasp.

"What's going on?" The playfulness filling his voice falls away, leaving a steeliness in its place. This is the contradiction that is Kingsley Rothchild. He can be soft and tender. Or forceful when necessary. Perhaps the latter should scare me, but instead, it turns me on.

Not only is he aware of it, he relishes it.

As much as I want to confide in him, I remain silent. If I tell him about my parents and nothing comes of it, I'll have stirred up a shit-storm for no reason. Everyone will be pissed off, and it will only create more bad blood between our families.

The entire town hates us for past misdeeds. Only now has it settled down, and that has everything to do with my relationship with Kingsley. In this realm, he's king. Whether or not it's a conscious deci-sion, everyone follows his lead. I know what it's like to have the student population of Hawthorne Prep turned against me. That's not something I want to live through again.

"Answer me, baby girl." His grip turns punishing, and a small cry leaves my lips. My heartbeat riots against my rib cage as arousal gathers in my core, flooding my panties with heat.

In the beginning of our relationship, the pleasure I derived from the hurt he inflicted disturbed me. It was impossible to wrap my brain around how something painful could cause so much arousal to flood my system. Was it normal to be so turned on by someone pinching my nipples, biting my lower lip, or tugging on my hair, all the while forcing me to surrender?

I have no idea.

Kingsley is the first person I've had a sexual relationship with. It's a brand-new world he's opened up. Whether or not it's right, I've made my peace with it. I don't care if it makes me a deviant or freak. I love the way he touches me. I love submitting to him. If that makes me weak, then so be it.

"There's nothing." I hoist my smile. "Everything is fine."

When I shake my head, the strands of my hair tug against my scalp. It sends another punch of need to the bottom of my belly. All right, so maybe the explosion takes place much lower.

"Hmmm." He scrutinizes my expression as if assessing me for the truth. Remorse slices through me. Even if I wanted to look away, I couldn't.

His face looms closer until his tongue can sweep over my lips. Unable to help myself, I open, only wanting to banish everything that has been haunting me for the last twenty-four hours.

Instead of kissing me, he whispers, "Don't ever lie to me, Summer. In order for this relationship to work, we need to trust each other. Once you've broken that trust, it's gone."

A shiver of unease creeps down my spine as my mouth turns bone-dry. I have no idea how to respond. When it comes down to it, I *am* lying to him by not admitting what I know. An omission of the truth is still a lie.

I'm saved from having to answer when a deep voice yells from down the hall, "Get a damn room, Rothchild!" Laughter reverberates off the walls as people turn in our direction.

Heat slams into my cheeks as I blink back to awareness.

How does he do that?

How is he able to make the world fall away around us?

"I'd love to," he responds without releasing me from the intensity of his gaze. It's as if I've been imprisoned and can't fight my way out.

When my teeth sink into my bottom lip, he groans. "The only

thing better than the way you're looking at me right now is when you do it from your knees."

I swallow as that image fills my mind.

His hand loosens from my ponytail before his large palms cup the sides of my skull. My eyelids flutter as his mouth settles over mine. The velvety softness of his tongue forces its way inside my mouth. It doesn't take much persuasion on his end. I'm more than willing to give him what he wants. *What we both want.* He tips my head for better access. A whimper slides free from my lips as he stakes his claim for all to see.

When he pulls away, his eyes are heavy-lidded and full of promise. "Don't ever forget that you're mine."

As if I could.

As if I'd want to.

My hands rise from the back of his neck, plowing their way through his thick hair before dragging his head down until his mouth is a breath away. My tongue darts out to trace over his lips. "Just as long as you don't forget the same."

A feral smile slides across his face. It's filled with darkness and all the carnal pleasure he's introduced me to. "I'll cry it from the fucking rooftops if that's what you want."

I have no doubt he would.

The excitement he's able to incite so effortlessly now riots deep in my core.

The two-minute warning bell rings, knocking me from the seductive web he so easily wove around me. It takes effort to dispel the sexual energy careening through my body and clouding my better judgment. Needing a bit of distance to clear my mind, I gently push him away. His attention never wavers as he reluctantly retreats, allowing me to escape his hold.

With a shaky breath, I grab my book from my locker and hug it close to my chest. "We should probably go."

"What's the matter?" He smirks knowingly. "Not looking to incur the wrath of Pettijohn bright and early on a Monday morning?"

Even the thought is enough to send a slight shudder of dread sliding through me. "God, no."

In an effort to escape the older teacher's unwanted attention, I do my best to fly under the radar and avoid her eagle-eyed scrutiny. That means making it to class on time, handing in every assignment promptly, and paying attention during lectures. So far, it's been working.

For the most part.

As we fall into line, walking to first hour, he leans toward me until his warm breath can feather against the outer shell of my ear. "You've got me all hot and bothered, girl. Don't be surprised if I find you during the day and fuck you senseless."

The breath I had unconsciously been holding hisses from my lungs as another wave of excitement crashes over me. I clench my thighs together to stifle the surge of arousal roaring through my blood.

I should smack him in the arm and tell him to go to hell. But how can I when the thought of him doing exactly that makes my knees weak and my pulse skitter? The attraction that rages between us could easily burn out of control yet, I wouldn't have it any other way.

4

With a few seconds to spare, we step over the threshold of the classroom and slide into our assigned seats. I settle at my desk as Kingsley drops on a chair two rows over.

He gives me one last simmering look before twisting around. I shift as need floods through me. I have a sneaking suspicion that I'll be walking around in a heightened state of arousal for the rest of the day.

Unless Kingsley makes good on his threat.

I'm distracted from those thoughts when Sloane saunters into the room with Aubrey, her trusty sidekick. Her blue gaze immediately fastens on Kingsley before she flicks it in my direction. The hatred that blazes from her is almost like a physical punch to the gut. Since day one, she's had it out for me. And in the month I've been here, it's only gotten worse.

With a flip of her long blond hair, she dismisses me as if I don't exist.

"Hi, Kingsley." She loiters near his desk, trailing her fingers along his arm before settling on the seat in front of him.

One.

Two.

Three.

Fou—

She spins around and thrusts out her breasts in one smooth motion. The rounded curve strains against the white fabric of her shirt. At any moment, buttons will fly. My ears prick, attempting to eavesdrop on their conversation. I hate myself for the jealousy that spikes unbidden through my veins.

"Hey," he responds, disinterest weaving its way through his deep voice as his gaze slides to mine.

Fury flashes across the other girl's face when she realizes his interest has been snagged elsewhere. Even though the pink-slicked smile never falters, the iciness filling her eyes is enough to freeze me on the spot.

Deep down, I know she's not a threat to my relationship with Kingsley. Sloane Carmichael is nothing more than a mean girl who thrives on intimidation. She gets off on threatening to socially crucify those beneath her. I can only imagine how much it infuriates her to know that she can't touch me without pissing off Kingsley.

As Ms. Pettijohn clears her throat, ready to get this show on the road, a girl with long auburn-colored hair hesitantly steps into the classroom. Her unusual blue-green eyes flicker over the sea of bored expressions. Uncertainty flashes across her pretty face before it's shuttered away behind a mask of indifference.

"Ms. Donahue, I presume?"

The girl dips her head. "Yes, ma'am."

Ms. Pettijohn points at the unoccupied desk across from mine. "You may take a seat right there. I'll get you a literature book after class."

"Thank you." With that, the new girl makes a beeline for the desk and settles on her chair.

It's hard to believe that I was the new girl at Hawthorne Prep a little less than two months ago. A shudder scuttles down my spine as memories engulf me.

I flash a smile in her direction, wanting to put her at ease. "Hi," I whisper, "I'm Summer."

"Everly." Her lips quirk into a grateful smile. "Nice to meet you."

"You, too."

When Ms. Pettijohn clears her throat, I glance at the front of the room. My gaze immediately crashes with her narrowed one, and I wince, dreading the none-too-gentle reprimand sure to follow.

"I do hope we're not interrupting your conversation, Ms. Hawthorne."

Warmth floods into my cheeks as I straighten in my chair. "No, ma'am."

"Wonderful." She pauses, and a few people turn in their seats to stare. "I trust you would approve of starting class since we have a great deal of instruction that needs to occur and a limited amount of time to impart it?"

I nod, not bothering to give a verbal response since we all know the question is more rhetorical in nature. Sloane swivels on her chair enough for me to see the delighted smile adorning her face. Thank goodness this is the only class we share. When I glance at Kingsley, he gives me a little wink. The tension coiled tightly in the pit of my belly gradually loosens.

The next forty-eight minutes drag as we do a deep delve into *Wuthering Heights*. Even though I adore the story and have read it more than half a dozen times, Ms. Pettijohn manages to suck every drop of pleasure out of Heathcliff and Catherine's relationship. It's a relief when the bell rings, signaling the end of the period.

"All right, everyone," the older woman says, "don't forget about the quiz tomorrow. Study as if your grade depends on it." There's a pause. "Because it does."

A groan ripples throughout the sea of navy blazers.

"Ms. Donahue." The teacher holds up the thick literature tome. "Here is your textbook. There are several novels that are required reading for the semester. Please consider purchasing them. The list is on the syllabus. As I'm sure you could surmise, we're midway through *Wuthering Heights*. If you don't own a copy, I highly suggest you get your hands on one."

Everly nods.

When another student captures Ms. Pettijohn's attention, I say, "If you need a copy, I can lend you mine. I've already read the story."

"Are you sure?" Surprise colors Everly's expression. "I'd really appreciate that. I'll order it after school."

I wave off her gratitude. "It's not a big deal."

"Excellent," Ms. Pettijohn cuts in before pointedly glancing at the clock on the wall. "You should both get moving to second hour."

A quick glance around reveals that all the other students have fled the room. Not that I can blame them. Normally, I'm one of the first to escape.

As we exit the room, Everly falls in line with me.

"What's your next—"

My voice is abruptly cut off when arms wrap around me from behind, hoisting me off the floor before swinging me in a tight circle. When I squeal, Everly's brows skyrocket across her forehead. For a heartbeat or two, I get lost in the feel of Kingsley and almost forget she's beside me. The urge to burrow against his warmth thrums through me.

Instead, I push my way out of his embrace before clearing my throat and waving a hand toward the dark-haired boy. "Everly, this is my boyfriend, Kingsley."

Other than family, no one knows we're secretly engaged. And that's exactly the way I want it to stay.

"Hi," she says, a friendly smile tugging at the corners of her lips.

Kingsley jerks his chin in acknowledgment. "Welcome to Hawthorne Prep."

"Thanks." Her gaze roams over the crowded hallway. "I'm not going to lie. This place is kind of intimidating."

"Yeah." I laugh, remembering how daunting it felt when Austin rolled the G-wagon through the wrought-iron gates for the first time, and we got a good look at the school. "I know the feeling."

"All right, babe. I gotta take off." Kingsley smacks a kiss against my lips. "I'll see you at lunch."

"Okay." It's oh-so tempting to melt against him. There might be conflict raging inside my head, but my body knows exactly what it wants.

Kingsley.

Everly and I watch him saunter in the opposite direction as we're swept away on a tide of students moving down the packed hallway.

When he disappears, Everly turns to me with a bemused expression. "So that's your boyfriend, huh?"

A little bubble of giddiness explodes inside me.

"Yup, that's him." As the words slide from my lips, I realize how much I like them. How much I like being in a relationship with him. It's what makes the situation with my parents so complicated. I wish the family business had nothing to do with us.

Unaware of the thoughts circling through my head, Everly's lips lift into a teasing smile as she nudges me with her shoulder. "You, my friend, are a very lucky girl."

I burst into laughter, and the auburn-haired girl grins, following suit. It feels good to have someone to laugh with. At Hawthorne Prep, where there are people eagerly waiting to rip me to shreds, I could really use a friend.

Changing the subject, I ask, "What's your next class?"

Everly pulls out her schedule and glances at the folded piece of paper in her hand. "Looks like it's AP psychology with Mr. Timmons."

"Bummer. I have him for sixth hour." I point at the intersecting corridor we're about to cross. "His classroom is that way." After we make the turn, the room is midway down the corridor.

Once we reach the door, our feet slow, and I throw the offer out there, wishing someone had done the same for me. "You're welcome to join us for lunch."

"Thanks." A smile of relief lights up her face. "I'd like that."

"Good." I glance at the ocean of students in their uniforms. Sometimes it doesn't feel like there's a friendly face in the crowd. "I know what it's like to be new here. They're kind of a cliquey bunch, but don't worry, it'll get better."

As long as your name isn't Hawthorne.

Interest flickers across her expression as she studies me. "When did you move here?"

"At the start of the school year." Even though it's been less than two months, sometimes it feels like forever.

"And you've already got *that* guy?"

"I guess so."

"Wow, girl," she says with a laugh. "You work fast. I'm seriously impressed."

She wouldn't be if she knew the real story behind our relationship.

"Okay," Everly says, "one last question before I head to psych."

I raise my brows.

"Does Kingsley have any hot friends?"

A snort escapes as my lips quirk into a smile. "Guess you'll have to meet me for lunch and find out for yourself."

With a grin, Everly points a finger at me as she walks backward to the classroom door. "Challenge accepted, I'll be there."

With Kingsley's arm slung around my shoulders, we head to the cafeteria. Our blazers have been shed, and we've rolled up our long sleeves. Lunch is a less formal affair with scarcely any adult supervision. That used to scare the crap out of me.

"Hey, Summer, wait up!"

I turn to find Everly jogging to catch up with us. Her wavy auburn hair bounces around her shoulders, and her cheeks are stained with a hint of pink. She really is striking with all that long red hair, unusual turquoise-colored eyes, and a dusting of freckles across the bridge of her nose.

"Hi!" I greet, happy she joined us. Even though I've been here since August, I haven't made any girlfriends, and I really miss the ones I left behind in Chicago. We keep in touch, but it's not the same. Plus, there's the whole *Team Summer* or *Team Sloane* thing going on. Obviously, a lot of the girls are *Team Sloane*. And I can't necessarily fault them for that.

At least, I try not to.

Sloane has been the queen bee of Hawthorne since kindergarten. I moved here a hot minute ago and my family has been public enemy number one for generations. Overcoming the family brand hasn't been easy. What I've learned is that memories are long around these parts.

Everly's attention slides from me to Kingsley before bouncing back again. "Thanks for the invite." She tucks a stray lock of hair behind her ear. "I woke up this morning in a cold sweat at the thought of having to eat lunch by myself."

The need to reassure her surges through me, and I untangle myself from Kingsley before looping my arm through hers. "See? Nothing to worry about."

A smile curls around the edges of her lips. I've just met Everly, but so far, I like her. If given half a chance, we could be friends. The babble of voices intensifies as we near the cafeteria. Once we turn the corner and head inside, Everly's footsteps falter as she takes in the vast space with widened eyes.

"Wow," she murmurs in awe, "this is gorgeous."

Much like the corridors, rustic wood beams cross the vaulted ceiling. Heavy chandeliers ringed with thick white tapers are suspended in place from high above. An arched stained glass window on the far wall allows sunbeams to flood the space, giving the expansive room a warm, colorful feel. Gold-leaf framed pictures of when the school was built dot the walls. Tables are arranged in three neat rows, allowing all four grades of students to dine together so everyone is on the same schedule.

For a second, my mind tumbles back to what it felt like to walk into the lunchroom for the first time. Austin and I hadn't *just* been the new kids. We'd been the hated Hawthornes. It takes effort to shake loose the discomfort trying to take root in the pit of my belly.

"You know what's ironic?" she muses. "I attended an exclusive prep school on the Upper East Side that my father paid fifty grand a year in tuition, and it wasn't nearly this fancy." She looks genuinely confounded by her surroundings. "Remind me again that we're in the middle of nowhere."

"We're in the middle of nowhere," I parrot back.

"Yeah," she says in bemusement, "that's what I thought."

"I grew up in Chicago and attended public school my entire life," I add with a chuckle, "so this was a definite culture shock."

I point at the hot lunch line and give her a rundown on the type of food served as we wind our way through the rows of polished wood tables to the one reserved for Kingsley and his friends.

Everly doesn't take notice of it because she's much too busy checking out her surroundings, but people's heads swivel as she walks past. As the new girl, she would immediately draw attention. The school is fairly small with around five hundred students, but her vibrant beauty draws the eye and holds it. She's like a flame dancing in the darkness.

"I didn't realize I should have packed a lunch." Everly glances at my brown paper bag with concern as we stop near the table.

"No problem." I point at the dark-haired boy and a few of his friends who have veered toward the hot lunch line. "Kingsley will help you out. Or I can come with you. I don't mind."

"I'm good." She waves a hand. "Thanks for all the help, Summer."

"No problem," I say as she takes off. As soon as she sidles up to Kingsley, he introduces her to a couple of the guys he's standing with.

I watch to make sure Everly is all right before dropping my lunch onto the table and settling on the bench.

"Who's the new chick?"

Surprised by the question, I glance at the blond boy sitting across from me.

Duke Carmichael.

I've noticed him before. It would be impossible not to with all that messy blond hair he's constantly shoving away from whiskey-colored eyes. Instead of playing football like a lot of these guys, he's on the lacrosse team. Austin has mentioned him a few times. They lift together in the weight room.

And just to be clear, he looks like it. His biceps are massive. It would be a challenge to wrap both of my hands around one of his upper arms and have the fingers touch. There have been times when I've wondered if the sleeves of his crisp white shirt would burst right off him.

I've never witnessed him lose his temper, but I've heard the whispers. What I've noticed is that he's always watching, taking in what's being said without constantly having to weigh in on a topic. I'm not sure what to make of the guy. He's obviously in with the popular crowd but seems somehow removed from it.

Aloof.

That's the word that springs to mind. This is probably the first time he's spoken two words to me.

"Her name is Everly." I glance up from the lunch I'm unpacking onto the table. "She's in Pettijohn's first hour with us." I do a quick mental rewind and realize that Duke didn't show up to lit class this morning.

"Huh." His gaze slides from mine before coming to rest on the auburn-haired girl across the room. Other than the calculating look that fills his eyes, I have no idea what he's thinking. What I do know is that I've never seen him take an interest in anyone since I've been here. Sloane and her minions may flirt with the guys at this table, but they steer clear of Duke, which only reinforces the gossip I've heard.

I toss a glance over my shoulder to see if Everly has noticed the interest she's drawing. And not just from Duke, but a lot of other guys. A bright smile curves her lips, making her even prettier than I originally suspected. She's loosened up and looks more at ease and less nervous. I'm glad I could help make her first day run a little smoother.

A few minutes later, Everly settles next to me with a tray. Her brows draw together as she points at the food. "I can't believe the school uses real Lenox china."

Her reaction makes me chuckle. "Yeah, I know. It's a little over the top."

"Are you kidding? *Everything* around here is over the top." She looks around again, amazement filling her face. "I wasn't expecting Hawthorne Prep to be so...*sophisticated.* I mean..." She waves a hand to encompass the space. "It's in the middle of the country."

Before I can summon a response, a deep male voice barks, "What's that supposed to mean?" Both of our heads jerk toward the boy sitting across the table. "Hicks aren't allowed to have nice things?"

I blink to make sure that Duke is the one who made the loud comment. By the way he's glaring at Everly, there's no mistaking it. I'm a little dumbfounded. I had no idea he was paying attention to our conversation. I mean, why would he? Instead of trying to smooth over the tension that simmers in the air, I gape slack-jawed at the blond-haired boy with the brooding eyes.

I cringe when Everly whispers, "That's not what I meant."

"Really?" A thick brow rises, changing his normally docile appearance to a strangely menacing one. "'Cause that's the shit that came out of your mouth."

What in the actual fuck?

All the color drains from Everly's face before it roars back to life again. Bright red stains flag her cheeks. They almost match her auburn-colored hair.

Anxiety eats away at me as I glance at Kingsley, but he's deep in conversation with the guy on the other side of him. He's not paying the least bit of attention to our conversation.

I'll admit to being momentarily thrown off, but I'm not going to allow Duke to scare Everly away. "That's not what she meant."

Sparks of resentment fly from him. I don't understand the intensity of his reaction. Where is this coming from?

In a matter of seconds, Duke, a boy I've never conversed with, has blown our lunch to smithereens. The one I feel most sorry for is Everly. She's visibly squirming on her seat, and it makes me angry that this guy is being such a giant dick for no apparent reason. He doesn't know her. And she doesn't need shit from him on her first day of school. He continues to glare like he's waiting for her to offer up a defense so he can pounce before ripping her to shreds. It's the most bizarre interaction I've ever witnessed. I wish he would back off and leave her alone.

"Then maybe she should keep her big trap shut instead of insulting people who have spent their entire lives in this town."

In an attempt to defuse the situation, I say, "You're overreacting."

"Am I?" His steely gaze never deviates from Everly.

"She didn't mean the comment like that, all right? Leave her alone."

His gaze jerks to mine, and a sliver of fear scampers down my spine. But I'll be damned if I allow him to see how much this encounter has shaken me. Twenty minutes ago, I had never spoken to Duke Carmichael. Now, I realize he's one more person at Hawthorne to be avoided. One glance at Everly's ashen features tells me that she realizes it, too. I reach out and lay my hand over her fingers, which are twisted together in her lap. When I give them a reassuring squeeze, she glances at me before forcing a smile to her lips. After a few silent moments, her gaze reluctantly slides to Duke who is still focused on her.

Seriously, what's his problem?

It's a relief when Austin settles on the bench next to him.

"Everly," I say, wanting to draw her attention away from the angry blond boy, "this is my brother, Austin."

It's almost as if she has to rip her gaze from Duke. Once her focus shifts, she gives my twin a forced smile that doesn't quite reach her eyes. All the bubbliness filling them a handful of minutes ago has vanished. Duke has chased it all away, and that pisses me off.

"Nice to meet you." Austin glances at me with a quirk of his brow as if to ask where all the strange suffocating tension is emanating from.

"You, too." Everly's narrowed gaze bounces back and forth between us before she asks, "Are you twins?"

I smile, wanting to lighten the mood. "Yup."

The change in topic does exactly what I was hoping it would. Some of her anxiety falls away as Austin peppers her with a few questions, drawing her out of her shell and helping her to relax.

For the rest of lunch, the three of us talk, but it's almost impossible to ignore the guy sitting across from us. Even though Everly puts on a good show and avoids eye contact, I can tell she's bothered by the strange confrontation. Her earlier happiness never quite returns.

6

It's not a surprise when Kingsley slips into my bedroom later that night. As conflicted as I am about what my parents have set in motion, it doesn't stop me from craving what only he can give me.

"Missed you, baby girl," he growls, hauling me into his arms.

The hard-sinewy strength of his body pressed against mine is all it takes to have me melting. "I missed you, too."

The confession isn't a lie. The more time we spend together, the stronger our bond grows. It's not something I have control over. When his mouth crashes against mine, it silences the riotous thoughts swirling through my head. All I want is to forget about the future and focus on the boy in my bed. The one who drives me to distraction with his touch.

Without prompting, I open, giving him the access he demands. The way our mouths fuse and tongues tangle is enough to have desire curling in the pit of my belly. A groan works its way from deep in his chest as his hands graze the length of my body. His lips tease a fiery trail to my chin, nipping at the delicate flesh of my throat. My mind clicks off as he forces me to my back, his mouth dancing along my collarbone before hovering over my chest. His tongue darts out to lap at one taut nipple, drawing it between his lips.

It's almost as if there is an invisible thread connecting the tip of my breast to my core. The deeper he tugs on me, the more I throb with painful awareness. A whimper slides free from my lips as I bow my back, attempting to get closer. Within a matter of seconds, I'm shifting beneath him, restless with anticipation.

"Do you like that?"

It's a question he already knows the answer to. When my response isn't given quickly enough, he bites the hard bud with his teeth.

I yelp as a rush of pleasure-infused pain throbs through me before settling in my core and igniting a deep ache. Cool night air rushes over my wet flesh as he releases the hard point and lifts his head. When his lips crash with mine, his tongue thrusts into my mouth and our teeth scrape. At times, it feels as though he's trying to devour me in one hungry gulp. As if he can't get enough. This is one of those times.

"Answer me," he growls.

"You know I do."

His teeth sink into my bottom lip and another flash of pain explodes before he sucks the bruised flesh in his mouth, releasing it with a soft pop.

"I want to hear the words."

So much arousal careens through every cell in my body that it's almost too much to handle within the confines of my skin. The way he carefully stokes my excitement to life leaves me mindless with need. Like I'm nothing more than an animal, driven by instinct.

His lips are everywhere as he hovers over my body, sucking the other taut peak into his mouth. Once he releases me, he licks a path down my rib cage. The velvety softness of his tongue swirls around my navel. His teeth nip at my flesh, sending a thousand shivers of need coursing through me as he continues his descent.

Once he reaches my lower body, he maneuvers between my legs, spreading them wide to accommodate the broad set of his shoulders. His fingers splay against my inner thighs, pushing them apart until

I'm stretched impossibly wide. The first time he did this, it embarrassed the hell out of me. The intimacy was enough to send me up in flames. No longer do I feel that way. How could I possibly when there is so much pleasure to be had? The way he's able to use his mouth should be illegal. Or, at the very least, come with a warning label.

I squirm beneath his hot gaze. Shards of silvery moonlight filter in through the unadorned windows, giving him enough light to look his fill. And he does, taking his sweet damn time while doing it. I can almost feel the way his gaze burns into me. It's like a physical caress that leaves me breathless for more.

"You're so fucking pretty," he murmurs. "Do you know that?"

Before I can formulate a response, his thumb slides over my core. A thousand tiny shock waves riot through me. It's like a heavy stone being tossed into a calm pool of water. The ripples of pleasure originate in the center before spreading outward until they reverberate in my fingertips and toes.

"I love your pussy." As he presses a tender kiss against me, his tongue darts out, grazing the delicate flesh. "And the way you taste. I could eat you up all night."

The stark image he paints in my mind has a fresh wave of arousal crashing over me.

Another moan punctures the silence of the room when his fingers glide over my outer lips before separating them so he can inspect every intimate inch. He drags his tongue over me again before it circles the tiny bundle of nerves that pulses with painful awareness. He laps at it until my fingers claw the sheets and I'm arching my back. With relentless determination, he propels me toward an orgasm until I'm nearly mindless with the hot licks of pleasure that scorch my insides.

"Kingsley," I whimper, "I need you."

His lips quirk against my damp flesh. "I know exactly what you need, baby girl. And you'll get it when I'm damn good and ready."

The way he torments me makes the arousal thump with agonizing awareness. It's almost more than I can withstand.

"Please," I gasp, unable to stop myself from pleading, "please make me come."

"Mmm," he growls, "you know how much I love when you beg."

When his teeth scrape against my clit, it propels me over the edge until I shatter, screaming out my orgasm. Even after my body turns limp and my muscles sink into the soft mattress, he continues to feast as if he will never be satiated.

It takes a couple of heartbeats to crash back to earth and regain my senses. There's only one thing I like more than when Kingsley makes me come. And that's returning the favor. It's sexy as fuck to watch him splinter apart beneath my fingers.

I might be new to the game, but I'm a quick study and have learned what drives him over the edge. As much as he loves being buried inside me, he loves when I'm on my knees, staring up at him while worshiping him with my mouth.

As I catch my breath, he kisses his way up my body until he's able to hover over me.

"Open," he demands gruffly.

My lips part as he licks at the top and then the bottom. Need sparks to life deep inside my core. When my tongue peeks out, he strokes it, sucking me deep inside him. No one has ever kissed me with such intensity. Slow, steady strokes that slide against mine and ignite a firestorm of need. Even though I've only just come, I want more.

My legs wrap around his waist as the blunt tip of his cock nudges my entrance. With every thrust of his hips, he penetrates my heat, sliding deeper inside me.

"Are you ready for yours?" I ask, knowing if I don't do it now, I'll be lost to the pleasure he's so intent on showering me with.

A grin curls around the edges of his lips. "I'm always ready for what you want to give me."

My palms flatten against the chiseled lines of his chest, shoving until he slides from my body and rolls onto his back. He stacks his hands behind his head, all the while watching me with thinly veiled interest. In an effort to draw out the pleasure, I take my time in straddling him so that the lips of my swollen pussy are splayed wide against his erection. I remain still, allowing him to soak up the warmth of my heated flesh before rubbing myself over the thick length.

It only takes a few moments for his eyes to grow heavy-lidded. "You're such a fucking tease," he snarls, voice sounding as if it's been scraped from the bottom of the ocean.

Ha!

Kingsley has no idea how much of a tease I can be. He's unleashed the monster I never realized was lurking in the darkness.

I linger over him until our faces are so close that his warm breath can feather against my parted lips. When he shifts beneath me, growing impatient, a sly smile curves my mouth. His eyes narrow as he attempts to nip at me. Before he can make contact, I pull away with a grin before sliding from him. My hands go to his larger ones, dragging him from the bed. He raises his brows when I pull him through the door that leads outside to my private balcony. With the cool night air slapping at us, I position him against the wrought-iron railing that frames the compact space.

On my tiptoes, I press kisses to his perfect cupid's bow of a mouth. As he sinks into the caress, I slide down his body, licking over his firm jaw to the thick column of his throat. I pay homage to his shoulders before moving to his chest. I graze one flat nipple with my lips before giving the same attention to the other. When a groan rumbles up from his chest, I continue downward over his ribs and taut abdominals until I arrive at the V of chiseled muscle leading to the part of him that is silk-encased steel. I drop to my knees so I'm eye level with his erection.

Long.

Thick.

And gorgeous.

Not in a million years did I ever imagine being so obsessed with a penis. I'd always assumed they looked the same. That theory has been completely blown out of the water by Kingsley's cock. I love flicking the tip with my tongue and drawing him deep into my mouth. I love the way he throws his head back and groans out his release. The way his fingers sink into my scalp, holding me in place as if he can't bear the thought of not being brought to climax.

His joy is my own.

And vice versa.

Which he has proven dozens of times.

As I tip my head and meet his glittering gaze, a predatory smile settles on his face. He reaches out, tracing the contours of my lips with the pad of his thumb before gently pushing it between them. My tongue slides over the blunt tip as I draw him deeper into my mouth and suck on it. A rumble of pleasure reverberates from his chest as he pulls the digit from me. His hand wraps around the thick length of his cock before he brings it to my lips.

"Kiss the crown, baby girl."

Those five words send a flurry of arousal to my core, where it explodes like a firework. With my gaze locked on his, I press my lips to the glistening head. When my tongue darts out to taste the pearly drop of moisture gathered at the slit, he jerks his dick away.

"Did I say you could do that?"

"No." Wetness gathers in my pussy. The power he wields as if it's his God-given right turns me on.

"You get what I give you, only when *I* decide you can have it," he growls. His deep voice sends a million sparks of need careening through me.

"Please," I whisper, wanting to feel the slide of him against my tongue and filling my mouth, pushing so far down my throat that I might gag.

The way he fists his dick has me growing agitated. He pulls his hard member toward his belly before jutting out his hips. "There are other parts that need worshipping first."

He threads the fingers of his other hand through my hair and pulls me close. My tongue slips out to lap at his clean-shaven sac. I hate to admit just how much I love the silky-soft feel of it.

That's weird, right?

Except it's not. It's erotic as hell.

The need to please him rushes through me as my tongue dances over one heavy ball, showering it with tender attention before moving to its twin.

My hands grip his thighs as the tempo of his breathing picks up. "Goddamn but I love your mouth. You know exactly how to use it."

Desire spikes through me as another groan slides from his lips. When I've licked every part of him, he releases his hold, and I sit back on my heels, eager for what will come next. His eyes remain at half-mast as he brings the tip of his cock to my mouth, tracing over it with a featherlight touch. Painting it with salty moisture before placing the mushroom-shaped crown against the seam of my lips.

"Open."

As I follow his directive, he places the blunt head on the flat of my tongue before carefully thrusting inside. The taste of our combined arousal explodes on my tongue as my mouth closes around him, drawing him inside as his other hand tunnels through my thick strands before setting a steady rhythm. A snarl of pleasure escapes from him as his gaze captures mine. My hands drift from his muscular thighs to his firm backside.

"That feels fucking amazing, baby."

He strokes my mouth, sliding deeper with each drive of his hips until he's gliding down my throat. I force my muscles to relax and suck air in through my nose. It doesn't take long for his fingers to bite into my scalp and his thrusts to become frenzied. His head falls back, revealing the thickly corded muscles of his neck. The pleasure unfolding across his features spurs me on until my name is a fervent chant on his lips before drifting on the breeze that wafts over us.

Greedy for everything he has to give, I milk every drop until his hard length softens. Only then do I allow him to slip free. The wetness from my mouth glistens on his cock. Unable to resist the sight, I press another kiss to the tip before nuzzling it with my lips and nose.

"Goddamn, that was good," he rasps, cheeks stained with a dull flush under the silvery moonlight that slants across us.

I gasp when his hands slide under my arms, and he hauls me to my feet as if I weigh nothing at all. He lifts me until our faces are aligned, and my legs can tangle around his waist. Once my arms entwine around his neck, his hands drop to my ass.

"You ready to fuck?"

God, yes!

I nod, greedy for everything he's willing to give me and then some.

"Good, 'cause I need back in that sweet pussy."

With that, he stalks inside the room. A handful of minutes later, I'm groaning out my pleasure.

KINGSLEY

With my arms stacked behind my head, contentment floods through me as I stare sightlessly at the ceiling. Summer is curled up against my chest. Her breathing has turned deep and even. For the first time in I don't know how long, everything feels right. *Summer* feels right. Maybe I fought this arrangement at the very beginning, but no more. I'm fully on board with it.

I've never felt this way about a girl.

Is it love?

Who the hell knows? It's a little too soon to slap a label on anything. What I do know is that it's barreling in that direction.

When my belly growls, I realize I might have satiated one appetite but not the other. I never grabbed anything to eat after practice. There was one thing on my mind, and that's the girl draped across my chest.

Luckily, the food situation is easily rectified.

With that decision made, I shift Summer's naked body from mine so I can slip from beneath her. For a heartbeat, I still, making sure I haven't roused her. We fucked for a while, so she's gotta be tired. The girl drifted off to sleep almost immediately.

When her breathing continues without interruption, I drop a light kiss against her bare shoulder blade and roll from the side of the bed before grabbing my boxer briefs and hauling them up my thighs until the waistband snaps against my abdominals. A quick glance at the digital clock on the nightstand tells me it's half past midnight. It's doubtful anyone will be up at this late hour.

And if they are?

Who the hell cares?

Summer and I are practically engaged. The contract has been signed, sealed, and delivered with a copy securely tucked away in my father's safe.

After Eloise's untimely interruption Sunday morning, they've been made aware of their daughter's activities. Had it been up to me, I would have told them weeks ago. I don't particularly like sneaking around behind their backs, especially when there's no need for it. Summer belongs to me. If we want to have sex, then we'll goddamn do it. There's no reason for it to be some big secret.

For fuck's sake, the girl is eighteen years old. I'm amazed she managed to hold on to her virginity for as long as she did. I'm the only guy to be inside her body, and as far as I'm concerned, that's the way it'll stay for the rest of our lives. I shake my head as that strange thought takes root.

For the rest of our lives...

Something so permanent should scare the crap out of me.

What does it say that it doesn't?

Exactly.

I hesitate for a moment and consider throwing on my shorts and T-shirt. But what's the point? All I'm doing is sneaking down to the kitchen to grab something to eat. Then I'll be heading back upstairs to sleep. Quietly, I slip from the door and pad through the second-floor hallway before creeping down the staircase. Once my bare feet hit the cold marble of the tile floor in the foyer, I turn toward the back of the house before skidding to a halt. A dim light emanates from the kitchen.

Hmm.

Either someone forgot to turn it off before going to bed, or one of the Hawthornes is still awake.

"I need this over with," a soft female voice says, shattering the stillness that has settled over the house.

Eloise.

My guess is that she's conversing with her husband, which means both of Summer's parents are awake. My belly rumbles as I consider my options. I'm starving. It feels like my stomach is seconds away from making a meal of its own lining. That being said, I sure as hell can't waltz into the kitchen after midnight in my boxers like I own the joint. That would go over like a ton of bricks. Maybe I haven't said anything to Summer, but I want her parents to like me. At some point in the not so distant future, we'll be family.

Guess I'm shit out of luck as far as foraging around in the fridge goes. I either return home for sustenance or wait until breakfast to fuel my body. Given a choice between Summer and a late-night snack, I'll choose the ebony-haired girl every time. I fucking hate sleeping without her. It's only been a month, but I've gotten used to having her slender body wrapped in my arms. Something about the sound of her steady inhalations is strangely soothing.

As I swing around to retrace my steps, Griffin confirms his presence. "Roland thinks he might have found a way to toss out Mom's affidavit. Without that, Keaton doesn't have a legal leg to stand on in court."

My footsteps falter. There is no damn way they're talking about Rose Hawthorne's accounting of how Herbert Hawthorne killed my great-great-grandfather, Gerald Rothchild. Are they seriously attempting to circumvent the contract after they agreed to the terms?

I drag a hand through my hair as their conversation circles viciously through my head. As much as I don't want to believe it's true, there's no denying what I heard.

Everything inside me deflates as anger sets in.

Why am I even surprised?

In all honesty, I should have expected it. They're Hawthornes. And in my experience, Hawthornes are nothing but liars, cheaters, and murderers.

I inch closer to the kitchen, needing to confirm their treachery. Whatever they're up to, Dad will want to know about it.

"I'll never understand how your mother could have done this." Eloise sighs.

"It's my fault. I should have realized she wouldn't give me a dime without attaching strings." His voice drops before softening. "With any luck, we'll be able to get Summer out of this situation."

My heartbeat speeds up at the mention of their daughter's name.

Wait a minute...does she know about this?

"I should never have agreed to the contract in the first place," Griffin continues. "If I'd been smart, I would have held Keaton off for as long as possible. Instead, Summer will be tied to a man she never wanted, forced to spend the rest of her life in this miserable excuse for a town."

"You're doing everything you can to get her out of it," Eloise soothes, "and that's what matters."

"You explained the situation to her?" he asks.

"I did." Her confirmation blows a fucking hole right through my heart. "She wants this over with as much as we do."

"I should have told her about it myself," her father mumbles. "I didn't want to get her hopes up, only to be let down if it doesn't turn out the way we want it to."

And here I thought it wasn't possible to feel any more pain.

Not only does Summer know about this betrayal but she's also on board with it.

The bitterness that crashes over me is almost enough to drive me to my knees. My fingers curl into my palms until the short nails puncture the flesh. The urge to smash my fist through the plaster wall pounds through me. That girl has been playing me this entire time. I think about how we just fucked in her room. The way she took me in her mouth and sucked me dry. Her gaze pinned to mine the entire time she was on her knees. There had been so much emotion churning in her dark, velvety depths.

I'd really thought it meant something.

Bitterness gurgles up in my throat, but I swallow it down, keeping the sound buried deep inside where it will never see the light of day. The last thing I want to do is to tip the bastards off.

What has been proven tonight is that I'm a dumbass for allowing myself to get caught up in a pretty girl with an even prettier snatch. A mixture of humiliation and fury burns through me like molten lava, destroying all the fragile emotions attempting to take root.

The rage that blinds me is all-consuming, and it takes a few moments for the thick haze to clear as I blink back to awareness and realize Summer's parents have fallen into a heavy silence.

I can't stay here any longer. If I do, I run the risk of storming into the kitchen and losing my shit. It's almost mind-boggling how fast my reality has shifted. A couple of hours ago, there didn't seem to be anything that could kill my feelings for Summer.

And now...

Now hatred rushes in to fill every cell of my being.

"I was so foolish," Griffin mumbles. "I thought this would give Summer and Austin a better life. An advantage we couldn't give them in Chicago." His voice breaks. "And look what happened..."

"Don't worry, we'll fix it."

"I don't think I'll ever be able to forgive myself for putting Summer through this ordeal."

"Oh, Griffin." Eloise's voice softens. "She's already forgiven you. Once we're able to end this nonsense, we'll put it behind us and forget it ever happened." There's a pause. "We'll leave Hawthorne, of course. There's no way we can stay here."

"I know," he sighs. "Roland is working on it. We should have brought him on earlier and saved ourselves the headache."

"What about Keaton?" she whispers, fear weaving its way through her voice.

She's smart to be concerned. Once he learns of their treachery, he'll bury them alive.

"I have a meeting set with Roland on Thursday. He'll lay out all the options and direct us on how to proceed. For the time being, it's a waiting game."

"Then we can get the hell out of here and never come back," she whispers wistfully.

"I think that's what we all want."

My gut twists. I've heard more than enough. Any lingering doubts have been laid to rest. Silently, I slink through the shadows to the second floor. My mind riots with each step that brings me closer to the girl sleeping soundly in the bed we fucked in.

She knew.

She's known the entire time. As far as I'm concerned, that makes her as culpable as they are. Summer strung me along, allowing me to believe she gave a damn while her parents were busy working behind the scenes, attempting to cheat my family out of what's rightfully ours.

And I fell for it.

All she had to do was spread those pretty legs, and I fucking fell for it.

My hands shake with unspent fury as I push open the bedroom door. It barely squeaks on its hinges as I step inside and secure it before leaning against the wood. My gaze strays to the beauty sleeping soundly, exactly the way I left her. The thick mass of her inky black hair is spread out across the snowy white pillowcase. Her pale skin almost glows in the moonlight as it filters in through the open windows. The sheet has slithered down her body, revealing the dusky tips of her breasts.

She's so fucking gorgeous that it's actually painful, and I have to physically stop myself from gravitating toward her. From the first moment I saw Summer, I wanted her. Everything about this girl called to me like a siren song. Even after I discovered her true identity, I found it impossible to stay away. That knowledge should have been enough to kill my feelings.

But now?

Any bit of tenderness has vanished.

There's nothing.

Actually, that's a lie. I feel a deep-seated hatred that she could play me so effortlessly. She pretended to want me, allowing me inside her body, all the while knowing exactly how this charade would end. A fresh wave of resentment roars through my blood as I watch her from across the room. My fingers tighten into fists, and for a heartbeat, I close my eyes and welcome the hot rush of fury that licks at me, singeing everything in its path. When they flicker open again, every delicate emotion I'd ever felt for her has been eradicated.

How fucking dare she sleep so soundly when my entire world is crashing down around my head?

Traitorous little bitch.

It's entirely too tempting to close the distance between us and wrap my fingers around her throat, all the while pressing against her fragile flesh until the pulse flutters madly beneath my grip. I want to watch her eyes pop wide as I demand the truth.

How fucking satisfying would that be?

Know what I want even more?

To bring Summer Hawthorne to her knees and make her wish she'd never heard the Rothchild name.

Once upon a time, she accused me of playing games.

Oh, the fucking irony of it all. If her deceit didn't cut so deep, I would be on the floor rolling around with laughter.

Unable to stare at her prone form a moment longer, I swing away before gathering up my clothing. Once dressed, I slip through the door that leads to her private balcony. As I do, images from earlier rush through my brain, tangling insidiously around me. It takes effort to shake them free before I stalk across the lawn to my property.

The only joy I have right now is in knowing that tonight will be the last night of sound sleep she has before I make her life a living hell.

8

When the alarm buzzes the next morning, I stretch and grab the phone from the nightstand before turning it off. My lashes flutter open, and I blink to awareness, rolling over and reaching for Kingsley. Normally when I wake up, my head is pillowed against the solid wall of his chest, and his arms are enveloped around me, anchoring me to his warm body.

And for that moment, before reality can press in on us, I revel in the feel of him. The safety I've found in his presence. And I thank whatever higher power there is that he crashed so forcefully into my life. Maybe I'm confused about everything else, but never that.

Never my feelings for the dark-haired boy.

It's all the other bullshit that I'm attempting to unravel in my head.

I reach out, stroking my fingers across the cool sheets. Kingsley is always here when I wake up in the morning. Most of the time, I have to kick his ass out of bed.

My brows draw together as I sit up and glance around the empty room. The door to my private bathroom is wide open. There's a stillness to the space that tells me he's not here. Further inspection has me realizing that the clothes he shed in a hurry last night are gone.

That's odd. Why did he take off without waking me up to say goodbye?

My mind tumbles back to the night before. The last thing I remember is falling asleep in his arms after we had sex.

I grab my phone and fire off a quick text.

Where did u go? Missed waking up with you.

As I collapse against the pillows, I stare at the screen and wait. When a response doesn't seem forthcoming, I realize I need to get moving. Even the idea of being late to Ms. Pettijohn's class is enough to have me breaking out into an itchy case of hives. There's not much I wouldn't do to avoid incurring the wrath of the older teacher. She has all the charm of a fire-breathing dragon.

I shoot off one last text so we're both on the same page.

Pick me up for school?

Then I throw off the covers and head to the shower. Twenty minutes later, I'm dressed in my tartan skirt and white button-down shirt. My hair bounces around my shoulders as I head down for breakfast. With a step into the hallway, I glance at the phone in my hand.

There's still no response.

I don't get it.

Kingsley always texts back. As I move through the second floor, I press his contact info, deciding to call. Instead of ringing, his phone goes straight to voicemail.

Which is...*strange.*

Is there a problem?

Something going on I'm unaware of?

Why isn't he responding?

It's so unlike him.

Even though it's stupid and I have zero reason for concern, a little knot of tension blooms in the pit of my belly. Since spending the long weekend at his family's beach house in Door County, we've been inseparable. Kingsley Rothchild has quickly become one of the most important people in my life. The thought of something being wrong has me sick with anxiety.

My feet grind to a halt when I find my brother in the kitchen, wolfing down a fresh stack of pancakes.

"What's going on? Normally, you're not even out of bed yet." I make a beeline for the cherry wood cabinet and grab a mug before filling it to the brim with piping hot dark brew.

My brother shrugs before shoveling another oversized forkful into his mouth.

"Want some pancakes, sweetie?" Mom gestures to the plate next to the stove. "I made a few extras."

I snort, giving my twin a pointed look. "Doubtful they'll stay *extra* for long."

Mom cracks a smile. We both know Austin has an enormous appetite. "I'm sure he can spare a pancake or two for his favorite sister."

"I think what you meant to say is his *only* sister," I cut in.

My twin shakes his head before pointing his fork at our mother. "No can do." He pats his flat belly. "I'm a growing boy."

"If you're not careful," I snark, "you'll start growing horizontal instead of vertical."

His teeth flash in the light that filters in through the window. "You're just jealous."

Truth.

It's not fair that one individual can pack away so much food and look the way he does. The only thing I'll concede is that Austin works out in the gym and on the practice field like he's already a professional athlete. If he doesn't make it to the NFL, it won't be from lack of effort.

"Thanks for the offer, but I'm not all that hungry." I've never been a big breakfast eater. Mom knows this but asks every morning just the same. It's a little dance we do.

"Where's Dad?" I glance around the sunlit kitchen and realize he's conspicuously absent. Lately, we've been trying to make more of an effort to eat breakfast together as a family. Since Austin stays after school for football and Dad has been pulling late nights at the office, it's the only time the four of us are in one place at the same time.

"He had an early morning meeting," Mom says, busying herself with the pancakes on the griddle.

Unease scampers down my spine as I add sugar to my oversized cup of coffee. "Oh?" I give her a bit of side-eye, trying to get a read on her thoughts, but her face remains impassive. I can't decipher if Dad's meeting has anything to do with the Hawthorne-Rothchild agreement. A burst of nausea explodes in my gut, and I grimace. These secrets will eat me alive if I let them. If Kingsley discovers what my parents are up to, he'll be furious, and I can't blame him for that.

Austin's dark eyes narrow as if he can sense the sudden tension in the atmosphere. "What the hell is going on now?"

Not wanting to tackle that particular question, I lift the mug to my lips for a sip of java.

Mom hoists a smile and shakes her head as if to say—*whatever do you mean?* Her mannerisms become overly animated, which is a dead giveaway that she's attempting to cover something up.

When it becomes apparent that Austin isn't buying what she's attempting to sell, Mom switches tactics and waves a hand dismissively. "It's nothing, really. Your father hired a lawyer from New York. He's hoping a fresh pair of eyes might help iron out a few details with the company."

What she's really saying is—*All right, move it along now. There's nothing to see here.*

Unfortunately for Mom, her response has the opposite effect on Austin. His suspicions have only been roused further. He's like a bird dog who has caught a scent.

"Uh-huh." That's all my twin grunts as his speculative gaze returns to me. It's as if he's attempting to work out a complicated math problem in his brain. I can almost see the wheels turning.

I've spent the past two days trying very hard *not* to think about the shitstorm my parents have unwittingly unleashed. They don't understand the tenuous position they've put me in. I either betray them or Kingsley. There is no middle ground. What I now realize is that I'm partly responsible for the road we're careening down. When Mom dropped the bomb regarding their plans to fight the contract, I should have admitted my feelings for the next-door neighbor boy.

Instead, I'd remained silent.

I won't deny a part of me detests the thought of being forced into marriage. Who I spend my life with should be my decision. If I end my relationship with Kingsley down the road, I should be allowed to walk away. The family company should not be the reason I'm stuck in a marriage. And that, in a nutshell, is the crux of the issue. If my parents could have figured it out before the contract had been signed, I would have been all for it.

A frustrated puff of air escapes from my lips because nothing can be done about it now. As those thoughts swirl through my head, my gaze drops to my phone. The twinge of concern in my belly blooms into something more.

It's been nothing but radio silence from Kingsley. If he would shoot back a simple text, I'd know we were good and could relax. Instead, my nerves continue to stretch and lengthen. I'm on edge, and the caffeine jolting through my system only makes it worse.

"I'm going to catch a ride to school with you," I say with a casualness I no longer feel. For the past two weeks, Austin has had the G-wagon all to himself.

My twin's brows rise at that bit of information. He's not thrown off by my blasé attitude. "Trouble in paradise already?"

I should have known he would seize on the implication.

"Don't be ridiculous," I scoff.

Mom snags my gaze and raises her brows.

I'm surprised when she says, "For the time being, pulling back is for the best."

"Pulling back from what?" Austin questions, voice sharpening as he homes in on the cryptic statement. His narrowed gaze bounces back and forth between the two of us as his fork clatters to the empty plate. "Someone better tell me what the hell is going on around here before I lose my shit."

"*Language,*" Mom snaps, straightening to her full height. If there's one thing she can't abide, it's Austin's potty mouth. Although, my twin has been swearing for years, and our mother is constantly chastising him for it. Not that it's done any good. The proverbial horse is out of the barn as far as his colorful vernacular is concerned, and it isn't coming back anytime soon.

Austin rolls his eyes, not in the least bit cowed by her rebuke. "Then answer the question."

When Mom presses her lips into a flat line, he pounds his fist against the table. "I'm so freaking tired of all the secrets around here!" He jerks to his feet, towering over both of us. "I thought we were done with all that BS, and now there's more!" His angry gaze drills into Mom before shifting to me. "Is this how it'll be from now on? Only *certain* people in this family will be privy to insider information?" There's a pause. When neither of us attempts to fill the suffocating silence, he snaps, "You know what? Maybe I should have moved back to Chicago when I had the chance."

My teeth sink into my lower lip as remorse surges through me. If it bothers me to hold back from Kingsley, it's even worse with my brother. Before moving to Hawthorne, we never kept anything from each other. But the past six weeks have changed our relationship. Secrets have mushroomed up all around us, and everyone is guilty of keeping them.

"I'm sorry, Austin." Mom flattens both palms against the granite as if to prop herself up. As if the weight of what's going on is slowly crushing her to the floor. "Your father and I aren't trying to keep anything from you. It's just..." Her voice trails off as if she's not sure how to finish the thought.

When it comes down to it, that's exactly what they're doing, and my brother realizes it.

Austin pins me in place with a hard-edged glare. I can't blame him for being pissed off and hyper-sensitive about the situation. The last secret nearly splintered the four of us apart. "I don't want to hear any more crap. You either tell me what's going on, or I'm out of here."

A frustrated puff of air escapes from my lungs. Ever since Dad inherited the family company and moved us to Hawthorne, there have been too many surprises simmering beneath the surface.

It shouldn't be like this.

If Mom won't tell Austin what's going on, then *I* will.

Before I can do exactly that, Mom beats me to the punch. "Your father is trying to figure out a way to break the contract with the Rothchilds."

Austin's dark brows skyrocket into his hairline. "Don't you think you should have figured that out *before* you bargained away my sister's life?"

Mom's eyes widen as her mouth gapes open. She's not used to Austin speaking to her in such a disrespectful manner. Our relationships have changed, and not necessarily for the better. Ever since we were forced to uproot our lives, Austin has become surlier. I can't blame him for it. The move has been especially rough on him. In Chicago, he was treated with god-like reverence as a star on the football field. Here in Hawthorne, his new teammates haven't exactly welcomed him with open arms.

More like the opposite.

Ignoring the statement, she says in a clipped tone, "New information has come to our attention, and we're doing our due diligence by exploring it."

My brother's unrelenting gaze shifts to me, pinning me in place. "And you're good with this?"

I jerk my shoulders, unwilling to say differently. It's a complicated question. I'm doing my best to sift through my feelings and figure it out.

With a quick shake of his head, he grunts out his disgust before picking up his plate and dumping it in the sink. As he strides from the room, he barks over his shoulder, "Be ready in ten."

Mom watches him leave before glancing at me. It's only then that I notice the exhaustion that fills her eyes and the tiny lines bracketing her mouth. "What's gotten into him?"

Even though our situation at school has improved, and we're no longer treated like lepers fresh from the colony, Austin isn't happy living in Hawthorne. He'd rather be in Chicago, playing football with his former teammates.

Jasper Morgan, AKA the douchebag, still has the starting quarterback position with Austin playing backup. My brother is a talented player who spent the past three years as QB for the varsity team. He's been on the radar of college scouts since his freshman year of high school. So, to move to Nowheresville, Wisconsin, and get stuck playing backup for a less talented guy doesn't sit well with him. Now add that Jasper is the one who filled his locker with cow shit and provoked him into a fight that led to a three-day out-of-school suspension, and you have the perfect recipe for a volatile situation.

Austin is no stranger to brawling. Over the years, he's grown accustomed to defending himself because of his dyslexia. He's unwilling to let a sleight pass by, and he doesn't know how to turn the other cheek.

Well...maybe he knows. He just refuses to do it.

"Moving to Hawthorne has been difficult," I say by way of explanation. "A lot has happened in a brief period."

Too much.

Her brows slide together as she stares at the now empty doorway with contemplation. "Maybe we should have allowed him to move back to Chicago."

My heart lurches at the idea of being separated from my twin. As relieved as I am that it never came to fruition, she's probably right. But it's too late to do anything about it now. It's October, and the football season is well underway.

"When we were offered this opportunity, it had seemed like a fresh start for all of us. And now..."

And now it's turned to complete shit.

When Grandma Rose passed away, leaving both the estate and multimillion-dollar company to Dad, it had seemed like an opportunity of a lifetime. A chance to escape the rat race in Chicago and enjoy life in the country.

Unfortunately, it hasn't turned out that way.

Little did we know that everyone in town would hate us or that the Rothchilds would threaten to take the company away, bankrupting my family.

"If we find a way out of the contract, the Rothchilds will crucify us. You think the way everyone treats us is bad now, but it'll be a thousand times worse. All we'll be doing is confirming their thoughts about this family."

A heavy pall settles over the room as Mom lifts the mug to her lips before taking a sip. Her attention strays to the golf course beyond the window. "We would have to leave, Summer. Your father is trying to figure out how we could do it and still run the company."

Wait a minute...what?

Leave?

The thought of walking away from Kingsley has my throat closing up until it feels like I'm being strangled from the inside out. Barely am I able to push out the question. "When will Dad know?"

"I'm not sure. In a day or two." She shrugs. "And then the four of us will sit down and discuss the situation openly. No more secrets, I promise."

I draw my bottom lip into my mouth before chewing on it. I don't want to break the contract if it means destroying my relationship with Kingsley. When he finds out about this, it'll annihilate the little bit of trust we've managed to build.

"Summer?" Mom says, cutting into my thoughts.

"Hmm?"

She searches my face, sifting through all the emotions flickering across it. "I'm sorry about all of this. Your father and I shouldn't have agreed to the terms of the contract. It wasn't fair to you. There has to be another way for us to work everything out between our families. It's not like we're trying to rescind their share of the company. We just don't think you or Kingsley should be part of the deal. Once we can prove there's nothing for Keaton to blackmail us with, we can sit down with the lawyers and negotiate a compromise that is fair to both parties. That's all we're trying to do."

When she puts it like that, it makes perfect sense. The deal struck regarding Hawthorne Industries shouldn't have anything to do with us. It should be about the company.

"It's still possible the lawyers might not find a way out of the contract, right?"

"It could go either way," she agrees. "For the time being, we have to sit tight and wait." There's a pause. Her voice dips, becoming more hushed. "You haven't mentioned any of this to Kingsley, have you?"

"No." If this all comes to light, will he see it the way I do? Would he agree that the company and our relationship should be separate?

As much as I want to be with him, it feels important that I have a choice in the matter. I'm aware that my rationale doesn't necessarily make sense, but it does to me.

"Good." The tension in her face diminishes, softening the little lines around her eyes. "I realize you're having sex and perhaps developing feelings for him, but don't forget that it was his family who forced you into this situation."

Disbelief bubbles up in my throat.

Is she serious?

It's oh-so tempting to add that they also had a hand in forcing me into this predicament but I decide to hold my tongue at the last minute. There's no point in heaping more guilt onto my parents. It won't change anything.

From the driveway comes the blast of a horn.

Eager to end this conversation, I place my mug in the sink and make a beeline for the front door. "I need to go. I don't want to be late." Once I get to school, I'll find Kingsley and figure out what's going on. Hopefully, my mind is spinning for no reason, and this is nothing more than an overreaction on my part.

Mom hoists her smile. "Try to have a good day, sweetie."

"I will," I say with a wave, escaping to the entryway where I grab my backpack before heading to the shiny black G-wagon parked in the weathered brick drive.

It seems like with every day that passes, life becomes more complicated. I'm not sure how much more I can withstand.

9

As soon as I open the door, music pours out at an earsplitting decibel. My ass has barely slid onto the passenger seat next to Austin before he steps on the gas and rockets out of the drive. I give him a bit of side-eye and grab the oh-shit bar as he swings out of the subdivision and speeds toward the school.

His face is set in grim lines.

I turn down the radio instead of trying to yell over it. "What's the matter?"

"Seriously?" With a scowl, he shoots me a disbelieving look before his attention snaps back to the black ribbon of pavement stretched out in front of him.

I wince and realize that he's still upset about the earlier discussion in the kitchen.

"I'm sorry, Aus. I found out about their plans the other day."

"And you didn't say anything to me?" he snaps. "I'm really fucking tired of all the secrets. Every day, it's some new bullshit."

Sadly, he's not wrong. That's exactly the way it feels.

"You're right," I admit, "I should have told you. I'm sorry."

My apology has the desired effect, and his anger recedes as we pull into the long drive of Hawthorne Prep before passing through the elaborate wrought-iron gate that wraps around the hundred-acre property.

"It burns my ass that Mom and Dad didn't bother telling me about this themselves," he begrudgingly admits. "I'm always the one left in the dark."

"I know, but it wasn't meant like that." Somewhere in the back of my mind, I acknowledge it's the secrets that will rip our family apart. And I don't want that to happen.

"It never is," he mutters, pulling into a parking space and cutting the engine. He swivels toward me. Now that the brunt of his anger has dissipated, he searches my face. "I'm a little surprised you're good with this."

Yeah, that's the thing...

"I'm not sure that I am," I admit nervously before glancing away.

Austin knows me better than anyone. All he has to do is read my expression to know what is in my heart.

"You like him, don't you?" His words are low, laced at the edges with resignation.

I could deny it, but what would be the point? Much like him, I'm tired of the lies.

"Yeah, I do." It's almost a relief to release the truth into the world instead of continuing to hide it.

His brow furrows as he digests that bit of news. Maybe he suspected it, but to hear it confirmed is another matter entirely. "If that's the case, then why the hell are you going along with their plan?"

"That's not what I'm doing," I mumble, guilt slicing through me as I shift on the butter-soft leather seat before glancing out the windshield. My gaze scans the thick crowd of students for one in particular. The boys are dressed in navy blazers, white button-downs, and perfectly pressed tan pants while the girls are outfitted similarly with the exception of short navy, green, and gold tartan skirts in place of the khakis.

Nowhere in the sea of teenagers do I find Kingsley's dark head.

Where is he?

"That doesn't make sense. If you like the guy and are fine with being a child bride, then you should have been straight up with them."

I roll my eyes. "I am *not* a child bride."

"Whatever." He snorts. "You know what I mean."

A pent-up sigh of frustration bursts from my lips. Yeah, I do, and that's part of the struggle. "I'm not sure how to explain it. I like Kingsley. And the more time I spend with him, the more my feelings grow, but that doesn't mean I want all of my choices snatched away from me at the ripe old age of eighteen. I don't want to feel like a prize awarded in some stupid agreement between our parents. I want us together for the right reasons, not because we were trapped by circumstances outside of our control." When I finally run out of steam, my body sags against the seat as I glance at him. "Does that make sense?"

"Yeah." His voice softens as understanding fills his eyes. "It does." He reaches out and wraps his larger hand around mine before giving it a gentle squeeze. "I'm sorry about all this bullshit you're going through. I had assumed you were cool with it." He jerks his shoulders. "You seemed, I don't know...*happy*."

Air leaks from my lungs. He's not wrong about that. Over the past couple of weeks, I've been content. But still...

In the back of my brain, the knowledge that we've been forced into this relationship eats away at me. And no matter what I do, it refuses to go away.

"I worry about the future. We're only eighteen years old. For goodness' sake, we're still in high school! A lot can change over the next couple of years. I don't want to be stuck with someone for the rest of my life who doesn't want me."

"I didn't think about it like that." His hand tightens around mine. "Who knows, maybe it would be for the best if they can find a way out of this stupid contract." He drags a hand down his face. "Fuck, Summer. I don't know how to make anything better. All I know is that it's a mess."

I sputter out a laugh. Leave it to Austin to sum up the situation perfectly. "You got that right."

A heavy silence stretches between us before he clears his throat, drawing my attention to him. "Does Kingsley know what's going on?"

I shake my head.

His lips flatten into a tight line. "If Mom and Dad find a way out of this contract and Kingsley discovers that you knew about it, he'll go apeshit."

Yeah, that's *exactly* what I'm afraid of. Austin's confirmation only makes my pulse skitter as a fresh wave of anxiety crashes over me.

"I know," I whisper, barely able to force out the admittance before worrying my lower lip with my teeth. "Why does everything have to be so complicated?"

A soft puff of air escapes from his lips. "You realize everything has been a massive clusterfuck since Grandma Rose kicked the bucket, right?"

How could I not?

Rather ironically, she had zero involvement in our lives when she was alive. Now that she's dead, she's a specter that refuses to be banished. It's a cosmic joke of epic proportions, except no one's laughing.

"Yup, I have."

"Fucking Grandma Rose," he mumbles with a shake of his head.

The sentiment has my lips quirking. Sometimes, I wonder if her last dying wish had been to turn our lives upside down.

"Guess we better get this show on the road," Austin says with a quick glance in my direction. "You ready to do this?"

I jerk my head into a nod. It wasn't so long ago that I dreaded walking through the doors of Hawthorne Prep. Today, that's not the case. Those first few weeks were a nightmare. There is no way I could have survived the entire year under those stressful conditions. And my brother would have most certainly got his ass expelled.

After we exit the Mercedes, Austin clicks the locks before tossing me the keys. Since he stays after for football practice, I usually drive home by myself. For the past two weeks, he's been catching a ride with Kingsley. I wouldn't exactly say they've become friends, but we're neighbors and our families are now locked in an agreement, so I guess it behooves both to make the best of the situation.

"Thanks." I slip the key chain into my backpack before hoisting the strap over my shoulder.

"Summer," a female voice calls out, "wait up!"

I swing around only to find Everly jogging through the parking lot to reach us. Her long auburn hair bounces around her shoulders, glinting in the sunlight. Guys turn, watching as she moves seamlessly through the crowd.

"Hi!" I greet as she falls in line with us.

Other than Kingsley, no one has gone out of their way to be welcoming. I have no idea if that has to do with us being Hawthornes or if this is the special treatment all new residents are subjected to. What I do know is that it's nice to have a girlfriend again. Especially after contending with Sloane and her cohorts.

Austin jerks his chin at the pretty redhead in acknowledgment. "Hey."

From beneath my lashes, I watch Austin for telltale signs of interest. My brother isn't a long-haul type of guy. And I've lost more than my fair share of girlfriends over the years because of him. Or maybe they were never my friends to begin with. I'm hoping that won't be the case with Everly.

When I don't pick up any *I'd-like-to-get-in-your-pants* vibes from Austin, I glance at Everly and am pleasantly surprised to discover the same amount of disinterest radiating from her.

"Hi," she says with a smile, promptly dismissing him as we walk up the wide stone steps to the front entrance.

And then we're pulling open the doors and getting swallowed up by the tide of students making their way to their lockers.

"Did you study for the lit quiz?" she asks.

"Not really." I shoot her a grimace. "I've read the story so many times that I'm pretty sure I can get away with winging it."

"I'll catch you at lunch," Austin cuts in as I stop in front of my locker.

I give him a quick wave as he strides away. Everly's attention stays glued to him until he disappears down the corridor.

"Your brother is a real hottie," she says conversationally. I get the feeling it's more of an observation than a roundabout way of telling me that she's interested.

A smile springs to my lips as I grab my books from inside my locker. "My advice is to steer clear. I hate to say it, 'cuz I love him and everything, but the guy is kind of a manwhore. And even though we just met, I like you way too much to see you get chewed up and spit out."

I hold my breath, waiting to see how that comment will play out. From experience, it'll go one of two ways. If she gets huffy, then I know Everly was never interested in developing a friendship with me. If she—

When a burst of laughter escapes from her upturned lips, the tension filling me evaporates.

"Oh, trust me, I'm not interested. I'm more than happy to admit that he's pretty to look at, but the guy has dangerous stamped all over him. Which is exactly the type I avoid at all costs." She cracks a grin. "But I appreciate the warning. I'm sure it's not the first time you've had to issue it."

"It's not." I can't help but return the easygoing smile. "A lot of girls look at him as a challenge."

"Been there, done that. And have the T-shirt to prove it."

"Ohhh..." I chuckle, eyes widening. "I sense a story."

"Here, I'll give you the SparkNotes version—it doesn't have a happy ending. Anyway," she says before quickly changing the subject, "I ordered a copy of *Wuthering Heights* last night, so I'll be able to return yours in a couple of days. Thanks again for letting me borrow it."

"It wasn't a problem." I slam the metal door shut.

Everly keeps up a light chatter as we walk through the corridor to her locker. I'm only half-listening as I search the area for Kingsley. I don't remember seeing his red Mustang parked in the lot when we arrived. I pull my phone from my blazer pocket and glance at it for the umpteenth time.

There's still nothing. It's been almost an hour and a half since I fired off the first text, and he still hasn't responded. Even though I can't imagine what could be wrong, it feels like something is off.

The two-minute warning bell rings as Everly shoves her messenger bag into her locker and grabs her books for first hour before we hightail it to class. As soon as I step over the threshold, my gaze flies around the room, but he's conspicuously absent. My brows draw together in concern as I slide into my assigned seat, and Everly settles on the one across from me. There's less than a minute before the bell rings, and Kingsley continues to be MIA. I slip my phone from my pocket and send one last text before Ms. Pettijohn passes out the quiz.

Now I *am* worried.

What if something happened to him?

Like an accident.

Should I reach out to his dad? I don't even have Keaton's number.

I'm at a loss as to what to do.

As the bell rings throughout the building, signaling the start of class, Kingsley strolls into the room and takes his seat. Relief rushes through me as I sag on the chair. Why did I allow myself to get so jacked up? Clearly, everything is fine. He probably overslept and was running late.

"All right, everyone," Ms. Pettijohn begins, "it's quiz time!"

Groans ripple throughout the room.

Now that Kingsley is here, I wait for him to turn around and flash me a familiar grin or wink. Any gesture that will prove that we're good and my downward spiral was nothing more than a strange case of self-induced paranoia. One minute slowly ticks by, and Kingsley's attention stays focused at the front of the room as our teacher finishes passing out the one-page quiz. When sixty more seconds creep by, and he doesn't acknowledge my presence, I realize it's not a bout of paranoia after all.

Something is definitely wrong.

But what?

10

Confusion swirls through me as I mentally pour over the events of the past twenty-four hours with a fine-tooth comb.

I don't get it.

Why is Kingsley ignoring me?

Last night, we had sex, and I fell asleep with his arms banded around me. What could have changed between now and then?

Nausea rises in my throat until I can practically taste it in my mouth. This is so reminiscent of the first day of school that my body breaks out into a cold, clammy sweat. I fold my arms around my middle, trying to calm the nerves that prickle beneath the surface of my skin. Whatever is going on between us has to be a misunderstanding. There's no other explanation for it. As soon as we can talk, I'll clear it up, and everything will be fine.

When the quiz lands on my desk, I stare at it blankly. My brain refuses to compute the words on the paper. By the time Ms. Pettijohn collects them ten minutes later, I have no idea what questions were asked, and I certainly don't remember what I scribbled down in response. My guess is that I bombed it in spectacular fashion. I've never failed anything in my life, let alone a quiz on a book I've read so many times that I could recite it in my sleep.

The bell rings, and I jump from my seat, making a beeline for Kingsley. As I step in his direction, Ms. Pettijohn summons me to the front of the room. The dark-haired boy doesn't even glance at me as he slips into the hallway with Duke.

His cold dismissal has my heart crashing to the bottom of my toes.

It's like I don't exist.

For a moment, I hesitate, staring at the doorway. I'm tempted to ignore her and go after him. Except...I already know that it won't be worth the trouble I'll find myself in. My feet drag as I head to the front of the room where Ms. Pettijohn waits with her arms folded across her chest.

"Can I assume there was a problem today with your attention span, Ms. Hawthorne?"

I dip my head. "Sorry, ma'am."

She arches a severely penciled-in brow. "Let's not make a habit of woolgathering in my class."

"I won't."

"Very well then." By way of dismissal, she shoos me away with a flick of her fingers.

I don't need to be told twice. Her hand hasn't even fallen to her side, and I'm shooting out the door and swinging into the hallway. Even though I search the immediate vicinity, I don't see Kingsley anywhere.

Not that I thought he would wait...

Okay, so maybe I did.

Everything in me deflates as I expel a breath and head to my locker before gathering my books for second and third hour. The rest of the morning passes by as if in slow motion. I feel the tick of every second. Every millisecond. It's excruciating. I sit in class, foot tapping, staring at the clock, waiting for the fifty-minute period to draw to a close. And then I spend the next five minutes scouring the halls for Kingsley. Normally, I see him between classes, but so far this morning, he remains elusive, almost as if he's deliberately avoiding me.

By the end of fourth hour, I'm a complete mess. The thought of trying to choke down my lunch makes me want to hurl. Out of habit, I grab the bag from my locker before meeting up with Everly. Not wanting her to suspect anything's wrong, I plaster a smile across my face. This isn't a situation I can delve into with my new friend.

As we head to the cafeteria, I keep an eye out for Kingsley. It's like he's vanished off the face of the earth. What has become disturbingly clear is that he's avoiding me, and I can no longer fool myself into believing otherwise.

The moment I step into the cavernous space, my gaze falls upon the table Kingsley and his friends have claimed as their own. Already football players are crowded onto the long stretch of twin benches. They're talking and laughing as if everything is normal and my world isn't slowly being tipped upside down. I'm not sure if I'm relieved or not to find Kingsley conspicuously absent. The last thing I need is a confrontation with him in front of the entire school. When we finally have a conversation, it needs to be in private.

Unaware of the thoughts that circle through my head, Everly heads for the table packed with athletes. Reluctant to explain why I'm hesitant to sit there, I trail halfheartedly behind her. Instead of buying lunch like she did yesterday, Everly holds a brown paper bag in her hand.

Tension fills me as we settle at the far end of the table. From the corner of my eye, I glance at Kingsley's friends, half-expecting them to rip me to shreds. It only makes me realize how precarious my situation is and how much protection Kingsley afforded me. It's almost frightening how easily I forgot what it felt like to be hated by these people.

A few of the guys acknowledge our presence with a chin lift before going back to their discussions. Football season is well underway, and most of the conversations consist of the team they'll be playing on Friday.

It's almost a relief when Austin settles next to me with his tray. "Hey."

Other than my brother and Everly, I'm surrounded by people who aren't really my friends. It's a little bit like swimming with sharks. Even though there's relative calm, you're constantly on edge with the realization that the situation has the potential to turn deadly at any moment. A stress headache brews at the back of my skull.

"Hi," I murmur.

His narrowed gaze searches my face. A few seconds of eye contact is all it takes for a silent communication to pass between us. Unaware of the tension that brews beneath the surface, Everly unpacks her lunch and eats her PB and J. I don't bother going through the motions of emptying mine. It remains untouched on the table in front of me.

When the guy next to Everly engages her in conversation, Austin whispers, "Did you talk with him yet?"

The *him* in question doesn't need further elaboration.

Kingsley.

I shake my head.

A troubled look passes over his face as his lips flatten into a tight line. Although that doesn't stop him from wolfing down his cheeseburger and fries. There isn't much that gets in the way of Austin's appetite.

"Hawthorne," I jump to attention when one of the guys at the far end of the table yells, "where's Rothchild?"

All eyes turn to me with interest as they collectively wait for a response.

My mouth turns cottony as I attempt to swallow down my nerves. "I'm not sure."

They might be oblivious to the circumstances surrounding the deal struck between our families, but everyone knows we're together. It only makes me wonder what would happen if that weren't the case. Would these people continue to accept us, or would Austin and I be relegated to outcast status in a school founded by our family?

It's a scary prospect. One I don't want to contemplate. Although instinct tells me that I'll have to. Sooner rather than later.

11

The second half of the day passes much like the first. Kingsley remains elusive, and the tension brewing inside me ratchets up until it becomes almost unbearable. At any moment, I'm going to splinter into a million pieces. I have no idea if he was here for anything other than first hour. I stopped texting after I realized he wouldn't respond.

It's like he fell off the face of the earth.

Or maybe I did, and I haven't realized it yet.

How is it possible that we had sex last night, doing things to each other that I would have never imagined I'd be comfortable with, only to end up like this twelve brief hours later?

It doesn't make sense. No matter how many ways I come at it, I'm at a loss. I don't know where we go from here. Am I supposed to stop by after football practice and demand answers? How much longer do I sit on my ass and wait for Kingsley to clue me in on what changed?

My brain races as I slide behind the wheel of the Mercedes and drive home. The obnoxious beat of the music blasting through the sound system isn't enough to take my mind off Kingsley. I pull into the drive, surprised to find Dad's pearly white Volvo SUV parked near the garage. I've become used to the long hours he puts in at

Hawthorne Industries. To find him home at three o'clock in the afternoon now seems out of the norm.

A strange feeling of foreboding fills me as I sit in the car and stare at the sprawling stone mansion. It takes effort to shake it away as I grab my backpack and head to the front door. As I turn the handle and push open the heavy wood, raised voices fill the air and have me skidding to a halt. Unease crawls across my skin.

"You've fucked with my family for the last time, Hawthorne! When I'm done with you, there will be nothing left!"

There haven't been many occasions to hear Keaton's voice, but I would recognize the deep timbre of it anywhere. After our bizarre first encounter, it's been singed into my memory.

Why is he here?

"What did you really expect?" Dad shouts back in a voice that echoes off the high ceilings and leaves me cringing. "That we would just hand over our daughter?"

"The terms were laid out clearly in the contract. If they were so repugnant to you, then you shouldn't have agreed to them. Quite frankly, I would have been more than happy to take you to court and bury you under a mountain of debt."

He knows.

Keaton knows that Dad was looking for a way out of the contract.

But how?

How did he find out?

It's tempting to back out of the foyer and pretend I haven't stumbled upon this volatile situation. As difficult as it is, I force my feet forward. The two male voices continue to escalate, rising higher as I put one foot in front of the other until I'm hovering at the threshold of the dark wood panel study. I've never been a fan of this space. It reminds me too much of Hawthorne Prep.

My gaze sweeps nervously over the room as I loiter in the doorway. Mom is planted near the oversized fireplace with her arms crossed tightly against her chest. Concern flickers in her eyes as her teeth sink into her bottom lip.

"You all but pressured us into it! We weren't given enough time to look for other options!"

Dad stands unnaturally erect next to her. His face is bright red as he stabs a finger in Keaton's direction. A fine sweat beads on his brow as he continues to bellow. A rush of concern floods through me. Rarely have I witnessed Dad lose his temper. Even under the direst of circumstances, he always maintains an unflappable control.

"This is exactly what I expected from you, Hawthorne." Malevolence glitters in Keaton's dark eyes as if he's pleased by the sudden turn of events. As if this is what he wanted all along. Perhaps the end goal was never for me to marry his son. He was looking to inflict as much pain as possible.

A movement catches the corner of my eye, and I turn my head until my gaze collides with the fourth person in the room.

Kingsley.

He watches me from where he's taken up sentinel near the window. His narrowed, mahogany-colored eyes drill into mine. The coldness swirling in them slaps at me, and I almost take a hasty step in retreat. Even after Kingsley discovered I was a Hawthorne, he never stared at me with so much ill-concealed contempt or hatred.

Panic careens down my spine. I had spent all day obsessing about what was wrong, and now I know. Somehow, he discovered what my parents were up to. It's obvious from the animosity wafting off him in heavy suffocating waves that the fragile bond we had painstakingly built has been destroyed.

My attention jerks from Kingsley to Keaton as he takes a step toward my father. I gasp when he plows both hands into Dad's chest, knocking him back a couple of steps.

"Tell me when the Hawthornes have ever done what's right?" A vicious smile stretches across his thin lips. "Which is precisely why I had everything in place to take the company from you. My lawyers will have you tied up in litigation for years. Death will seem like a preferable option when I'm done with you. You've got my promise on that!"

When Keaton reaches out again, Dad slaps his hand away. "Go ahead and try it, Rothchild! I wouldn't hang everything you have on the affidavit you've been waving around for all to see. My mother was eighty years old. I have two doctors willing to testify she wasn't in her right mind the last couple of months of her life. Whatever she said is nothing more than the ramblings of a sad, lonely woman who regretted the choices she'd made."

"You son of a bitch!" A flush steals across Keaton's cheeks as his eyes flash with rage. "Your family stole from me, and I'll be damned if I allow you to do it again!"

Mom and I both scream when Keaton yanks back his arm and swings at Dad, who barely manages to sidestep the attack.

"Stop it!" Mom shouts. "Both of you!"

Neither takes their gazes from the other as they circle around the small space like caged animals.

"You damn well know what happened all those years ago," Keaton growls. "You know what your family did to mine."

"Well, that's the thing. No one knows for sure what really tran- spired," Dad says stiffly. "It's nothing more than speculation on your part. And after this stunt, that's the way it'll remain. I was willing to be reasonable, but no longer."

"Not only will I ruin you," Keaton vows, "I'll destroy the little whelps you spawned. I won't be happy until I wipe every last Hawthorne off the face of the earth."

"Leave the children out of it," Dad roars, spittle flying from his mouth. "I told you before that we could settle this like civilized adults, but you refused to listen. There's no reason to drag Summer into your half-cocked schemes. Do you think this is what she wants for her life? To be forced into a marriage with your son? She wants nothing to do with him."

Oh, God. That's not true!

My wide eyes cut to Kingsley. Pain flashes across his expression before it's quickly shuttered away, almost as if it had never been there. His attention remains focused on the two older men.

That's not how I feel, and I don't want Kingsley to think it is. My tongue darts out to moisten my lips. "Dad—"

"Not now, Summer!" He swipes a hand in my direction, cutting me off.

This is all my fault.

When Mom admitted to what they were planning, I should have immediately shut it down. Now it's too late. The wheels have been set in motion, and there's no stopping them. It's like a runaway train barreling down the tracks.

Once again, my gaze is drawn to Kingsley. His expression is set in hard lines, and his jaw is clenched. Regret rushes through me, threatening to swallow me whole. No matter what I say, he won't believe me.

"Is that really what you think?" The dark chuckle that slides from Keaton's lips has alarm bells ringing in my head. "Your whore daughter has been spreading her legs for a month now." His eyes glint triumphantly. "Before the contract was ever struck."

The high color that fills Dad's face drains away before slamming back into his cheeks. "You're lying!"

"What? You don't believe me?" Keaton smiles before thrusting a hand in my direction. "Just ask her. I'm sure Summer would be delighted to give you all the juicy details."

Heat radiates from my face as Dad swings toward me with disbelieving eyes. I take a hasty step in retreat as he skewers me in place. I'm like a butterfly pinned to a Styrofoam board. All I want to do is sink into the floorboards and escape the oppressiveness that fills the paneled room.

"Summer?" he whispers, pausing for a beat as his gaze searches mine. "Tell me it's not true."

Humiliation burns through me as I remain silent. I don't think my father has ever looked at me with so much disdain.

"Come now, my dear, don't be shy. Tell your father how my son has spent the past month sleeping in your bed." When there's a pause, I send up a little prayer that Keaton won't say anything more. "So, let me get this straight," he drawls, "you've been telling your parents that you're against this arrangement when, in actuality, you've been begging Kingsley to fuck you?"

The air gets sucked from my lungs until nothing is left.

Keaton grins when my eyes pop wide. "Perhaps your parents didn't realize what you two were up to, but I've made it my business to know where my son sticks his dick."

Throughout his father's tirade, Kingsley remains stoically silent with his expression devoid of emotion. Perhaps I made a mistake in not being truthful with him, but I was always honest about my feelings. My guilt lies in not wanting to be bartered away like property. As I continue to stare, I can't help but wonder if he ever felt anything or if it was nothing more than a game. Maybe I'm the one who got played after all.

"Answer the question, Summer," Dad chokes out, snapping me from my thoughts.

I yank my gaze from Kingsley, barely able to meet Dad's shocked one. This isn't the way I imagined him finding out about my relationship. I had assumed Mom clued him in as to what she walked in on Sunday morning. From his stunned expression, that isn't the case.

"Have you been sleeping with him?" he barks again.

The growing silence turns deafening. The sound of my own breathing fills my ears until it's like the roar of the ocean crashing onto rocks. I remind myself that I'm eighteen years old. My guess is that this has more to do with *who* I had sex with rather than the actual deed itself. "Yes, I have."

Color rushes into Dad's cheeks. A bead of sweat rolls down the side of his face. It seems at odds with the coolness of the room. He presses his lips together and jerks his gaze from mine.

"Dad," I whisper brokenly, hating that I've disappointed him.

When I take a hesitant step in his direction, he holds up a hand and staggers in retreat as if he doesn't want me any closer. "No."

"Not quite the vestal virgin you purported her to be, huh?" Keaton snickers, amusement flashing in his eyes. "Or does your disgust lie in the fact that it was a Rothchild who defiled her?"

Oh God...

Why can't he shut the hell up?

Hasn't he caused enough damage for one day?

I glance at Kingsley, wishing he would do something about his father, but his face remains inscrutable. I'm tempted to close the distance between us and smack him. Or pound my fists against his chest. Anything to solicit a reaction. How can he stand there and allow Keaton to say such vile things about me?

Unless it really *was* all a game.

The thought is enough to gut me.

My father wedges two fingers beneath the collar of his starched blue dress shirt, attempting to pull it away from his throat. When that doesn't work, he loosens the top two buttons with shaking fingers. His breathing becomes labored as he paces the confined space like a caged animal before dragging a hand through his short, silvered hair.

"Dad, please..."

Why is Keaton Rothchild so intent on destroying our family?

I understand what the Hawthornes stole from them. But we, personally, weren't the ones to do it. We're innocent in all this.

In an effort to de-escalate the situation, I take a tentative step toward Dad and lay a hand on his shoulder. "Maybe you should sit down for a moment."

"I'm fine," he growls, shaking off my touch.

"I'm sorry." Tears fill my eyes as my hand falls reluctantly to my side. "I didn't mean to hurt or embarrass you."

His breathing turns harsh as he rubs his chest. Pain flashes across his face before vanishing.

"Griffin?" Concern threads through Mom's voice as her brow furrows. "Are you okay?"

"I'm fine," Dad snaps, waving off her concern before spinning toward Keaton. "Get out of my house! Anything that needs to be said can be done through our..." His eyes widen as a burst of panic explodes across his face. *"Through our..."*

His voice dies as one hand clutches at his chest, and he gasps for air. His fingers twist, clawing at the perfectly pressed cotton of his shirt.

"Dad!" I leap forward as he topples over like a tree. I reach out, attempting to slide my arms around him. Instead of stopping his

descent, I get taken down. I'm no match for his girth. He crashes onto the wood floor with a thump, and the wind gets knocked out of me.

For one brief second that stretches for eons, utter silence swamps the room. My heartbeat gallops in my ears as I gape at my father's ashen face. He stares back sightlessly as his mouth hangs open.

And then all hell breaks loose.

"Griffin!" Mom screams, dropping to her knees. She clutches his arm before pressing her fingers against his neck. *"Summer, call an ambulance!"*

Unable to stop staring at my father, I drag my arm from beneath him and scoot back on all fours until my back slams into the paneled wall. My brain clicks off, no longer able to process my surroundings. I can't shake myself from the strange stupor that has fallen over me.

"Summer!" Mom shouts, louder this time. The panic filling her voice has my own hurtling to the surface. *"Call 911!"*

Oh God.

I need to call an ambulance.

Something is wrong with Dad.

A sob threatens to escape as I crawl toward the door. My body trembles as I rise unsteadily to my feet and stumble toward the foyer where I dropped my backpack when I walked through the door only fifteen minutes ago. Tears streak down my face as I rip open the zipper and frantically rifle through the bag.

"I've already called," says a deep voice. "They're on the way."

My head jerks up to meet Kingsley's hard-edged stare.

Before I can utter a sound, he swings away, leaving me alone in the foyer. Ice seeps into my veins as I stare into the study. Mom is hunkered over Dad, pressing on his chest. Her voice wobbles as she counts off compressions before pinching his nose and breathing into his mouth.

One, two, three, four, five...

12

Mom, Austin, and I sit huddled on an uncomfortable fabric bench in the waiting area of the emergency room. There's a handful of other people who have taken up sentinel like we have, waiting for news regarding a loved one. It feels like we've been here forever, and we still don't know what's going on with Dad.

The past sixty minutes continue to play on a vicious loop inside my head. Nothing I do makes it stop.

Stepping inside the house and hearing the raised voices.

Dad and Keaton arguing about the contract.

Keaton gleefully informing Dad that I've been sleeping with his son.

The disappointment and shock that had filled my father's eyes.

Him clutching his chest and toppling over.

Oh God...

Is this really happening, or have I become trapped in a nightmare?

Dad is only in his late forties. I'm not saying he's in the best shape of his life and could run a marathon, but for the most part, he eats right and exercises when time allows. He's always been strong and healthy. There's no reason he shouldn't pull through this.

Yet that does nothing to alleviate my concerns.

It took the paramedics fifteen minutes to arrive at the house. And during that time, Mom never stopped administering CPR. Dad was still breathing when they rushed in, converging on him before checking his vitals, securing him on a stretcher, and loading him into the back of an ambulance. Mom and I jumped into the Volvo and followed.

On the way to the hospital, I left a message on Austin's phone before calling the school. Luckily, Mrs. Baxter was still working in the office and was able to get a hold of the head football coach. Five minutes later, a teammate was driving Austin to the only hospital within a sixty-mile radius. We arrived twenty minutes ago, and Austin rushed through the emergency room doors not ten minutes after that.

Mom swipes at the tears that leak from the corners of her eyes with trembling fingers.

"He'll be fine." Unsure how to comfort her, I rub soft circles over her back. "Dad is a fighter." The idea of losing him is almost unfathomable. He's the backbone of this family. How could we possibly survive without that?

She jerks her gaze to mine before blinking back more wetness and nodding. "He's been under so much pressure lately."

Ever since he took over Hawthorne Industries, he's been putting in longer hours and skipping meals or grabbing fast food. And trying to find a way out of this mess...

It's all taken a toll.

Austin jumps to his feet, pacing in front of the bench with a long-legged stride. "Why won't they tell us what's going on?" He swings around, prowling ten feet before spinning in a tight half-circle. "Is it so damn hard to give us an update?" He stops and glares at the desk on the other side of the room. "This is complete bullshit."

"Language," Mom murmurs, but her words lack conviction. It's more of a reflex than anything else. A tiny bit of normalcy in a world of chaos.

"Sorry," Austin mutters before drawing himself up to his full height. "I'm going to check with the nurse at the desk. I'll be back in a minute."

My brother doesn't stalk more than three steps when an older man in scrubs pushes out through an oversized metal door. He stops at the desk and speaks briefly with the woman before she glances in our direction. My mouth goes bone-dry as I scour his face for clues. Every step that brings him closer makes my heart pound faster until each beat becomes agonizing. My hand rises to rub gently at the spot.

"Mrs. Hawthorne?" His light blue gaze strays first to Austin and then to me before settling on our mother.

She rises unsteadily to her feet, hands clutched together in front of her until the knuckles turn white. "Is Griffin all right?" Her tongue darts out to smudge her lips. "Are we able to see him now?"

Emotion flickers in his eyes, but it's there and gone before I can decipher what it means. A pit blooms at the bottom of my belly as my nerves stretch to their breaking point. At any moment, they'll snap.

He gestures to a room off to the side that had, until now, gone unnoticed. "I'd like to speak with you in private."

Any color filling her face drains away as she jerks her head into a tight nod.

"Mom?" I say, popping to my feet, "should we come with you?"

Fear pools in her bloodshot eyes as they dart to me. "Let me speak with the doctor alone."

My teeth sink into my lower lip until the metallic taste of blood fills my mouth. The need to reach out and stop her from leaving thrums through me as if that has the potential to alter the outcome. Or, at the very least, prolong the inevitable.

Somewhere in the back of my mind, I realize we're standing at the precipice. Once she crosses it, nothing will ever be the same. There's no going back. I want to keep her with us for as long as possible.

My brother takes a step toward her. "Mom—"

"Austin, please," she whispers, her voice cracking on his name. "Let me figure out what's going on. Then we'll talk."

His wide shoulders slump under the heaviness of the moment. It feels bone-crushing in its intensity.

"Yeah, fine," he mumbles.

Silently, we watch as the doctor leads Mom to the private room before holding open the door. Once she walks past, he shutters them away. I don't realize there's a thin sliver of a window until Mom is standing in front of it. My breath gets trapped in my lungs. Even though I can't see the doctor, I know her gaze is pinned to him. She jerks her head and continues staring. From this distance, I see fresh tears well in her eyes. Within moments, she buries her face in both hands.

No.

No.

No.

This can't be happening.

Austin slips an arm around my shoulders before hauling me close. "He'll be fine, Summer. He has to be."

As desperate as I am to believe my brother, somehow, I know he's wrong. Once again, our lives are about to change, and there's nothing we can do to stop it from happening.

13

ardiac arrest.

The official cause of Dad's death.

It's been six days since he passed away.

Six.

The last image I have of my father is when the paramedics loaded him into the back of the ambulance. He was still breathing when they arrived at the hospital and rushed him into the emergency room. Unfortunately, that's where his heart stopped. They spent twenty minutes trying to resuscitate him but weren't able to bring him back.

Stretched out on my bed, I stare blindly at the ceiling, unable to comprehend his death. How can he be gone? My mind spins. It's almost impossible to fathom how we got to this place. Six months ago, I'd never heard of this shit town. Our lives had been in Chicago. And Dad had been fine.

Alive.

And now...

He's not.

And I'm trapped in a nightmare.

One I can't wake from.

Three days ago, we held the funeral. Mom's sister, Aunt Trish, flew in from California, and friends and work colleagues drove up from Chicago. Employees from Hawthorne Industries also attended, paying their last respects. Everly showed up with her father. I hadn't realized he was the New York lawyer Dad hired. I suppose I should have put two and two together. It meant a lot to see everyone celebrate Dad's life. We reminisced and told funny stories that made me smile through the tears.

It was only after the service that I noticed Kingsley and Keaton in attendance. The idea that either was at the church to offer condolences felt like a slap in the face. It took all of my effort to keep Austin from losing his shit. Thankfully, they left as quietly as they'd crept in.

The time that has unfolded since is a blur. Each new day feels like a formidable mountain that needs to be scaled. It hasn't even been a week, and I'm already exhausted. I have no idea how we're supposed to carry on. How do we pick up the shattered pieces and continue without Dad?

Life has become a thorny mess with more questions than answers. There is no longer anyone to go to with our concerns. Mentally, Mom has checked out. Once the shock of Dad's death wore off at the hospital, she started sobbing and couldn't stop. How do you reach someone steeped so deeply in grief? In desperation, we called the emergency room doctor from the hospital, and he prescribed something to help calm her nerves. Instead of weeping continuously, she now sleeps like the dead.

At times, she's so groggy she doesn't remember Dad is gone. Having to explain what happened all over again is gut-wrenching. Since she was in no frame of mind to plan the funeral, Aunt Trish helped. Mom sat as still as a statue in the first pew of the church and didn't interact with anyone.

Austin returned to school two days after Dad died, but I haven't been back since.

How can I leave Mom alone?

At this point, she's barely functioning, and it's a scary sight to behold. The only reason she's eating is because meals are brought to her bedroom. Half of the time, they go untouched.

It's the chiming of the doorbell that knocks me out of my turbulent thoughts. With a quick puff of air, I haul myself from the bed before glancing at the clock on the nightstand. It's only four in the afternoon. Austin is still at football practice, and there's no way Mom will leave her room to answer the door.

I wrap my hoodie around my body as I pad into the hallway and down the sweeping staircase to the foyer. It's early October, and there's a definite chill to the air. I have no idea if Mom has turned on the heat for the house. I should probably check.

From the moment Austin and I were born, Mom has taken care of us, and now she can barely fend for herself. That knowledge leaves me feeling lost and adrift. Without Dad and with Mom knocked out of commission, there is no one to count on. No one to turn to for help. The enormousness of our lives has now fallen on me.

And the weight of it is crushing.

Aunt Trish offered to return for a couple of weeks, but she wasn't able to take the time off from work after the funeral. Plus, she has three kids of her own who are in elementary and middle school. It's not like she can leave them alone for weeks on end. They need their mother, too. And she lives in California, which is practically across the country. Since Hawthorne isn't exactly a bustling metropolitan, the closest airport is hours away. It only makes the logistics more complicated.

As the bell peals for a second time, I pull open the door only to find a strange man standing on the other side of the threshold. "Can I help you?"

Since Dad died, there have been a slew of flower deliveries. That assumption is blown out of the water when I realize he's not holding a vase full of fresh blooms or a plant.

"Good afternoon," he says cordially, "I'm looking for Eloise Hawthorne."

The guy is dressed in a suit and holds a manila envelope in his hand. I don't recognize him, but it's possible he's from Hawthorne Industries and is here dropping off paperwork. Dad might be gone, but the company, unfortunately, continues on. It's just another thing I'll have to deal with.

I hug the door a little closer to my body. "She's not available right now."

"That's a problem. I have documents that need to be hand delivered and signed for." Along with the packet, he holds a small electronic device.

With a frown, my brows draw together as I stare at the envelope. "Who is it from?"

"Sorry, miss, I'm not at liberty to say." He retreats from the front porch. "I'll try again tomorrow."

"Wait!" I don't know what the envelope contains, but what if it's important? "I'm Eloise's daughter. Is it possible for me to sign for it?"

His footsteps falter. "Are you over the age of eighteen?"

"Yes."

Silently, he mulls it over before shrugging. "Sure, I guess that would be fine."

He holds out the electric pad and stylus for me to scrawl my name. As soon as I return the device, he hands over the package.

"Have a nice night." With that, he leaves me standing in the doorway.

I watch as he slides behind the wheel of a fancy black sedan before pulling out of the driveway. Only then do I glance at the thick packet in my hand. Mom's name and address are typed on a white label on the front of the envelope. I flip it over, unable to find a return address.

That's odd.

My hands tighten around the package as I trudge up the staircase to the second floor. Whatever this is, it must be important for someone to go through all the trouble of hand delivering it. At the top of the stairs, I turn to the right and move toward my parents' master suite. Thirty steps bring me to the closed door of Mom's bedroom. Unsure what I'll find, I press my ear against the thick wood and listen for sounds of life.

There are none. It's been this way for almost a week. I realize

Mom is going through a tough time. We all are, but I need her to snap out of it and take control.

I raise my fist and hesitate before rapping my knuckles against the door.

When my knock is met with silence, I add a little more force to it and try again. "Mom?" I pause for a beat. "Are you awake?"

Guilt rushes in for disturbing her, but all she does is sleep. At some point, she needs to rejoin the land of the living. We can't continue like this for much longer.

When my second attempt goes unanswered, I wrap my fingers around the handle and push the door open before taking a peek inside. The normally bright and spacious room is shrouded in shadows. As my eyes adjust to the gloom, I spy Mom curled up in the middle of the bed. She's burrowed beneath the covers as if she's a small child hiding from the monsters in her closet. If not for the slight snoring, I'd be concerned that she had done something stupid.

This is the first time I've had to deal with this kind of all-encompassing grief. It's nothing short of terrifying, and it only makes me realize how powerless I am to help her or make the situation better. The only thing I know how to do is take charge and hold our lives together until she can surface from the depression she's fallen into.

I could wake her up, but what then?

Will she remember that Dad is gone, or will I have to explain it to her all over again? Honestly, I don't have the energy for that. I chew my lower lip before creeping out of the room. Whatever is contained in the envelope can wait until morning. I'll talk to her at breakfast before she numbs the pain with another dose of medication.

It might not be a bad idea to look over the paperwork first. Then I can bottom line it for her. With that decision made, I return to my room and settle on the bed before sliding my finger under the flap and lifting the sheath of papers from the envelope.

Dread curls like a wisp of smoke in my belly as I realize where the correspondence originated from.

Keaton Rothchild.

Even though every other word is legal jargon that makes comprehension difficult, what becomes clear is that he has every intention of moving forward with the lawsuit.

Unless...

The Hawthornes fulfill the original terms that were agreed upon with the caveat I live under their roof. A trapdoor springs open, and I'm sent into a freefall. The letters on the thick sheet of paper swim before my eyes.

How can he demand this of me at a time like this?

Dad is dead.

How much more will he extract from us?

I already know the answer.

Everything.

He'll squeeze us for every drop, and even then, he'll be greedy for more.

My mouth dries as a wave of dizziness crashes over me. Hoping that I misread the document, I pore over it a dozen more times. Even though I want to crumple the papers and throw them in the garbage can where they belong, that's not an option.

Maybe I *should* wake Mom. She needs to know what new demands Keaton is making. My knees turn to jelly as I rise to my feet and take a tentative step toward the door before stumbling to a halt.

But...then what?

Will she be able to protect me?

How will she fight this?

The woman can barely rouse herself enough to get out of bed and use the bathroom. She's functioning with only scant moments of clarity. What if this new demand pushes her further over the edge?

There's no way I can allow that to happen. Loneliness and grief flood through every cell in my body as I sink to the bed. Since Dad died, I've tried so hard to be the strong one. To keep all the turbulent emotions tamped down where I can pretend they don't exist, but I won't be able to do it much longer. It's taking too much of a toll.

With a broken sob, my head falls into my hands as the hot sting of tears leaks from the corners of my eyes.

I don't think I've ever felt this lost or alone in my life.

1 4

It's after seven o'clock when Austin walks through the door after practice. Each day, the time gets later and later. My guess is that he's trying to avoid the house altogether. I don't blame him for wanting to escape, but I can't be the only one holding down the fort.

I pace the length of my room, waiting for the shower to stop running. Then I give it ten more minutes before forcing myself to walk down the hallway and knock on his door. "Aus?"

Not waiting for a response, I poke my head inside. His hair is still damp as he digs through the contents of his backpack before tossing a few books onto his bed.

He glances up as I step inside the space. "Hey, what's up?"

It takes effort to blink away the tears and not crumple to the floor. In the end, what good would it do?

Not a damn thing. I'm trapped. If I fall apart in front of Austin, it'll only make matters worse. The last thing I need is for him to fly off the handle or threaten retribution.

When I remain silent, unable to produce a sound, he straightens to his full height. His thick brows furrow as he inspects me with more care. "What's wrong?"

Everything.

"Stupid question," he mutters, shaking his head before dragging a hand down his face. "You know what I meant."

"Yeah, I do." I hoist my lips into a thin smile and close the distance. "Need any help with homework?" I ask, desperate to prolong the inevitable discussion, even if it's only for a few moments.

He doesn't take the bait. "Nah, I got it covered."

I exhale a long breath, knowing what needs to be done, but still, that knowledge doesn't make it any easier.

"Summer?" His voice drops as urgency fills it. "Did something happen?" His gaze falls to the tan envelope in my hand as if only now noticing it. "What's that?"

My fingers tighten around the packet. "A delivery from Keaton."

That name is enough to have storm clouds gathering on Austin's face. "What does that asshole want now?"

I wince at the bitter rage that whips through his voice. This is more difficult than I expected. An hour ago, I had stupidly convinced myself that my brother would accept the circumstances and agree there was nothing to be done, but now...

Now I realize that won't be the case.

In true Austin fashion, he'll fight it tooth and nail. He won't want to lose anyone else to the Rothchild family. It's up to me to make him understand that this arrangement, at least for the time being, is our only viable option unless we're willing to lose everything.

Voice devoid of emotion, I lay out the facts. "Keaton has every intention of moving forward with the lawsuit, which means taking the company from us, unless we fulfill the original terms of the contract Mom and Dad signed."

Austin's mouth falls open. "You're shitting me, right?"

If only I were.

I gulp down the growing nausea that churns inside because releasing the words into the atmosphere makes it more real.

"Wasn't it enough that he took Dad from us, now he's taking you, too?"

I cringe as he roars out the question. In the deafening silence of the shadowy room, it echoes hollowly in my head.

"What other choice is there, Aus? We can't afford a lawsuit, not with Dad gone and Mom checked out the way she is."

He folds his brawny arms across his chest. "What did Mom say about all this?"

I glance away and admit, "The envelope arrived a couple of hours ago. She was sleeping, and I haven't had a chance to tell her."

"For fuck's sake, Summer! You need to talk with her first instead of taking this into your own hands."

"What's she gonna do about it?" Frustration roils until it reaches a boiling point. "Does Mom seem like she's in any kind of condition to fight the Rothchild family?" I throw an arm toward the other side of the house. "She's so overmedicated that she doesn't even know what day it is."

His anger evaporates as his body deflates. Maybe my brother is reluctant to acknowledge it, but he realizes that what I'm saying is the truth. It's a shit situation we'll have to figure out on our own.

When Austin doesn't immediately come back with an argument, I take a cautious step toward him before reaching out and squeezing his arm. "For right now, it's the only solution. At the very least, it'll buy us time to figure out our next step."

"Fuck," he grumbles before plowing a hand through his hair. "I don't like it."

Does he really think I do?

Nothing could be further from the truth.

"Me, neither."

"As much as I hate to admit it, maybe you're right." His body vibrates with barely restrained agitation. "We agree to the terms for the time being and figure out something else. Dad had a team of lawyers working on this. Hopefully, they'll come up with a solution. It's not like Keaton is forcing you to marry his asshole son tomorrow."

I gravitate toward the window and stare up at the inky sky. It's too early for the stars to be visible. And even if they were, there wouldn't be any solace to be found in the tiny pinpricks of light.

"Summer?" Austin's voice turns sharp, piercing my thoughts.

Now I have to finish it. Much like ripping off a Band-Aid, it's best to do it quickly. I exhale and push the rest out in a rush. "One stipulation is that I live at their house."

"With the Rothchilds?" he asks incredulously.

I swing around to face him. "Yup."

"What the hell for?"

I shrug and force my expression to remain bland. "I would imagine they don't want us plotting and scheming against them." I give him a thin smile since that's exactly what we're intent on doing.

Austin growls before spinning away and slamming his fist into the plaster wall near his bathroom door. *"Goddamn them!"*

I stifle a sharp yelp before slapping a hand over my mouth. Austin has always been the more volatile twin, while I've been the calm, pragmatic one. "Are you—"

"I'm fine," he barks, shaking out his hand with a wince.

My teeth sink into my lower lip to keep silent. Coddling him won't do a damn bit of good. He needs to work off his anger, or it'll fester like poison beneath the surface, and then he'll blow like a geyser. And more than likely do something much worse than damage a wall.

He stabs a finger at me. "Over my dead body are you living there!"

"What choice do we have?" My shoulders fall under the overwhelming weight of the world that attempts to press me down. My reservoir of strength is quickly being depleted. At this very moment, I'm scraping the bottom of the barrel. "Mom can't handle a lawsuit. And we have no way to fight this by ourselves."

Concern fills his eyes. "Are you really going to be able to deal with living over there?" There's a pause before he adds, "Interacting with those bastards every single day?"

Definitely not.

Rather than admit how frightened I am, I lie through my teeth. "I'll be fine. They won't hurt me."

Much.

A shiver scampers down my spine as I recall the look of hatred in Kingsley's eyes.

Austin slumps onto the bed before cradling the sides of his skull in his hands. For a sliver of a moment, he reminds me of the child he once was. "What am I supposed to do, Summer? Tell me how to make this better."

My heart lurches painfully under my breast. It's always been difficult for me to glimpse Austin's pain. If given the choice, I'd put myself through hell to ease my brother's way. We're family, and that's what family does. They take care of each other.

In three swift steps, I eat up the distance between us and wrap my arms around his shoulders. "There's nothing you can do to change this. Just take care of Mom."

"Fine," he murmurs brokenly.

I draw in a deep breath, relieved this conversation has been put to rest. "I need to get over there."

"Tonight?" His head snaps up. *"They're making you leave tonight?"*

"If I'm not standing on their doorstep with my belongings at precisely nine o'clock, Keaton will call his lawyer and start the proceedings." It takes effort to separate myself from him before heading to the bedroom door. I don't want to leave any more than he wants me to. Unfortunately, the Rothchilds have other plans. "I've already packed everything up."

"Summer?"

Austin's voice has me halting over the threshold before swinging around to face him. "Yeah?" It takes every bit of strength I have to keep the turbulent emotion from breaking loose.

"I love you."

I press my lips together and jerk my head into a tight nod. A thick lump of emotion clogs my throat as wetness gathers in my eyes. "I love you, too."

Once the door is closed behind me, I pause and allow the tears to slide down my cheeks.

15

With my suitcase in hand, I press the doorbell at the Rothchild mansion. A muffled chime echoes throughout the cavernous space. Only now do I realize that I've never stepped foot in Kingsley's house. He's always come to me. Either sneaking into my room at night or picking me up for school in his Mustang. I'm unsure what to expect. Even though the house is a monstrosity, I know it's just the two of them. His sister, Harlow, is at a boarding school in Europe. And his mom...

I have no idea where she is. Kingsley doesn't talk about her, and the one time I asked, he quickly shut down the conversation and changed the subject.

The front door swings open, and I'm surprised to find the older woman from the beach house. When I remain silent, unsure what to say, she raises her brows in askance. Does she recognize me from that morning months ago when she threatened to call the police unless I vacated the property?

I really hope not.

"Can I help you, young lady?" she snaps, unfriendliness bleeding through every syllable. This is exactly the demeanor I remember.

I wince and force myself to say, "Um, yes. I—"

Her narrowed gaze falls to the black suitcase parked beside me. "I suppose you're Summer Hawthorne. I was told to prepare a room for your arrival."

She makes it sound like I'm here for a holiday when, in actuality, I'm nothing more than a glorified prisoner.

"Don't just stand there gawking," she barks when I remain silent. "Grab your bag, and I'll show you to your accommodations."

Holy crap. If rudeness had a face, the dour one before me would be it.

I glance longingly over my shoulder, tempted to make a run for it, but I get the feeling this woman would give chase and tackle me to the ground before dragging me inside.

My fingers tremble as they wrap around the handle of my suitcase before hauling it over the threshold. Once I'm inside the foyer, my gaze travels around the spacious interior. No matter how fancy our house is, this is a hundred times more so.

A sparkling crystal chandelier drips from the vaulted ceiling. It looks more like an impressive work of art rather than a utilitarian piece that gives off light. My gaze skitters to the intricate wrought-iron railing that wraps around the second-floor gallery, giving the area an open and airy feel.

The older woman clears her throat, drawing my distracted attention to her.

"Sorry," I mumble before following her up the sweeping staircase. What has become clear in the two minutes I've been here is that the Rothchild mansion is more museum than house. This place is easily fifteen thousand square feet of sprawling, perfectly decorated space. While it's spectacular, it's not exactly what one would call homey. There's a definite chill to the air mimicked by its owner. Or maybe vice versa.

Landscapes in gold-leaf frames are carefully arranged on the wall. I glance at a few as I drag my suitcase up the stairs. I'm more into astronomy than art history, but I'd stake money on these being original works that cost a small fortune.

Kingsley told me that his family owns a chain of stores named

Rothchild's. Like fifty of them. The flagship is in Hawthorne, but the rest are scattered throughout the Midwest.

It's glaringly apparent that the Rothchilds don't lack for wealth, which means that extracting a pound of flesh from my family is the driving force behind this lawsuit. Maybe my great-great-grandfather murdered Gerald Rothchild eighty years ago, but to go to these lengths to settle almost a century-old score seems diabolical.

I'm huffing and puffing by the time we reach the second-floor landing. It takes a moment to catch my breath before scurrying after the older woman as she turns to the left, walking with military precision past numerous doors. My shoes sink into the plush rugs that are strategically placed over the long stretch of dark hardwoods. I don't realize that one wheel on the suitcase is wonky until I drag it for what feels like a block. Finally, she stops in front of a closed door and waits for me to catch up.

Her hand wraps around the brushed nickel hardware. "This will be your room for the duration of your stay."

That doesn't sound ominous at all.

I nod as she thrusts open the door and steps over the threshold. My eyes widen as they rove over the interior. Again, I'm awed by the opulence. The ceiling is ridiculously high, soaring at least twenty feet. If the room wasn't so palatial, the king-sized bed with its tufted headboard trimmed with a silver-colored wood would overwhelm the space. The wall behind it is tiled in square mirrors set in a diagonal pattern. Matching silver nightstands flank the bed. A thick white carpet covers a portion of the marble floor with tall windows that stretch from floor to ceiling. During the day, I can only imagine the sunlight that must pour in.

There's a short staircase on the other side of the bed. I'm curious where it leads. Perhaps an escape hatch?

I almost snort.

More like wishful thinking.

The sumptuous surroundings are almost enough to distract me from the fact that I've been forced into this living arrangement.

"Do you have any questions?"

Startled out of my cursory inspection, I swing around with a million perched on the tip of my tongue. Instead of giving voice to them, I shake my head.

She takes a step toward the hallway before stopping. "Forgive me, but it just occurred to me that I failed to introduce myself earlier. I'm Mrs. Fieber, house manager for the Rothchild family. If you need anything, all you have to do is ask."

Even though the offer has been issued, Mrs. Fieber doesn't strike me as the kind of woman who would welcome questions, comments, or demands. She looks like she should be commanding an army through enemy territory. Or maybe working at a maximum-security prison. For some reason, that image sticks in my brain.

When I stare mutely, she raises her severely plucked brows, and I jerk my head into a tight nod. Without another word, she strides to the door before closing it firmly behind her. Now that I'm alone, the breath rushes from my body until my lungs are completely emptied.

It's tempting to fly across the room and shake the door handle to confirm my prisoner status. Am I trapped in this gilded cage or free to come and go as I please? Maybe that should have been my first question.

I force myself to the sleek silver bench at the end of the bed before collapsing on top of it. My gaze wanders around the room, soaking in all the elaborate details. My brain is operating on sensory overload. It's almost too much to absorb. Anything more and I'll splinter apart. And much like Humpty Dumpty, I'll never be put back together again.

A mirthless chuckle slides from my lips.

Fucking Grandma Rose.

This is all her fault.

Dad is gone, and I'm being forced to live with the Rothchilds. At some point, I'll marry Kingsley so my family can keep ownership of Hawthorne Industries. I don't give a crap about the stupid company. I never did. I wish it were possible to walk away, but Keaton won't allow that to happen. And neither will the specifications of Grandma Rose's will.

Thoughts of my father are enough to leave me gasping for air. A tightness develops in my chest before slowly spreading throughout my body like a virus. It feels as if I'm being suffocated from the inside out. I open my mouth, but I'm not able to draw in enough oxygen, and my head grows light. Little spots dance before my eyes.

The spacious room turns oppressive as the walls press in on me.

I need to get out of here.

It's unsteadily that I rise to my feet before staggering to the balcony door. With fingers that tremble, I grab the handle before yanking it open and stumbling onto the porch that stretches across the back of the house. Stone balusters line the perimeter with tall potted plants that are strategically spaced out across the width. Chairs are arranged in small clusters with a few loungers and cafe-style tables that allow for relaxation, while surveying the property and the golf course beyond the trees. With the darkness that has fallen, that's not possible.

My fingernails claw at the railing as I squeeze my eyes shut and inhale deep gulps of air. Blackness swirls around me, threatening to suck me under. When my knees weaken, my grip tightens.

Don't pass out.

Don't pass out.

Don't pass out.

I chant the mantra and concentrate on regulating my airflow until the muscles in my chest loosen and my breathing isn't so agonizing. Only then does the laughter and voices floating on the breeze push their way into my consciousness. I force my eyes open and survey the scene below. Much like our house next door, there's a custom pool, hot tub, and cozy seating arrangement. Orange flames twist and dance from the firepit as moonlight slants across the concrete. The perimeter is illuminated by tiny lights that dot the darkness.

I blink as my eyes adjust to the inky blackness, and the people below coalesce before taking shape. At least a dozen are reclining over the chairs and the curved sectional that surrounds the firepit. I'm not able to make out all the faces, but the ones I can see, I recognize from school.

It's the dark-haired boy sprawled on a plush armchair who snags my attention. Once my gaze locks on him, glancing away becomes impossible. Even in the shadowy darkness, I'm aware of the moment his interest is drawn to me. The energy we always generate careens through me, lighting up every cell in my body. Maybe I don't want to feel the spark of attraction, but it's there, humming beneath the surface. Once my gaze is captured, Kingsley doesn't relinquish his hold as he lifts a green bottle of beer to his lips before taking a long swig. I can almost imagine the way his thickly corded throat constricts with each swallow of golden liquid.

With my attention focused solely on him, I don't immediately realize there's a girl nestled on his lap. My breath becomes wedged in my throat when she tosses her head back. Long blond hair cascades around her shoulders as it catches the firelight.

Sloane.

Of course it would be her.

Bitterness gathers inside me, which makes no sense. My feelings for this boy should have been extinguished. It's disconcerting to realize that they aren't. That it's possible for him to lash out and hurt me.

Even though the evening has plunged into the low sixties, a thin T-shirt clings to Sloane's curvy breasts as her long, sun-kissed legs peek out from tiny shorts. As if to drive the knife in deeper, she burrows against the wide expanse of his chest before slipping her arms around his neck.

The pain that explodes in my heart feels as excruciating as a gunshot wound. I know precisely what it's like to be so close to him that you feel as if you are one. If I squeeze my eyes tight, the scent of his woodsy cologne would wrap around me, shielding me from the world.

Only now, he's the one I need protection from.

That thought is enough to snap me out of the trance that had fallen over me. It's carefully that I retreat from the railing. When the connection between us is finally severed and the party below disappears, I step inside the bedroom, shuttering myself away. After locking the balcony door, I sag against it and wonder how I'll ever survive this.

16

My eyelids fly open as a heavy weight settles on top of me. With a gasp, I stare into narrowed eyes that are inches from my own. It's enough to send the breath rushing from my lungs.

Kingsley.

My palms flatten against the sinewy strength of his naked chest as I attempt to push him away. No matter how hard I shove, he doesn't budge. Kingsley outweighs me by a solid hundred pounds. It's like trying to move a brick wall. Frustration bubbles up at my own powerlessness, and I ball my hands, pummeling his chest, wanting to inflict as much damage on him as he so easily does to me.

His lips curve into a smirk at my feeble attack. In the blink of an eye, he shackles my wrists with his fingers and drags them above my head before pinning them near the tufted headboard.

"Get off!" I growl, attempting to buck him from my body even though I know deep down it's not possible.

"What's wrong, baby girl?" He lowers his face to mine until he can nip at the curve of my jawline. His mouth grazes my cheekbone before settling at my ear. "You don't want me anymore?"

"No!" There's a hitch in my voice I'm unable to disguise.

"Liar." Even though I can't see the curve of his lips, smugness weaves its way through his voice.

"Why are you here?"

"Isn't that obvious?" There's a pause. "You belong to me, and I'm taking what's mine."

A thick shudder works its way through my body. I don't know whether it's from fear or longing, and I'm too chickenshit to find out. Deep down, I'm frightened of the truth. Then I'll have no choice but to admit I still want him. "Go fuck Sloane," I hiss.

He laughs, and the deep timbre of it grates against my core, unintentionally setting off a million little sparks. "That sounds suspiciously like jealousy."

"Don't flatter yourself." He's right, damn him. Not only do I hate myself for not being able to hide it better but also him for needing to point it out.

"Is that so?" Challenge fills his voice, and only then do I realize my misstep. "Maybe I should prove what a little liar you are."

I press my lips together, refusing to get drawn into his insidious games. He's proven time and time again that I'm no match for him. Kingsley always wins at all costs. He won't be satisfied until he completely obliterates me. In my weakened state, it won't take much.

When I remain silent, he yanks my wrists together. His fingers are long enough to secure both with one hand to free up the other. The knowledge of what is sure to come is enough to renew my struggles.

In a matter of weeks, his touch has become an addiction. One stroke of his lips or fingers across my flesh, and I lose all sense of reason. It's demoralizing to realize that as much as I want to hate him for everything that has happened between us, between our families, I'm not there yet.

Will I ever be?

Calloused fingers shove at the soft cotton T-shirt I wore to bed. The fabric slides up my belly, rib cage, and over my chest until I'm exposed to his searching gaze. A steady stream of moonlight floods into the space, illuminating our bodies in a silvery glow.

His nimble fingers zero in on one breast, tweaking the nipple until it stiffens beneath his relentless touch. Tiny sparks of arousal burst to life. My body is like dry kindling. It won't take much for it to catch fire. If he keeps this up, it'll only be a matter of time before I go up in a blaze of glory.

And Kingsley understands this. It's that knowledge that spurs me into action, and I squirm beneath him, attempting to evade his intimate touch. My teeth sink into my lower lip, wanting to keep the guttural sounds buried deep inside my chest.

I can't stop him from taking what he wants, but I refuse to give him anything more than that. I'll be damned if he sees exactly how much he still affects me. When it comes to Kingsley, my body has always been traitorous. No matter what happens between us, I can't stop wanting him. It's disconcerting to realize that might never change. That I will always be held captive by this boy.

When I refuse to give him the reaction he seeks, a growl rumbles up from deep within his throat as he pinches one of the tiny buds. Unable to stand the pain-infused pleasure he's forcing upon me, a whimper escapes.

Why does it have to be like this between us?

A combustible energy impossible to extinguish.

Kingsley's face drops to my chest. He circles the stiffened peak with the tip of his nose before drawing it deep into his mouth. The sharp tugs send ripples of ecstasy through my body, making my core throb with need. I can't help but shift impatiently beneath him as my hips roll against his. With a painful jerk of his lips, he releases my nipple with a soft pop before his fingers pluck at the other.

I want to scream as pleasure unfurls inside me. All he's done is toy with my breasts, and I'm already on the verge of losing it. Over the past month, Kingsley has gone to great lengths to learn my body. He knows exactly what to do to stoke the flames. And I was so free with my responses, loving everything he did. Not once did it occur to me that he might turn around and use this information against me. I would have guarded my reactions better.

"Kingsley..."

"Mmm." His teeth flash in the moonlight. "You know how much I love it when you beg for my dick."

Oh God...

"No." My head twists from side to side, wishing I could take it back. "I'm not—"

"Are you sure about that?" A knowing chuckle slides from his lips. "The needy little noises you're making sound an awful lot like pleading to me. It's been much too long since I filled your mouth and pussy." His fingers wrap around the stiff little bud he's been toying with before giving it a vicious pinch.

Another burst of pleasure-spiked pain reverberates through me, forcing me closer to the edge.

"Do you miss my cock, baby girl?"

"No."

Liar.

With his gaze locked on mine, a wicked smile curls around the edges of his lips before he repeatedly nips at my breast. It doesn't take long until I'm squirming and whimpering beneath him. Desire pulses through me like that of a steady drumbeat. When I can't stand another moment, he sucks the tortured tip so deep into his mouth that it feels like he will never relinquish me.

Before I realize what is happening, he rips the shirt from my body before tossing it to the floor. With both hands, he cups my breasts, squeezing the softness. The hatred filling his eyes is almost jarring. I never wanted it to be like this between us. In the beginning, I had naïvely thought we could overcome the past, but it's become obvious that will never happen. There is too much ugly history that sits between us like a gaping chasm. The best thing we can do is leave each other alone.

"Why are you doing this?" I whisper.

His fingers still as he searches my eyes in the darkness. "Haven't you figured that out yet?"

I shake my head, bracing myself for his response.

"I'm going to ruin you for anyone else."

Laughter bubbles up in my throat. Doesn't he realize that I've already been wrecked?

"Now turn over." The heaviness of his weight disappears until he is no longer straddling my torso.

When I remain motionless, his hands lock around my hips before he flips me over and drags me down the mattress until I'm folded on my knees with my ass in the air. The side of my face hits the pillow, and a shuddering breath gets knocked from my chest.

A thin pair of cotton panties are all that bars him from full access.

His wide palms settle on each cheek before he gives them a rough squeeze. I close my eyes, desperately trying to block out his touch. If anything, it has the opposite effect, intensifying the sensation.

My muscles lock as I wait for the contact to turn punishing. It's only a matter of time before he lashes out, wanting to inflict as much damage as possible. Which is exactly why his gentleness confounds me. The way he caresses me, playing with my flesh, stoking the need that has been rioting dangerously beneath the surface, feels nothing short of amazing.

Kingsley once told me that he could be tender or punishing. He accused me of enjoying both, and he wasn't wrong. I like the pleasure-infused pain more than I should. It's almost as if he's trying to lull me into a false sense of security. I have to fight the natural inclination of my body to give in and enjoy the way he's stroking me.

Even knowing the game he's playing, it doesn't take long before my muscles are loosening beneath his fingers, surrendering to the masterful way he touches me. It takes a moment to realize that his hands have disappeared. As I question the coolness that now surrounds me, Kingsley grips the elastic band of my panties, and in one swift motion, he tears the material from my body.

A thick coil of tension settles in my core as his palm cracks one cheek before giving the same treatment to the other side. I press my lips together to stop the moan from escaping.

What the hell is wrong with me?

Enjoying this is all kinds of wrong. Yet that knowledge doesn't make a difference. No matter how he torments me, I enjoy it.

Would beg for it.

There's no point in lying to myself about how easily he's able to arouse me. As if to drive home the fact that he understands it as well, Kingsley smacks my backside a few more times with the flat of his palm until my cheeks feel like they're on fire. Only then does his hand flatten over me. The coolness of his skin dulls the fire radiating from within. Almost gently he massages the twin globes, and once again, my body surrenders to him.

He could do anything, and you would still fall apart beneath his fingertips.

It's a disturbing realization.

As he kneads my flesh, the thumbs of each hand graze the outer lips of my pussy. The touch grows closer until I can't stop from straining toward him. Somehow, he's able to break down all of my resistance until nothing is left. Until I am nothing more than a quivering mass of hormones greedy for his every caress. My brain is too clouded with pleasure to dwell on the ramifications of my actions.

On the next slow pass, his fingers sink deep inside me.

"I've missed this," he mutters.

For the first time in nearly a week, my mind clicks off, and I allow myself to soak up all the delicious sensations that ricochet through my body. It doesn't take long for an orgasm to build like a storm. When his fingers disappear, a whimper of protest escapes.

His hand migrates from my pussy to circle around the tightly puckered ring of muscle bared for his scrutiny. "I've missed this as well."

I've missed it, too.

Unwilling to give voice to those private thoughts, I keep them trapped inside where they can't do any further damage.

The thick finger buried inside my sheath now presses insistently against my anus. There's a slight burn as he breaches the barrier, pushing inside the tight space. When I whimper, he makes a soothing noise, rubbing soft circles across my lower back with his other hand.

The finger buried inside stills, giving me time to adjust to the intrusion. It doesn't take long for me to grow impatient. Only then does he surge forward. Nerve endings spark to life, and my eyes roll up inside my head as a throaty moan spills unwantedly from my lips.

"You like that, don't you?" Satisfaction brims in his voice. He knows what he does to me, how his touch affects me, how it teases out all the indecency within me before dragging it into the light.

"Yes." I don't bother to lie.

When he attempts to withdraw, my muscles clench around him, desperate to keep him locked inside me. Instead of pulling all the way out, he presses forward, sliding in deeper this time. It takes everything I have inside not to moan with ecstasy. He repeats the process, driving his finger farther with each new thrust. The rhythmic motion lulls my body into a contented state of bliss as he stretches the muscles with his finger. Once his thick digit is seated deep inside, his other hand wraps possessively around the curve of my ass as if to hold me in place.

"This is mine," he growls, squeezing my backside as if to claim ownership.

I hate that those words settle something deep inside me.

When I remain silent, his fingers bite into my flesh. "Did you hear me?"

"Yes," I yelp.

"Good." He deepens the penetration, his finger moving in a steady tempo as his other hand slides toward my clit before rubbing insistent circles against it.

"How much do you want me, Summer?" The slyness of his voice wraps around me, cocooning me in pleasure.

When I press my lips together, refusing to answer, the pressure on my clit increases, and I groan, moments away from splintering apart.

"Tell me," he demands, pausing as the finger filling my backside slides from me before surging forward again. A heartbeat passes as the intensity spiraling within becomes almost too much to bear. At any moment, I'll fall to pieces beneath his fingertips. "I want your words."

The breath lodges at the back of my throat as waves of ecstasy ripple through me. "So much," I reluctantly whisper, giving in to him. I'm so close to falling apart. Just a little bit more...

"Then beg for it."

No.

My teeth sink into my bottom lip, unwilling to allow a single sound to escape. No matter how much I want the pleasure he's capable of doling out, I refuse to plead. When I remain silent, the delicious pressure on my clit and anus increases, pushing me relentlessly closer to the precipice. As I'm about to dive headfirst over the cliff, he pulls back. It's like a ferocious storm gathering strength only to fall apart at the very last second before fading into nothingness.

And then it starts all over again. Climbing and building until it reaches a fever pitch.

"Do you want to come?" he murmurs, breaking the heavy silence that has fallen over us.

"Yes," I whimper, needing him to shove me over the edge so I'm able to forget for a few mindless moments that we are nothing more than enemies.

That we will *always* be enemies.

"All you have to do is say the magic words," he purrs.

A moan slips free as his fingers pick up speed. I can't take much more of this sweet torment.

I can't.

"Please." I hate myself for giving in to his demands.

"Please, what?"

I should have known it wouldn't be that easy.

"Please," I gulp, unable to stop the rest from tumbling out in a rush, "make me come."

His fingers turn relentless, and I squeeze my eyes tightly shut as intensity crashes over me. As I stand perched on the cliff, my orgasm seems imminent. The air becomes trapped in my lungs as every muscle coils tight with greedy anticipation. There has been no joy to be found over the last week. *I need this.* I need to feel the hot licks of pleasure pumping through my body, making me forget all the anguish. If only for a few fleeting seconds.

My fingers tangle in the sheets as I arch, and then...

Nothing.

When his fingers vanish from my body, my eyes spring open, and a strangled gasp falls from my lips as the force building disintegrates, leaving behind an ache so vicious that it borders on agonizing.

"On second thought, I'll follow your suggestion and find Sloane." A ruthless cruelty threads its way through his voice as he rises from the bed. "Sleep well."

He saunters to the door before pausing over the threshold. "Oh, and welcome to Rothchild Mansion." With that, he closes the door behind him, locking me inside the dark space.

Sexual frustration swells, but there is no outlet. Instead, it settles in my core. The stifled breath filling my lungs escapes in a rush as I flip onto my back and yank the covers over my naked body.

I'm an idiot for not expecting this. I turn onto my side and curl up into a tight ball, staring sightlessly at the wall of windows. Kingsley's new mission in life will be to break me.

And I can't allow that to happen.

17

*S*ix o'clock rolls around much too fast. I've barely closed my eyes, and the alarm is going off the next morning. As tempting as it is to skip school, that's not possible unless I'm in the mood to repeat senior year, and honestly, I'd rather slit my throat than spend any more time than necessary at Hawthorne Prep.

For just a moment, I stare at the vast stretch of ceiling that soars over my head. It's been exactly one week since Dad died. A deep pang of sadness fills my heart.

How have seven days already slipped by?

The first couple were shrouded in numbness. There had been a funeral to plan and Mom to take care of. A flurry of activity that seemed unending. Now that Dad has been laid to rest in a family plot outside of Hawthorne, the world is once again pressing in at the edges. The arrival of Keaton's contract last night signaled that life refuses to be ignored any longer.

With a huff of breath, I throw off the covers and roll from the mattress. Even though the bed is comfortable, I tossed and turned after Kingsley left me high and dry.

All right, not so dry.

More like drenched and aching.

As much as I tried not to think about him, the insidious little voice inside my head kept wondering if he had followed through with his plans. Did he find Sloane and touch her the same way?

After everything that has happened between us, it should be a relief to have his attention turned elsewhere. But I'm ashamed to admit it's the opposite. He's the first guy I've ever felt this way about. If it were anyone else, I could walk away without a second thought. But I can't shut down the feelings that have been steadily growing inside me. The best I can hope for is that with time, they'll wither and die. With the way he's acting, it shouldn't take long.

With a stretch, I head to the bathroom. The private en suite makes mine at home look like a dump. It's at least three times the size, with sleek marble tile and expensive finishes. The shower is a glass enclosure with jets that line the interior walls. There's also a massive soaking tub spacious enough for half a dozen people. It's like a mini swimming pool. Normally an amenity like that would thrill me, but I'm unable to summon up the enthusiasm.

Once finished with the shower, I blow-dry my hair before pulling it up into a ponytail. Five minutes later, I'm dressed in my school uniform. It's almost startling when I catch a glimpse of my reflection in the mirror.

Holy crap, I look like hammered horseshit.

Why am I surprised that my features are so drawn and pale? This week has been a fucking nightmare, and now, with my new living arrangement, it won't improve anytime soon.

If ever.

I grab my makeup bag and dab a bit of concealer under my eyes before rubbing it in. Then I add a smidge of bronzer to my cheekbones for color. Last comes the lip gloss and mascara. With a critical eye, I assess my image for a second time.

Sure, it's better, but that's not saying much.

Once all of my emotions have been locked down tight, I grab my backpack and head for the door. I haven't ventured out of this room since Mrs. Fieber escorted me here last evening. Maybe I'm not a prisoner, but that's the way it feels. It's almost a relief to escape to Hawthorne Prep for the day.

A gurgle of laughter rises in my throat. That's something I never thought I'd say.

Instead of sauntering into the hallway, I hesitantly peek around the doorframe only to find it empty. The plan is to sneak home and check on Mom before grabbing a ride to school with Austin. With my ears pricked for the slightest sound, I slink through the open and airy second-floor gallery. It takes a couple of minutes to arrive at the staircase before jogging down the wide curving steps. My fingers trail over the wrought-iron railing as I hit the last tread.

The front door is less than thirty feet away. I can practically taste the freedom that lies beyond the threshold. As I reach for the brushed nickel handle, a deep voice cuts through the deafening silence, and all my hopes crash to my toes.

"Where do you think you're off to?" He pauses for a beat. "If I didn't know better, I'd almost think you were trying to sneak out."

My arm drops to my side as I spin around and face a rather bored-looking Kingsley who lounges against the far wall. He's wearing his crisp white button-down and perfectly pressed khakis. His normally short hair is longer than when we met at the beach in June and has been left carelessly disheveled. I tighten my fingers in an effort not to reach out and plow them through the thick strands, shoving them away from his eyes.

All the emotion I worked so hard to tamp down riots dangerously beneath the surface, threatening to break loose. As much as I want to despise him, I'm unable to do so. Kingsley Rothchild is like a poisonous drug pumping wildly through my veins. I crave him even though I know he's a detriment to my health.

If that knowledge doesn't make me a lost cause, I don't know what does.

It takes effort to snap back to the present and not lose myself in the sight of him. I straighten to my full height and say in halting tones, "I'm going to check on Mom and then catch a ride to school with Austin."

"Actually," he says, lips quirking with amusement, "that's not what you'll be doing." There's a beat of silence. "You'll drive with me."

And just like that, my temper explodes.

Goddamn him!

"No!" All the anger and frustration from the past week bubbles up like a geyser. Instead of stuffing it down, I allow it to boil over. So much has already been taken away, I refuse to lose my freedom on top of everything else. "You can't tell me what to do!"

A challenging light fills his eyes as he pushes away from the wall and saunters closer. "Wanna bet? You'll ride to school with *me* and only *me*. End of discussion."

I stomp my foot.

Who does this guy think he is?

He can't snap his fingers and demand that I fall in line. There is nothing for him to hold over my head or force me into compliance with. I open my mouth to tell him exactly that.

In the time it takes to blink, Kingsley has me pinned against the front door. I squeak in surprise, and everything on the tip of my tongue dissolves as his fingers tangle in my ponytail before winding the thick length around his hand. The other settles over my collarbone until his fingers can splay wide at the base of my throat. I wish it were only panic that I had to swallow down as arousal flares to life deep inside my core.

A knowing smile curves his lips. The thick tension building isn't a choice. It's weeks of conditioning.

"Maybe you don't understand that the paperwork your parents signed makes you mine." The grip on my hair tightens, drawing my chin upward. "To do with what I please. Or, in your case, *not*."

My teeth clench as resentment sparks to life. "It doesn't matter what my parents agreed to. You don't own me. You will *never* own me."

He presses closer until his warm breath can feather across the outer shell of my ear. "Not only do I own your ass." The hand at my collarbone drops between us before settling against my heated center and giving it a possessive squeeze. "I own this pretty little pussy, too."

I bite back the moan building deep in my chest.

How is it possible to detest his touch yet crave it at the same time?

There was a brief period when I felt protected and cherished in his arms. That is no longer the case. When I attempt to bat his hand away, his grip tightens on both my core and hair. I gasp when he yanks my head back, exposing the delicate column of my neck before his mouth descends, settling against the frantically beating pulse.

"Don't push me, Summer," he whispers. "Or I'll make you wear the T-shirts again, so everyone knows who owns you. It seems like you might need the reminder."

Ugh. I don't even want to think about the stupid shirts he forced me to wear at school.

Without a bra.

When I remain silent, he presses a kiss against the fluttering skin before dragging his teeth across it. The scrape ignites an inferno in my panties. I squirm beneath him as unwanted desire burns through my body. His fingers bite into me before one hand snakes underneath the thin cotton of my panties, thrusting deep inside my body with one smooth stroke.

"You might hate me, but that doesn't stop you from wanting my cock." Arrogance fills his voice. "If I wanted, I could have you on your knees begging for it."

"You're wrong." The forced denial doesn't fool either one of us. We both know his assessment of the situation is spot-on. I have yet to figure out a way to turn off my feelings for him, and until I'm able to do that, I'm vulnerable to his advances.

His body shakes with undisguised laughter, and it only drives home the ridiculousness of the lie.

"We both know you would let me take you right here in the middle of the entryway. You'd get so hot that you wouldn't even give a shit if my dad or the housekeeper walked in while I was fucking you."

The bastard is probably right. One stroke of his fingers and I come undone. Trust me, I hate myself for the weakness.

He drags his fingers from my drenched body and steps away

before straightening my skirt. "Unfortunately, we don't have time to screw around."

When I stand frozen in place, he points at the floor. "Grab your backpack, and let's get moving."

My gaze drops to my feet, and I realize my school bag has slipped from my shoulder during the exchange. Carefully, I lower myself to the tile floor. As my fingers tighten around the padded strap, Kingsley presses his hand against my shoulder until I'm forced to my knees. My head jerks up in silent question.

A smirk simmers around the corners of his lips as his eyes darken with lust. My gaze becomes trapped in his heated one, rendering me powerless to look away. My mouth turns cottony as I crane my neck, attention focused solely on him. His knuckles brush over the curve of my jawline, and an unwanted shiver of desire dances down my spine.

"There's nothing I like more than when you're on your knees, worshiping your king."

When his cock jerks inches from my mouth, a fresh wave of arousal crashes over me.

How is it possible to still want him this much?

What the hell is wrong with me?

Even though the cold marble is unforgiving beneath my knees, I don't make a move to rise. I'm barely even breathing.

"Ahem."

It's the clearing of a throat that has me jerking to awareness, dispelling the thick haze of lust that had descended. Embarrassment floods through me as I scramble to my feet and clutch the bag to my chest as if that will protect me against this boy.

Ironically, nothing will keep me safe from Kingsley.

With a bland expression in place, he swings in a semicircle. I cower behind his back, unwilling to peek around his shoulder. It's humiliating that someone saw me on my knees in front of him.

"Here is the coffee and protein bar you requested."

"Excellent," he says as if nothing happened. "Thanks, Mrs. Fieber."

After the footsteps fade from the foyer, Kingsley turns to me. Only this time, there's a travel mug in one hand and a bar in the other. "You'll have to eat breakfast in the car."

Unsure what to make of the strange gesture, I stare at the offerings. Much to my mother's consternation, I rarely eat breakfast. The container of coffee, on the other hand, I'm all but dying for. I can practically taste the bitter brew on my tongue before it slides down my throat, warming me from the inside out. Except I'm reluctant to take anything from him. Kingsley is the last person I want to be indebted to.

When it becomes apparent that I won't accept them, he invades my personal space. "Take it, Summer." He pushes both the bar and coffee toward me. "Haven't you figured out that this isn't a battle you'll win?"

Of course I have, but that doesn't mean I'm going to simply roll over and give in without a fight.

Although...I'm not going to lie—the coffee is calling to me with its siren song. Arabica, if my nose isn't deceiving me. I guess there's no reason to punish myself by refusing his offer of java.

Decision made, I swipe the travel mug and bar from him before greedily taking my first sip of the dark liquid. I wince as it scalds my tongue, but it tastes so damn good. And I wasn't wrong, it's arabica. If anything, it'll help sharpen my wits when dealing with Kingsley.

Clearly, I'm in desperate need of that.

I'm almost surprised when he doesn't gloat. Instead, he grabs his backpack along with the keys from a large silver bowl on top of the polished wood credenza before yanking open the front door and waving me through as if he were raised with manners.

Ha! More like raised by wolves.

Feral ones.

I glare before taking another deep drink. When he arches a brow, I stalk through the wide opening to his glossy red convertible parked in the circular drive. Unlike our weathered driveway, Kingsley's is decidedly fancier. There are gray bricks formed to make enormous squares. Each configuration is edged with a perfect row of neatly trimmed grass. The center of the drive overflows with a manicured garden.

Once at the vehicle, Kingsley reaches out, popping open the door. I wish he would knock off the gallant behavior. Gestures like these only confuse the hell out of me. He needs to act like the asshole he truly is. It'll make it so much easier to annihilate the feelings that continue to plague me.

As much as I would like to ignore the kindness, my own manners won't allow me to do so. "Thank you," I mutter begrudgingly before sliding onto the black leather.

"Ouch." Humor laces his voice. "Was that as painful as it sounded?"

He has no idea. Before I can fire off a snide comment, he closes me inside the tight space, then saunters to the other side and settles next to me. Within a matter of moments, he's turning the key, and the engine is purring to life. I place the coffee between my knees before dropping my backpack to the floorboards and yanking open the zipper. The protein bar gets shoved into the pocket for later.

Or maybe never.

Screw Kingsley Rothchild. He can't tell me what to do.

Before I can straighten, he plucks the coffee from my knees, swiftly transferring it to the other hand.

"Hey!" My head jerks up as I glare. "What are you doing?"

"Making sure you eat." He grabs his aviators and slides them onto the bridge of his nose. "Finish the bar, and you'll get the coffee. Simple as that."

"I'm not a breakfast eater," I growl with frustration.

I've spent less than fifteen minutes in his presence, and I'm already tired of him telling me what to do. He may think the contract my parents signed makes him the boss of me, but he's wrong.

"Guess you're gonna start." He doesn't wait for a response. "Even if it's a crappy bar." From behind his mirrored sunglasses, his gaze drifts over my body like a physical caress. "You've lost weight."

"Whether or not I have is none of your damn business," I shoot back. Seriously, who does this guy think he is?

"Wrong. It's *my* business to be all up in *your* business."

Grrrr.

"Go to hell," I snap.

With a smirk, he shifts toward me and strokes his thumb over my lower lip. "You still don't get it, do you?" Instead of knocking his hand away, I sit transfixed by the possessive look that fills his eyes as he stares at my mouth. "I'm the one in control. I'm the one who makes the decisions. If I tell you to do something, you do it. Understand?"

Gahhhh.

I hate the way he scrambles my senses.

When I fail to respond, he continues. "Now, are you going to be a good little girl and eat your breakfast, or should I dump your coffee out the window?"

What!

That threat has me blinking out of the stupor that had fallen over me. "You wouldn't dare!"

His teeth flash in the morning sunlight as it climbs over the horizon. "We both know that I would."

He's right, we do. If there's a way to piss me off, he'll find it. I hate that he holds so much power over me.

Without another word, he stabs the button on the door handle and the glass disappears, allowing the chilly morning air to sweep through the interior. Kingsley twists off the top before holding the container outside the vehicle. "What's it gonna be?"

Goddamn him!

"Tick tock. You have three seconds to make a decision, or I'll make it for you. Although, you won't be happy about it."

"I hate you!" I hiss in an effort to delay the inevitable.

"Two," he continues as if I didn't say anything at all.

"Why are you such a jerk?"

"One."

He turns his arm so that the mug makes a slow rotation.

Before one precious drop can fall, I yell, "Fine! I'll eat the stupid bar!"

I hate him.

Hot tears sting the back of my eyelids as I wrench open the zipper of my backpack and dig through the pocket until my fingers close around the slim bar. Unwilling to watch him take pleasure in my capitulation, I stare straight ahead before ripping off the wrapper and shoving the pressed granola into my mouth. I taste nothing, swallowing the first piece and forcing down the rest. Once it's gone, I shift on my seat and glare before throwing the empty package at his chest. "Happy?"

"Ecstatic."

"Give me the coffee," I demand.

With a self-satisfied smirk, he hands over the mug. I snatch it from him before he can change his mind. With my back to him, I stare broodingly out the window and take a deep drink of the dark beverage. By the time I settle against the leather, we're pulling out of the subdivision and onto the main country road that leads to Hawthorne Prep.

If this is a sign as to how the rest of the day will go, I'll never make it through unscathed. Kingsley will fight me at every turn to make my life hell.

And there's not a damn thing I can do about it.

18

By the time we roll through the gated drive onto school property, I'm more than ready to escape Kingsley's insufferable presence. Even though we have first hour together, I need the ten minutes before the bell rings to collect myself, or I'll lose it. The moment he parks the Mustang at the front of the lot, I grab the handle, ready to bolt. Before I can pop the door and escape, Kingsley's fingers tighten around my upper arm.

"Not so fast."

Exasperation burns through me like molten lava, scorching my insides. My brows slam together as he shackles me in place. It's almost impossible to ignore the electricity zipping through my veins. "Excuse me?"

"You'll stay by my side."

I draw in a deep breath, attempting to calm everything that riots painfully inside.

No!

No!

No!

"You stopped me from going home this morning," I grit between clenched teeth. "I need to talk with Austin."

"You can see him later."

A scream builds in my chest. Any moment, I'm going to open my mouth, and everything will pour out. *"King—"*

His hand snakes out before wrapping around the back of my neck and tugging me toward him until his warm, minty breath can feather over my lips. "That's right, I'm your king, and you'll do what I say. Got it?"

A whimper slides from my lips as his grip tightens.

"Mmm, I love the little noises you make. They get me hard. Wanna feel?"

"Stop," I whisper, trying to keep the tremble in my body from working its way through my voice.

His teeth snap, nipping at my bottom lip. The sting of the encounter leaves me panting before he draws the fullness into his mouth. As I'm about to self-combust, he releases the plump flesh. A zing of arousal shoots through me.

"Is that what you really want?" A wicked glint enters his eyes. "For me to leave you alone?"

"Yes."

No.

I don't know.

Why does he muddle everything inside my head? Decisions that should be easy now seem riddled with complications.

"Such a little liar," he says, pulling away before flicking his finger against the tip of my nose. "I underestimated you once. It won't be a mistake I make again."

The heartless comment is like a bucket of freezing water dumped over my head. Any heat that had gathered between my legs vanishes. I stay rooted on my seat as he exits the Mustang. It's the slamming of the car door that jolts me from my stupor. A shiver works its way through me as I grab the door handle for the second time and pull it open, rising unsteadily to my feet. Kingsley waits near the hood of the car. Even though I want to fly past him, I force my feet to shuffle in his direction. When I'm within striking distance, he throws a muscled arm around my shoulders and hauls me close.

Too close.

The woodsy scent of his aftershave assaults my senses, making me almost dizzy with it. All I want to do is inhale a big breath of him to savor. Confusion swirls through me. After everything that has happened since my father's death, how can the attraction be so powerful?

Is it even possible to turn off this strange need that courses through me?

"Smile, baby girl," he whispers in my ear, "everyone is watching."

From beneath the thick fringe of my lashes, my gaze darts around the impeccably manicured front lawn. He's right. Most of the students we walk past turn to gawk at us.

No, not us.

Me.

Their open perusal only heightens my growing discomfort. These people aren't my friends. And neither is Kingsley. It would behoove me to remember that. We're enemies forced to act out this tragic farce. Possibly for the rest of our lives.

"Here's the thing," he continues blandly, interrupting the frantic whirl of my thoughts as we walk toward the main entrance of the school, "every king needs a queen, but queens can be cast aside." When his breath drifts over my cheek, I stumble. "Don't ever forget that these are my loyal subjects, and they'll follow my lead."

I swallow down my growing nausea.

Sadly, he's not wrong.

Once inside the building, my pace quickens. I need to get away from him. As people congregate in the corridor, my gaze fastens on to my brother, who lounges near my locker. Relief floods through me at the sight of him. The moment he spots us, he pushes away from the metal door and straightens to his full height. From the harsh expression that falls over Austin's face, it's easy to see that his fury from last night has yet to recede, and he's spoiling for a fight.

If he looks hard enough, Kingsley will give it to him. Only the dark-haired boy at my side won't suffer the same consequences as my brother. That's something I can't allow to happen. No matter how tenuous the peace might be, I need to keep it.

Instead of walking by when we reach my locker, Kingsley stops about ten feet from my twin before jerking me into his arms. My breasts bump against the hard lines of his chest, and I steel myself, afraid of how the moment will unfold. We both know this little show of dominance is all about taunting Austin and provoking a reaction from him.

I hope my brother realizes it and doesn't take the bait.

One hand settles under my chin before tipping it upward. Barely am I able to draw in a full breath before his lips crash onto mine. When I gasp, his tongue slips inside my mouth to tangle with my own. For one fleeting moment, the world falls away, and the past ceases to exist. It's just the two of us. The only thing that matters is the here and now.

The stroke of his velvety softness against—

A squeak of surprise escapes from me when Kingsley is ripped away, and I'm left standing alone in the middle of the crowded hall.

"Leave her the fuck alone, Rothchild!" Austin snarls, sounding like a rabid animal.

The past week has pushed him past the point of no return. The tiniest of infractions will send him careening over the edge.

A knowing grin slides across Kingsley's handsome face as his voice turns threatening. *"Or what? What will you do?"*

When Austin takes a menacing step toward the other boy, I scramble to get between them. It takes all of my strength to shove my brother back a step and out of harm's way.

"Please," I plead, turning to him, *"don't."*

"Yeah, Hawthorne," Kingsley interrupts, humor dancing in his voice, "listen to your sister."

A deep growl of frustration rumbles up from Austin's chest as he pushes me back a step before lunging at Kingsley, who laughs and saunters down the hall toward his locker.

"I really fucking hate that prick," my brother grumbles.

"I know." I should echo the sentiment. Instead, I can't bring myself to voice the words.

Austin glares until Kingsley disappears from sight. Only then does his gaze soften as it returns to me, scanning my body from head to toe as if I might not be in one piece. "Are you okay?"

My guess is that he'll go after Kingsley if he finds one damn hair on my head out of place. Normally, I'm the one trying to smooth the way for him, but Austin is just as protective of me. To hear our mother tell it, we've had each other's backs since inside the womb.

"I'm fine," I say, brushing off his concern and hoisting my smile. It might not be possible to forget about Kingsley or this mess, but that doesn't mean I can't try.

One meaty hand reaches out and yanks me to him. A moment later, I'm enveloped in a tight embrace. "Missed you," he says gruffly. "The house is lonely as hell."

Everything in me wilts as I wrap my arms around him and tighten my hold. Yeah, my situation sucks, but Austin is the one I feel sorry for. He's been left behind, forced to take care of everything until Mom can pull herself together.

The longer I stay in his comforting embrace, the more emotion hurtles to the surface. And I can't have that. Everything needs to stay buried where it belongs. It takes effort to untangle myself from him. "How's Mom?"

His expression becomes inscrutable as he shrugs. "The same."

"Did you tell her that I'm now staying with the Rothchilds?"

"No." Guilt flickers across his face. "There wasn't time. She only roused long enough to eat a couple of bites of toast." He glances away as one hand goes to the back of his neck. "I have no idea if she even recognized me. She's so out of it."

I gnaw my lower lip and formulate a plan. "I'll stop home after school and tell her what's going on."

Concern flickers across his face. "Do you think it'll send her spiraling?"

I really hope not. My belly pinches at the thought of Mom deteriorating any further. Austin and I can only hold things together for so long. Not only does Mom need to snap out of it and take control, but she also needs to get me out of this mess before it's too late.

"Summer, you're here!" Everly's voice cuts through the chatter of the hallway.

I turn as she throws her arms around my shoulders and pulls me in for a hug.

"I'm so sorry about your dad," she whispers against my ear. "Are you all right?" She separates herself enough to search my gaze. Before I can respond, she winces and shakes her head. "Sorry, stupid question. Of course, you're not. How could you be?"

For the second time in a matter of minutes, emotion rockets to the surface. Uncomfortable with the possibility of it breaking loose and wreaking havoc, I disentangle myself from her. Instead of an actual answer, I give my new friend a tight smile. As much as I appreciate her kindness, I can't talk about my father.

Not here.

Not now.

Austin glances at the clock hanging in the hallway. "Come on, we better get moving, or we'll be late for first hour."

I nod, unaware that the two-minute warning bell has already rung and the congestion in the corridor has thinned considerably.

"See you at lunch?" he asks, searching my gaze for chinks in my armor.

Ugh.

Lunch.

"Yup, I'll be there." Even the thought of having to endure the thirty-minute period with Kingsley is enough to fill me with dread. After forcing me to walk in with him this morning, there's no way in hell he'll allow me to sit by myself.

I quickly twist the combination of my locker and grab my books as my brother takes off down the hall. My legs feel wooden as I force myself to first hour.

As soon as we cross over the threshold into Ms. Pettijohn's room, my gaze gets snagged by the dark-haired boy. It's a surprise to find him here, already lounging at his desk with his long legs stretched out in front of him and a slight smile curving his lips.

For a heartbeat, my mind tumbles back to the first time we met at the beach. How effortless everything seemed between us. How much I liked him and couldn't wait to spend more time together. I was crushed when my family ended up leaving unexpectedly and I wasn't able to say goodbye.

Guess the joke is on me.

"What is Sloane doing?" Everly whispers furiously in my ear.

The memories disintegrate into nothingness as the sight before me takes shape. I blink and find the blonde perched on the top of Kingsley's desk. The way she sits facing him, her legs straddling his thighs, gives him a perfect view up her skirt to her panties.

If she's wearing any.

The sight is enough to have bile rising sharply in my throat.

"Um, is she aware he's taken?" Everly sounds offended enough for both of us.

I should probably bring her up to speed on the situation, but an explanation stays lodged in my throat. The truth of the matter is that Kingsley is no longer my boyfriend. Maybe he never was. Maybe it was all a game.

Instead, I mutter, "Yup, she's aware."

"You need to go over there and stake your claim," she encourages. "I really hate girls that poach."

Stake my claim?

Ha!

Not a chance in hell. I wouldn't give Kingsley the satisfaction of thinking his behavior bothers me in the least. "It's fine. We all know where we stand." That's about as much of the truth as I can give her.

When I continue to stare, Sloan glances over before her lips lift into a triumphant smile.

"I don't know," Everly mutters. "She seems to think she won."

Well, if she wants to consider Kingsley a prize, then, yeah, I guess she did.

19

After fourth hour, Everly is waiting at my locker with her bagged lunch in hand. A pit the size of Texas sits at the bottom of my gut. After watching Sloane do everything possible to keep Kingsley focused on her during first hour, there's no way I can eat in the cafeteria. Worse than that, he seemed to welcome her fawning attention. It was enough to make me sick.

"You ready?" she asks.

My gaze darts away as I pull open the metal door of my locker. "If you don't mind, I'm going to work in the library instead." I pull my calc and psychology book from the metal shelf. "I've fallen behind and have a ton of work to catch up on."

Concern flashes across her face as her brow furrows. "Are you sure?"

"Yeah." I hoist my smile, not wanting her to worry. "I'm drowning in missing assignments. Thirty minutes should be enough to plow through a few of them."

"All right, if you change your mind, you know where to find me." With a quick hug, she takes off toward the cafeteria.

I release an unsteady breath as she turns the corner and disappears from sight before slamming my locker closed and heading to the library. Much like the cafeteria, the area is spacious with wood beams and gorgeous stained glass windows that allow sunlight to pour in. Rows of leather-bound volumes fill the shelves. The bookcases that line the perimeter stretch toward the ceiling, requiring one of the rolling ladders to reach the top.

With my head bent, I make my way through the maze of shelves to the very back corner. I need to regroup. Thirty minutes isn't nearly enough time to soothe all the hurt and confusion raging within, but it's all I've got.

Ever since I stepped foot on campus this morning, people have been staring like I'm a circus freak on display. I realize it's because my dad died, but it serves as an ugly reminder of my treatment during the first couple of weeks of school. Even though it's gotten better, a lot of students still avoid me. The Hawthorne family has been hated in these parts for generations and that isn't going to change overnight.

With a huff, I collapse onto a wooden chair and open my calculus textbook. I have five missing assignments that need to be turned in ASAP. Focusing on the first one forces me to stop dwelling on Dad and the state of my fractured relationship with Kingsley. For a few blissful minutes, the sorrow and grief recede enough for problem-solving skills to take over.

There's something therapeutic about working through the complicated equations. A slight sense of satisfaction fills me when I finish the first two and tackle the third. Who would have ever thought I would enjoy calculus? But you know what? In order to work out the computations, I have to concentrate. And to do that, I need to block out all the static in my head.

I'm about to wrap up the fourth problem when someone settles on the top of the table I'm camped out at. Khakis fill my line of vision as I stifle a gasp. There's no need to glance up. The delicate hair at the nape of my neck rises with awareness, tipping me off as to who I'll find.

Confirmation comes in the form of a question.

"Why isn't your ass in the cafeteria?"

My heartbeat picks up its tempo as I blank my features and force myself to meet Kingsley's gaze before waving a hand at the textbook splayed open in front of me. "I needed to catch up on some missing assignments."

"That's strange," he muses, "I don't recall giving you permission to work in the library."

Permission?

Did he really say that?

Heat slams into my cheeks as my temper ignites.

Who the hell does this guy think he is?

Stupid question.

"I don't need your *permission*," I snap. All the good vibes filling me are now long gone. A mixture of frustration and anger rushes through my veins.

"I own your ass," he reminds me with a smirk. "You need to ask permission for *everything*."

"Go to hell."

"Don't worry." He wraps his hand around my ponytail and forces my chin up. "I'll be there if I have to spend the rest of my life with you."

The poisonous barb is a direct hit. Pain explodes throughout my chest before radiating to every cell of my being. As impossible as it is, I swallow down the hurt, refusing to let him glimpse the damage he so effortlessly inflicts.

Why does the ugly comment even surprise me? I should be used to it by now.

"Then why go through with it?" I force myself to ask calmly. "Tell your father to tear up the contract."

When his grip tightens on my hair, I wince and keep my attention fastened on him. I'll be damned if I give Kingsley the satisfaction of cowering before him like a scared little girl. Maybe everyone else in this school treats him like the self-appointed king of Hawthorne Prep, but I refuse to fall in line. He's nothing more than a bully.

His mahogany-colored gaze sifts through mine. I get the feeling he's able to see way more than I'm comfortable with, and I shift on my chair.

With a grin, he shakes his head. "Nah, I don't think so."

"Why not?" Even though I knew it was a long shot, disappointment bursts like an over-inflated balloon. "If you don't want me, let me go."

Heat leaps into his eyes as he traces my lower lip with the tip of his index finger. "What? You think because I don't like you and no longer trust you, it means I don't want to fuck you senseless? Unfortunately, that's far from the case. Now that I've had a taste of that sweet pussy, I need more. And I'll have it whenever I want."

A shiver of unease scampers down my spine. As twisted as it is, my arousal ignites with his admittance.

His gaze glitters as a wicked grin flashes across his face. "What's wrong, baby girl? Getting turned on?" He pauses for a beat. "Got an itch you want me to take care of? Beg for it, and we'll see what happens. Who knows, maybe you'll get lucky."

"No, thanks. Not interested." When I shake my head, pain radiates throughout my scalp, and I flinch, instantly stilling as I remember the tight grip he has on me.

His warm breath drifts across my lips as he tilts my head. "Too bad I didn't realize what a little liar you were from the get-go. I would have done a better job of guarding myself against you." His lips twist with bitterness. "You live and learn, right?"

"I'm not a liar," I gulp, forcing down the nerves as his jaw clenches, fury igniting in his eyes.

"The hell you are." He snorts. "I was honest with you, Summer. I tried to make this shit situation work, and here you were, screwing me over from the very beginning."

His fingers tighten on my hair, and my chin rises a few more inches until my throat is bared. A whimper escapes from my mouth. A potent concoction of fear and excitement crashes through me, dampening my panties.

"You accused *me* of playing games, and it was *you* all along." The smirk that settles on his lips is full of menace and cruelty. Hatred vibrates off him in heavy waves that threaten to suffocate me. "Don't think I'll be fooled so easily again."

"That's not what happened," I whisper.

"No?" His brows rise. "Then explain it to me."

My tongue darts out to smudge my lips with moisture.

His gaze drops to the movement as rage mingles with desire. The intensity that wafts off him is almost frightening. "Do you have any idea how much it sucks to want you?"

Ignoring the question, I say, "I didn't know my parents were looking for a way to break the contract." Desperation and sadness surge through me.

Any lust that had crept over his features disappears as his expression turns threatening. *"Bullshit! You were aware of it from the beginning,"* he barks.

I flinch and shake my head as his words echo off the cavernous walls. I rack my brain, trying to remember if I passed by any students or teachers on my way through the library. Panic engulfs me. Even if people are occupying the space, none will dare to stop Kingsley. They'll turn a blind eye and walk away.

"I found out a few days before you did."

"And you said nothing?" His eyes narrow. "Not a damn word?"

Guilt floods through me as I admit, "I couldn't betray them."

"So you betrayed me instead?" The smile that flickers across his face doesn't quite reach the frigidness of his eyes. It's disconcerting how much the chilled look makes him resemble his father. "Then again, it wasn't really a betrayal, now was it? You were always looking for a way out. You led me to believe you were committed."

"That's not true!" The rest pours out in a rush. "I didn't think anything would come of it." My throat goes dry, making it impossible to swallow. "I figured it would all fall apart, and no one would ever find out that they tried to break the agreement. I didn't want to cause any more problems between our families."

"How did that work out for you?"

My shoulders slump. "Not well."

He lowers his mouth before tracing his tongue along the curve of my top lip. I can't stop myself from melting beneath the caress. My punishment is to forever want someone who loathes my very existence.

When he pulls away a fraction, I murmur brokenly, "I never meant to hurt you."

Only now do I realize how desperate I am for him to believe me. My father's death has wreaked havoc throughout my life. No longer is there anyone to lean on. As much as it pains me to admit it, I need him. I need Kingsley's strength to get me through this. As his lips hover over mine, I groan, wanting so much more. Is it possible for him to banish the grief that throbs through me like a living, breathing entity?

"You fucked me over and made a fool out of me," he whispers harshly. "When I'm done, you'll wish you'd never heard of this damn town."

I yelp when his teeth sink into my lip. Pain bursts through me, and the warm metallic taste of blood overwhelms my senses. His gaze drops to the red smear on my lip before he laves it with his tongue.

"I'll be staying after for football. When I get home, your ass better be there. Don't make me hunt you down."

He doesn't wait for a response as his grip loosens from my hair. Tears flood my eyes as he slides from the table, sauntering away. The little bit of solace I had found in the library has been shattered. And somehow, I don't think I'll ever find it again.

As the door slams shut in the distance, my gaze falls to the table and the brown paper bag that has been left behind in his wake. It only sends more confusion rippling through me.

At the end of the day, Everly drops me off at home so that Austin has access to the G-wagon after practice. The thought of my brother being on the same field with Kingsley after they almost came to blows this morning fills me with dread. Austin needs to keep his temper under control and not get into any more trouble. There's no way in hell that Kingsley will bail him out for a second time. If anything, the dark-haired boy will gun for my brother's expulsion.

With a wave, I watch Everly pull out of the driveway before heading into the house. I slip inside before closing the door and dropping my backpack to the marble floor in the entryway like I've done dozens of times.

For a fraction of a heartbeat, I close my eyes and allow myself to pretend that my life hasn't been blown apart at the seams. As I wait for Mom to call out an upbeat greeting from the study, I pray with all my might that the past week has been nothing more than a terrible dream. I'll wake up with Kingsley's arms wrapped around me before collapsing against him and sharing the details. When I'm finished, he'll smack a kiss against my lips, assuring me that everything is fine.

Instead, the house remains eerily silent. There's a staleness that clings to the air that never used to be there. When I finally open my eyes, the weight of the world presses down until I'm paralyzed with the heaviness of it.

Memories swirl around me, and I gravitate to the study. As I sag against the doorframe, resting my head against the smooth grain wood, my gaze falls on the empty desk, and sorrow crashes over me like a heavy wave, threatening to drag me under. How many times did I find my father sitting behind the antique piece of furniture, staring at his laptop while Mom was curled up on a wingback chair, enjoying a cup of tea as the afternoon sunlight slanted in through the window?

With one blink, the image dissolves, leaving behind an ache in its place. Unable to stand the debilitating grief that radiates through me, I turn away and head to the staircase. It takes effort to trudge up the curving treads. Once on the second floor, I turn toward the master suite only to find the door closed. Instead of knocking, I turn the handle and poke my head inside. Mom is a huddled mass in the middle of the king-sized mattress. My heart sinks as a feeling of powerlessness overwhelms me. I have no idea what to do for her or how to make the situation better. While Dad was stolen from us in the blink of an eye, it seems like Mom plans to drift away a little bit at a time. I'm not sure which is worse.

As I stare at the bed, my throat tightens until breathing becomes difficult. My fingers shake as they go to the top button of my shirt, needing to loosen the constricting material around my neck. It's like I'm being strangled from the inside out. My mind spins as a wave of dizziness crashes over me. I squeeze my eyes tightly shut and focus on my inhalations, willing myself not to fall apart. The turmoil continues to riot beneath the surface of my skin. It's getting increasingly diffi-cult to tamp down. I'm afraid of what will happen if it all bursts loose.

Who will be there to pick up the pieces?

No one.

I'm alone in this.

It's a devastating realization. I've never felt this overwhelmed or lonely in my life.

Since Mom is dead to the world, I give in, allowing myself five minutes to release some of the fear and anxiety that has become my constant companion. A few tears slide down my face as I silently rail at God.

Once my emotions have been purged, I blow out a steady breath and pull myself back together. There are only a few hours before I need to return to Rothchild Mansion. I've never known Kingsley to make idle threats. I wholeheartedly believe him when he says my ass better be there or else.

Since it's doubtful Mom has eaten anything other than the toast Austin made this morning, I return to the kitchen and rummage around in the refrigerator. But it's a barren wasteland. The food that remains has either reached the end of its shelf life or looks like a home grown fifth-grade penicillin project. I fire off a text to Austin, asking him to stop at the store after practice and pick up a few necessities.

I find a pound of ground beef in the freezer, along with a jar of spaghetti sauce and a box of noodles in the cabinet. It's not exactly the dinner of champions, but it'll do.

Thirty minutes later, I'm scooping noodles into a bowl, adding a bit of sauce, and sprinkling on parmesan cheese to finish it off. I grab a fork from the drawer and a bottle of water from the fridge before taking it upstairs.

The curtains are drawn, making the room dark and stuffy. I set the bowl and bottle on the nightstand next to the bed before gravitating to the windows and yanking back the thick brocade curtains until the late afternoon sunshine can filter into the room. Then I crack open the windows, allowing in a rush of fresh air. It's early October, and the temperatures are hovering in the low to mid-seventies. I inhale a deep breath, feeling less off-kilter than earlier.

As if Mom can sense the change in atmosphere, she shifts under the covers, flipping them off her head before blinking and glancing around. She has the look of an animal waking from a long hibernation.

When her slumberous gaze falls on me, I force a smile to my lips. "Hi, Mom. How do you feel?"

"Summer?" Drowsiness clouds her voice as she drags herself to a seated position. "What time is it? Shouldn't you be in school?"

Her disoriented state has my heart cracking wide open.

"School is over. It's almost four o'clock. Austin should be home in an hour."

"It's four in the afternoon?" She drags a hand over her face as confusion fills her eyes. "What day is it?"

I clear away the thick emotion that attempts to clog my throat. "Tuesday."

"Oh." Her brows pinch together. "I'm sorry, honey. How long has your dad been gone?"

If my heart weren't already breaking, that question would shatter it into a million pieces. She sounds so lost and bewildered, like a small child. It's unnerving to see her in this condition. "Seven days." A week exactly. Almost to the hour.

She nods as wetness gathers in her eyes. "Okay."

I blink to keep my own tears at bay. One of us needs to stay strong. And apparently that person is me. I point at the bowl on the nightstand. "I made spaghetti for dinner."

"You did?" Surprise colors her voice.

"Yup." I draw in a breath and force it out before hoisting my lips. "I can't guarantee it's any good, but it's better than nothing."

"I'm sure it's wonderful." An anemic smile settles across her lips as if she, too, is trying to bring a bit of normalcy to our relationship. "Thank you, Summer."

"It wasn't a problem."

"Maybe not, but I really appreciate it." She slides back against the pillows before picking up the bowl and using her fork to twirl the noodles around the silver tines.

As she takes a few bites, I settle at the foot of the bed. She glances at me, looking a little more like herself. The haziness has dissipated from her eyes. It might not be much, but it's a tiny step in the right direction.

"It's really good." Once she finishes half the bowl, she sets the ceramic dish on the nightstand and takes a drink from her bottle of water. "I don't know what I would do without you and your brother."

"That's not something you have to worry about," I reassure her. "We're not going anywhere."

I chew my lower lip as indecision flickers through me. I don't want to send her rocketing back to the bottom of the pill bottle, but I can't keep her in the dark much longer. She needs to know what's going on.

"There's something I have to tell you," I say hesitantly, trying to gauge whether I'm making the right call.

"What is it?" Her body stills as if waiting for the other shoe to drop. I can't exactly blame her for that. It's been a shit week.

Much like ripping off a Band-Aid, it's probably best to get it over with quickly.

"Keaton sent over the original contract that you and Dad signed last night, along with a new one." When she remains silent, I continue. "Unless Dad found a way out of it, there's nothing we can do. We have to hold up our end of the deal, or he'll sue us and take Hawthorne Industries."

She releases a pent-up breath from her lungs before admitting, "The lawyer he hired thought we had a fifty-fifty chance at getting Grandma Rose's affidavit thrown out."

My shoulders collapse as I digest that bit of information. "Then there's no way out of this situation." It's not a question. More like a death sentence.

"I'm not sure." She shakes her head before dragging a hand through her disheveled hair. "I don't think so."

The emotional dam held precariously in place breaks as all of my hope disappears. "One condition of the new contract is that I live at the Rothchild Mansion."

"What? No!" The bit of color filling her cheeks drains away. "He can't do that!"

A gurgle of laughter bursts from my lips. "Well, he did. Keaton threatened to sue us if I wasn't at his doorstep by nine o'clock last night, so I packed my bags and went over."

"I can't believe this is happening," she whispers in a strangled voice as a look of despair fills her eyes. "I don't know what to do."

It takes everything I have inside not to scream out my frustration. I'm eighteen years old. I need my mother to pull her shit together and figure this out. These aren't problems I should have to tackle on my own.

When she remains silent, I say in a voice devoid of emotion, "You need to get ahold of Dad's lawyer and make sure there's nothing else that can be done." Even though it hurts to push the rest out, there's no longer a choice. "Dad is gone, and you need to take care of this."

She squeezes her eyes together as a lone tear treks down her cheek. When she finally opens them, she looks more in control. There are flickers of the woman she once was, fighting to break through the impenetrable wall of grief. "I'll call him tomorrow."

A sigh of relief escapes as I cling to the tiny shred of hope she has given me.

I'm surprised when she asks, "Are you all right over there?" Worry flickers across her face, making the tiny lines bracketing her mouth more pronounced. "Has he...*hurt* you?"

Unwilling to reveal the truth, I shake my head and smooth out my features. The less she knows, the better. "I'm fine. There's a house-keeper who showed me around last night." Kind of. "And I never saw Keaton."

Unfortunately, the same can't be said of Kingsley.

Her shoulders loosen as she sucks her lower lip into her mouth before chewing it. "I'll get you out of this, Summer." Resolve fills her voice, strengthening it. "I promise."

I nod, relieved that I won't be left to molder away at the Rothchild estate. "Thank you."

"I'm sorry that your dad and I ever agreed to the terms." She swipes at another tear with the back of her hand. "I don't know what we were thinking."

I glance away, not wanting her to see the bitterness that fills my expression. I've often wondered the same thing. Before Dad passed away, all I had wanted was a choice over my future. My feelings for

Kingsley were never in question. It had more to do with our relationship being forever tied to the company and family history.

Now it's an entirely different story. If she doesn't find a loophole out of this nonsense, I could spend the rest of my life with a man who despises me.

The thought is almost enough to bring me to my knees.

The entire time I'm with Mom, I keep a careful eye on the clock, knowing I need to haul ass next door before Kingsley arrives home from practice. If not, there will be hell to pay. And I'd rather not deal with him any more than necessary. With precisely sixty seconds to spare before the clock strikes six, I slip through the front door of Rothchild Mansion. From somewhere deep inside the bowels of the house, a grandfather clock strikes six times. As I fly to the staircase, prepared to hide out in my room for the rest of the evening, I spot Keaton watching me from midway up the stairs and stumble to a halt.

He and his son share a strong family resemblance. They both have the same dark features, height, and athletic build. One difference is the cold calculatedness that radiates from Keaton's eyes, freezing me to the core every time I come in contact with him. It's the reason I've gone out of my way to avoid his presence. Now that I'm being forced to live under the same roof, it'll be more of a challenge.

"Ah, Ms. Hawthorne, so lovely to see you again." His lips lift into a thin smile that doesn't reach the iciness of his eyes as he continues toward me. "I trust you've settled in and are enjoying your accommodations?"

Not really.

The question is borne out of politeness rather than actual concern.

"Yes." I straighten to my full height and hold my ground even though I'm sorely tempted to turn tail and run. "Thank you."

"Oh, it's my pleasure." Once he reaches the last tread, the soles of his polished-to-a-high-shine wingtips strike the marble as he strolls toward me. "I must confess that it's nice to have a female in the house again."

I swallow, unsure how to respond to the bizarre comment. I'm almost tempted to ask where his wife is.

Alive and well?

Buried in the backyard?

It's not a comforting thought.

"I trust my son has played the part of gracious host and made sure you have everything you could desire?"

Ha!

Gracious host indeed...

It takes willpower to rein in the snort.

"Yup." I force another lie from my lips. I'm loath to ask anything of this man, but I have to at least try to appeal to his conscience.

If he has one.

"I hope you realize this wasn't necessary." When he quirks a brow, I rush to add, "Me living here. My parents weren't trying to cheat you out of your share of Hawthorne Industries. All they wanted was a fair resolution to the situation that didn't include forcing Kingsley and me into marriage."

He nods, a thoughtful expression flickering across his face. For a moment, I wonder if I've reached him and he'll allow me to return home. He and my mother can straighten out the company business between themselves instead of tangling their children up in the mess.

"I'm afraid, my dear, that your parents sealed your fate when they attempted to break the contract." He steps closer, invading my personal space. "I'm sure you can understand that I had no choice in the matter. I won't allow anything more to be stolen from my family." He reaches out, trailing his knuckles along the curve of my jaw. "You, unfortunately, are nothing more than a pawn." His pupils dilate. "Although, I have to admit that you're a very pretty pawn. My son is a lucky man."

Fear slithers through me as my mouth turns cottony. Both his touch and words have me jerking away as if I've been burned.

He smiles as his hand drops to his side. "Do not fret, Ms. Hawthorne. You'll find living here quite palatable. Mrs. Fieber is an excellent cook. Dinner is always served promptly in the dining room at seven."

Before I can tell him to go to hell, he saunters away, leaving me alone in the echoing foyer. The breath rushes from my lungs as I tighten the strap of my backpack against my shoulder and race up the stairs, trying to remember the way to the bedroom. Maybe I should have left a trail of breadcrumbs this morning.

It takes a few attempts before I finally stumble across the room that is now mine and slam the door shut before twisting the lock. Only then does the tightly coiled tension drain away, leaving me to feel weak in the knees.

It's so tempting to allow the tears to well in my eyes, but falling to pieces won't solve a damn thing. I have to keep it together. I take my backpack and head to the balcony before settling at one of the small tables and spreading out my homework. For the next couple of hours, I plow my way through two missing calculus assignments from last week and then spend the rest of the evening studying for an AP psychology quiz.

As submerged in my studies as I am, I can't help but nervously eye the time on my phone. When seven o'clock comes and goes, the tension gradually seeps from my body. After Keaton mentioned the evening meal, I was afraid they might force me to dine with them. It's doubtful I could deal with both Keaton and Kingsley at the same time. I'm barely able to handle them separately.

Around eight o'clock, I pause and stretch my hunched muscles, glancing around the outdoor space. The balcony off my bedroom at home is cramped, but it was enough to have a tiny cafe-style table and two chairs. This deck stretches across the entire back of the mansion.

About twenty feet away, I spot a telescope. Surprised by the discovery, I sit up a little straighter and study it from afar.

Curiosity piqued, I rise from the chair and pad to where the object is set up by a stone baluster before running my fingers over the sleek black metal. Even though money isn't an issue for the Rothchilds, this is an expensive model, designed for advanced astronomers. It looks shiny and brand new without a scratch on it.

At no time in the past month has Kingsley ever mentioned an interest in the solar system. In fact, when we've been in the backyard, I've always gotten the distinct impression he didn't know anything about astronomy.

For a split second, I consider the possibility that Kingsley bought this for me before dismissing it with a bitter laugh. He's gone out of his way to make it clear he can't stand the sight of me. If I had to guess, I'd say that his new mission in life is to make mine miserable. So far, he's succeeding with flying colors. This kind of generous action doesn't fit in with that MO. So, obviously, it was here last night, and I overlooked it.

It was dark.

I was upset.

It's easily explained away.

Unable to help myself, I remove the lens cap and gaze through the eyepiece. The sky isn't nearly dark enough to see properly. I'll return later this evening for a look. It's the splash of water from below that has me straightening to my full height before peeking over the railing.

My breath gets wedged in my throat when I find Kingsley arrowing from one end of the pool to the other. His muscular arms surge from the water as his feet propel him forward. The sinewy strength of his back flexes and shifts as he moves easily through the clear liquid. Even though there's a distinct chill to the air, I imagine his pool, much like ours, is heated.

As he reaches the wall, he flips over gracefully before pushing off the tiled edge and shooting forward. My fingers bite into the stone railing as I watch him swim from one end to the other. Something about his athletic prowess is captivating.

He really is the perfect male specimen.

Broad shoulders, powerful chest, and a tapered waist. Is it any wonder I fell so hard for the guy? The first time I saw him was like a punch to the gut. I don't think I ever fully recovered from that.

With him unaware of my perusal, I'm free to eat him up with my eyes. Even after everything that has happened between us, I find myself incapable of looking away. The sight of him mesmerizes me.

Once he finishes with his laps, he rises to his feet in the shallow end. Water sluices off his half-naked body, and my mouth turns bone-dry as I stare. The muscles of his biceps bunch as he raises his arms, plowing strong fingers through his hair, pushing it away from his face. His movements have my belly hollowing out. The attraction that pounds through me is undeniable. Much to my consternation, there isn't a switch to flip off.

It would be so much easier if there were.

Before I can consider backing away and disappearing into the shadows, his face lifts, gaze skewering mine. A shiver of desire explodes in my core and I squeeze my thighs together to extinguish it.

He remains still. We both do as the moment stretches and lengthens until sexual tension dances in the air. It would be one thing if it were only lust filling his eyes, but hatred and distrust flood through them. It's the last two emotions that crack my heart wide open. Silently I back away from the railing, breaking the connection before gathering up my books and disappearing inside to the relative safety of my room.

22

It's the scrape of sharp teeth against my aching clit that has a moan escaping from my mouth as I twist restlessly against the sheets. My fingers tunnel through thick hair, holding him in place as his tongue dances across my core. Pleasure suffuses every cell of my being as my body tightens, searching for release.

"Please," I whimper, arching against his seeking mouth.

"Tell me what you want."

It's those husky words that have me hurtling to the surface from what I assumed was a dream. My eyelids flutter open, and in the shadowy darkness of the room, I realize Kingsley's head is buried between my thighs. Unable to help myself, my fingers tighten around him, digging into his scalp. If I were thinking clearly, I would shove him away. But how can I do that when so much pleasure is crashing around inside me? Before I was even conscious, he stripped away all of my resistance.

It's not the first time, and it won't be the last.

When it comes to Kingsley, I am totally and completely at his mercy.

And he has none.

Especially where I am concerned.

He drags the velvety softness of his tongue across my flesh, and a thick shudder of ecstasy slides through me, pushing me to the edge of my sanity.

His head rises until our gazes can collide before he nips at the plump flesh. "I asked you a question."

There's no point in pretending. *"You,"* I admit. *"I want you."* That, at the very least, is the truth. Under the cover of darkness, our battle of wills no longer matters when my body is already splintering apart.

As if pleased by the response, his tongue skates over my throbbing clit. I groan and widen my legs, allowing him more access. Where he's concerned, I'm weak and pathetic. A slave to my hormones. Those thoughts are so disturbing that I do the only thing I can and shove them from my head, wanting to focus on the here and now. On the pleasure unfurling in my body. There will be plenty of time tomorrow to berate myself.

"Do you like that?"

"Yes," I whimper as his tongue continues to lap at me, carefully stoking the ecstasy until it's a raging inferno that threatens to scorch me from the inside out.

"Admit that you like the way I touch you."

"You know I do." As the truth slides from my lips, an orgasm explodes, and I scream out my release.

Kingsley torments me until every drop of joy has been wrung from my body. Just as my muscles loosen, sinking into the mattress, he grabs my hips and flips me over before jerking me to my knees.

With one large palm splayed at the center of my back, he drives deep inside my heat. I whimper as his other hand tangles in my hair, yanking my head back. His hips jerk against my backside. Every thrust of his cock sends my eyes rolling inside my head. Even though I came moments ago, pleasure sparks to life for a second time.

After the pain of the past week, this is the only thing that seems real. That makes me feel something other than grief, sorrow, frustration, and anger. When he's filling me, forcing me to submit, I can forget about all of it and concentrate on the animalistic pleasure.

His grip tightens on the length of my hair, and even though my scalp stings from the pressure, it only heightens the arousal pumping through me. Another orgasm, this one stronger, builds inside as he continues to thrust rhythmically.

It doesn't make sense for our bodies to be in such perfect synchronicity when we couldn't be any further apart. When his muscles tighten and his movements become more frenzied, mine follow suit, matching every thrust with a parry. The long guttural groan that escapes from him forces me over the edge. My inner muscles clench around his thick cock, squeezing it as he slams into me before collapsing with a huff of breath that feathers against my back.

For just a sliver of a moment, everything feels right between us. Instead of being leagues apart, his harsh breathing fills my ears. And just like our fucking, it feels as if we are in perfect harmony. As if we are two pieces of the same whole, finally coming together.

With him buried inside me, his body covering mine, it feels as if we might find a middle ground and work through our issues.

Is that even a possibility?

Can he shelf his anger long enough to hear me out?

To put himself in my shoes?

It was never my intention to lie. I was put in an untenable position. One I couldn't win. Either I betrayed Kingsley or my parents. Like everything regarding our relationship and family history, it's complicated. When it comes down to it, Kingsley had a choice in the matter. He could have walked away from this arrangement. Instead, he chose to go through with it.

He chose me.

But I wasn't given the same opportunity. It was—marry Kingsley or have the family company taken away and get buried alive under a mountain of debt.

How is that any kind of choice?

All I want is for him to see my side and cut me a little slack. He doesn't need to forgive me or even agree, just understand.

I moisten my lips. "Kingsley—"

The sound of my voice shatters the fragile peace that had fallen over us. He silently slides from my body, leaving me to feel empty and alone, before rolling from the bed. I bite my lip to keep from begging him to stay as he slips through the balcony door. Any hope filling me bursts like an over-inflated balloon, leaving nothing but despair and anguish in its place.

Whatever Kingsley and I once shared, if it was ever real, is gone. The only thing I can do is pray that Mom finds a way out of this mess.

23

I'm jolted out of a dead sleep by the incessant buzzing of my alarm. One hand snakes out from beneath the down comforter to swipe my phone from the nightstand. It takes effort to focus on the small screen.

What the hell?

How is it half past six?

Normally, my alarm goes off at precisely six, and that gives me enough time to jump into the shower and get ready for school.

Fuck!

With one swift motion, I toss off the covers and leap to my feet. As I do, a wave of nausea crashes over me. With a soft grunt, my hand flattens over my belly to still the sickness roiling inside.

It doesn't work. If anything, the illness only gets worse as I stumble to the bathroom, barely making it to the toilet in time before everything from last evening makes an encore appearance in the white porcelain.

Gross.

Once my belly has been completely emptied, I spend the next ten minutes dry heaving until tears sting my eyes. I grip the toilet basin as if hanging on for dear life.

Where the heck did that come from?

My limbs weaken as I stay hunkered in place, focusing on my breathing. As one minute stretches into two, and my stomach doesn't continue to revolt, I rise unsteadily to my feet before lurching toward the long stretch of marble countertop to run the faucet. With my hands, I rinse the acidic taste from my mouth before scrubbing my teeth. My gaze gets drawn to the reflection in the mirror.

Sheesh. I look terrible. I'm pale and more drawn than normal. There's a hollowed-out look in my eyes.

Is this stress, or am I coming down with something?

Like I need to deal with that on top of everything else.

I splash a few handfuls of cold water on my face before drawing in a deep, calming breath. Once all my emotions have been locked down tight, I head to the bedroom to dress. As I'm pulling the tartan skirt over my hips, my phone flashes with an incoming text.

I don't have to glance at the screen to know who it's from.

Five minutes. Then I'm coming up.

A growl of frustration builds in my throat. I'm tempted to hurtle my cell out the window. Unfortunately, destroying my electronic device won't stop Kingsley from stalking up the stairs, tossing me over his shoulder, and carrying me kicking and screaming to the car.

My guess is that he would probably get off on it.

Not bothering to dignify the message with a response, I tuck my shirt into the loose-fitting skirt and pull up the socks before sliding my feet into chunky heels. Then I grab my backpack and head for the hallway. As I race through the second-floor gallery, I spot Kingsley lounging near the front door with his phone in hand.

His head is bent, a wayward lock of mahogany-colored hair slides over his eyes. My heart spasms as longing bursts inside me. Those feelings only irritate me further. Whatever emotions he's sparked to life, I want them gone. I want to feel nothing where this boy is concerned.

When my phone chimes with a second text, I don't bother to read it. Kingsley must hear the high-pitched sound as it echoes off the cavernous walls because his head jerks up. The way his gaze licks over me feels very much like a physical caress. One that heats me from the inside out. My breath stalls, and I remind myself to exhale before descending the staircase. It would be an error in judgment to show him exactly how much he's able to burrow beneath my skin.

He grabs the same travel mug from yesterday off the credenza before passing it to me along with a peanut butter and chocolate protein bar. The aroma of freshly ground arabica beans permeates the air, and nausea explodes inside me again.

Instead of reaching for the offering, I shake my head and take a step in retreat as if to distance myself from the overpowering scent. "No, thank you."

"You need to eat," he says in a sharp tone. "You skipped dinner last night."

"Actually," I shoot back, "I ate with my mom." The mere thought of food is enough to make me nauseous. My belly spasms, and I'm half afraid I'll throw up all over the polished-to-a-high-shine marble floor. If I don't get out of here and into the fresh air, I won't be held accountable for what happens next.

"You look like shit," he comments with a slight frown marring his handsome face.

"Thanks." I suck in an unsteady breath before forcing it out again. "If you're finished sweet-talking me, can we leave? I don't want to be late."

He grunts in response as I stalk to the front door. I'm almost surprised when he doesn't force the breakfast down my throat. Once outside, the chilly morning air slaps at my overheated cheeks, immediately settling something deep inside.

In silence, I slide into the passenger seat as Kingsley starts the engine. Avoiding eye contact, I focus my attention on the greenery that passes by as he pulls out of the subdivision and onto the main road. What happened last night sits uncomfortably between us. Maybe it's easy for him to turn off his emotions and screw, but it's not like that for me. I can't have him inside my body and not feel *something* for him.

This is such a messed-up situation.

One I have no idea how to navigate.

As much as I want to discuss what happened, I refuse to broach the subject. I'm unwilling to risk being shut down for a second time. My pride has already been ground to a fine pulp beneath his heel. I can't take much more.

As we pull through the gate and onto school property, I clutch my bag, counting down the minutes until I can escape Kingsley's presence. I need to get my head on straight, and I can't do that when I'm forced to spend so much time with him. As he parks the Mustang and cuts the engine, I hoist my bag onto my lap and reach for the door handle.

His deep voice cuts through the silence of the car. "No more hiding out in the library. I expect to see you at lunch."

My fingernails dig into the leather as resentment builds in my chest.

Why can't he leave me alone?

Rather than argue and potentially cause a scene, I jerk my head into a tight nod. I'm not in any condition to fight him. Even though I woke up thirty minutes ago, my ass is still dragging. All the stress from Dad's death and the situation with Kingsley and Keaton have driven me to the breaking point.

It's a relief when he shifts away, dismissing me without another word before stepping from the Mustang. Unlike yesterday, he doesn't bother waiting for me to exit the vehicle before walking toward a crowd of his friends in the parking lot. Sloane separates herself from the same group before rushing toward him and looping her arms around Kingsley's neck. If I didn't know better, I'd think they were together.

For all I know, they are.

The thought of him fucking both of us at the same time makes me sick to my stomach. I want to curl up on the leather seat and pretend this isn't happening. Rather than give in to the impulse, I pop open the door and force myself to step onto the pavement before hurrying toward the front entrance of the school.

If Kingsley thinks he can inflict more damage by flaunting Sloane in front of me, he's got another thing coming.

155

24

"How are you holding up, girl?" Everly asks as we head to the cafeteria.

"I'm fine." The smile I paste on my lips takes effort. School is the last place I want to be. I dread seeing Kingsley because I know exactly what I'll find, and that's Sloane clinging to him like a barnacle. If that girl could fuck him in front of my face, solely to stake her claim, that's exactly what she would do.

Does she really think I care?

Or that I'll fight for him?

Ha! Nothing could be further from the truth. As far as I'm concerned, they deserve each other. The self-appointed king and queen of Hawthorne Prep.

Even though I keep my attention focused in front of me, Everly's concerned gaze flits over me, probing for details I'm unwilling to share.

"Are you sure?" She pauses for a beat, most likely waiting for me to spill my guts. "You look tired."

"I didn't sleep well last night." I shrug, not bothering to add the reason for it. My new friend hasn't asked many questions about Kingsley, but I have the feeling it's only a matter of time.

"The past two weeks have been brutal," she adds softly.

Every step that brings us closer to the dining hall has my nerves ratcheting up. I haven't felt this anxious since the first day of school. In a strange way, it feels as if I've come full circle. The only difference is that I now understand what to expect. The students of Hawthorne Prep are more vicious than barracudas. One word from Kingsley and they'll rip me to shreds without a second thought.

What did he tell me the other day?

Queens can be cast aside.

I'm waiting for him to do exactly that in a spectacularly public fashion.

As if sensing my growing unease, Everly loops her arm through mine. When I glance at her, she gives me a firm nod along with a stoic smile. It's like she knows we're going to battle, and her unwavering support is enough to bring tears to my eyes. Everly has no idea how grateful I am for her friendship. She came into my life when I needed her most. There's no way I could get through this without her.

"Thank you," I whisper, wishing there was a better way to convey everything that's in my heart.

As we step into the cavernous space, I tense, unsure how the situation will play out. It takes a moment to realize that no one is paying us any more attention than usual. The relief that floods through me is almost enough to weaken my knees. Unwilling to make eye contact with Kingsley, I focus on the floor as we walk to our normal table. I need to make it through the next thirty minutes unscathed.

That's it.

That's all I care about.

When Everly grinds to a halt, my gaze slices to her in question. Anger flashes across her face before she grumbles through stiff lips, "Let's sit somewhere else today."

My belly twists. I can only imagine what's prompted her to make the suggestion. I try to swallow down the thick lump of nausea that has settled in the middle of my throat.

Whatever you do, don't look!

Even though I tell myself not to do it, my gaze arrows to the table crowded with all the usual suspects. In the middle of the group is the king himself and perched on his lap is none other than Sloane. It's so reminiscent of the first day of school that I blink my eyes and tell myself that it's not déjà vu.

"Summer." Everly's fingers dig into my arm in an effort to shift my attention away from the scene. "Let's go."

The image has unfortunately been singed into my brain for all eternity. "Sure. Where do you want to sit?"

Everly scans the area until she finds a table with a few open seats before pointing. "How about over there?"

Honestly, I don't care where we go as long as I don't have to look at Kingsley and Sloane. The smell of mass-produced food assaults my nostrils, and my belly churns with a pang of discomfort. Maybe this isn't stress at all, but a case of the flu. I've spent most of the morning fighting nausea.

It's a relief when we finally settle at the end of the table on the outskirts of the cafeteria. Everly strategically positions herself so that she faces the football players, and my back is to Kingsley. She sets her bag down before pulling out her drink, sandwich, bag of pretzels, and a fruit snack.

Her brow furrows. "Didn't you bring a lunch?"

With a grimace, I shake my head. The thought is enough to make me vomit.

Everly pushes a small prepackaged bag of pretzels toward me. "Here, take this. I have more than enough."

Her gaze slides from me to something over my shoulder. After finishing off the last bite of her sandwich, she leans forward, closing the distance between us. I know what's coming, and I brace myself for it. I'm surprised it took her this long.

"I haven't wanted to be all up in your business, but you gotta throw me a bone here." She pauses for a heartbeat before blurting out the question I've been dreading most. "What happened between the two of you?"

"It's a long story." Where would I even begin?

"I'm sure it is, but I don't understand how your relationship unraveled so quickly. You two seemed solid." Scorn fills her eyes as her upper lip curls. "It's unbelievably shitty for him to do this right after everything with your dad."

A humorless chuckle slides from my lips as I shake my head. "It's so much more complicated than that." As much as I'd love to let Everly believe this is entirely Kingsley's fault, I can't do that. Yes, he's proven himself to be a total jerk, but the ownership for this particular fallout lies with me. I'm the one who fucked up.

When she raises her brows, I shrug, struggling to put it all into words. "There's a lot of bad blood between our families, and it's been that way for eighty years."

Surprise flashes in her eyes. "So, there's a whole Romeo and Juliet situation going on here?"

"Not exactly."

"Minus the suicides?"

Even though there's nothing to laugh about, a snort of humor escapes. "Along with a few other details."

"Hmm...star-crossed lovers," she adds dreamily, "that's kind of romantic."

She couldn't be more wrong about that.

"Trust me, there is *nothing* romantic about our situation." We were doomed for failure from the very beginning. It's almost painful to remember how hard I fell for Kingsley the day we spent on the boat. No matter how much I grieve, moving on from that feels impossible. I don't think I'll ever get over him.

Everly opens her mouth before snapping it shut as something snags her gaze behind me. She sits up straighter before muttering, "Incoming."

Please don't let it be Kingsley.

I can't deal with him right now. If he's looking to throw me to the wolves or slap a red bull's eye on my back, this would be the perfect time to do it. I flinch when a finger taps my shoulder. Somewhere in the back of my mind, I realize it can't be the dark-haired boy. There's no way he would ever be so meek as to hit my shoulder and wait for me to turn around. He's way more forceful than that.

I swivel and find Sloane. A smug smile curves her pink-slicked lips as she cocks a hip. "For some odd reason, Kingsley wants you at his table. So get your ass moving or he'll move it for you." She smirks before adding, "Frankly, I'd love to see that happen."

When I fail to respond, her blue eyes glitter with malice. After all the confrontations we've had over the past month and a half, she's loving that Kingsley is finally hers. What she doesn't understand is that she won by default. As tempted as I am to tell her, I keep the ugly comment to myself.

She closes the distance between us before whispering, "I knew you wouldn't be able to hold on to him."

"You must feel vindicated," I say, unwilling to get dragged into a pissing match. "Now he's all yours."

A haughty expression settles over her face. "That's the thing, Hawthorne—he was always mine."

"So...he was out on loan? Kind of like a library book?" I ask sweetly. There's only so much of Sloane's bitchy behavior I can take before losing it. Like Kingsley, this girl knows how to push my buttons to provoke a reaction.

Anger flashes in her eyes.

"Should I let you in on a little secret?" Before she can respond, I continue. "Enjoy him while you can. We both know he'll slip through your fingers before you can blink."

Heat slams into her cheeks. "You're nothing more than a jealous bitch," she snaps.

"Please, girl, that's more your MO."

Before Sloane can slap back at me, Everly cuts in, making a shooing motion with her fingers. "You've delivered your message like a good little lap dog. Now run back to your owner. I think he might have a treat for you."

Sloane's mouth gapes before she snaps it shut and straightens to her full height, glaring in Everly's direction. "You better shut your damn mouth before I do it for you."

Not the least bit intimidated, Everly rises to her feet. "Why don't you try it, and we'll see what happens?"

Clearly not expecting the snappy comeback, uncertainty flickers across Sloane's face before she presses her lips into a tight line.

There's a beat of silence as Everly's brows rise. "Well, I'm waiting for you to shut my damn mouth."

Holy shit!

Did she really just say that?

A gurgle of laughter escapes from my lips before I clap a hand over my mouth to stifle it. Sloane turns her glaring eyes on me. There is so much hatred blazing from them. It's enough to singe me alive.

"Fuck off," she growls. "Neither of you is worth my time." With that, she stomps away.

I stare after the blonde, enjoying one of the few victories I've managed to claim before turning to Everly with a mixture of amusement and awe. "You're kind of a bad bitch."

A reluctant smile quirks the edges of her lips. "The best thing you can do with a bully is put them in their place." Her gaze flicks from me before settling on something over my shoulder. "And that bully has just been knocked down to size."

Clearly.

"You realize that you've made an enemy today, right?" If Everly had escaped Sloane's notice thus far, that's no longer the case.

"I have no problem with that." She shrugs as her gaze settles on mine. There's not an ounce of regret in her eyes. "That girl can kiss my ass for all I care."

The image has a slight smile tugging at the corners of my lips. There's more fight in Everly than I first suspected. It'll serve her well at Hawthorne Prep. If I've learned one thing, this isn't a place where the weak thrive or survive.

More like the opposite.

I gnaw my bottom lip as my mind turns to the reason Sloane sauntered over in the first place.

Kingsley.

Maybe Everly was able to chase Sloane away easily enough, but that won't be the case with the dark-haired boy. There's a cost for defiance, and I'm not sure I want to pay the price.

"He can't make you do anything," she says as if reading my thoughts. "He doesn't own you."

Her words echo hollowly in my head.

He doesn't own you.

I want to laugh. Or maybe cry. The sad truth of the matter is that he does. Kingsley's family *does* own me, but how can I explain that to Everly? I can't imagine the look of horror that would flash across her face if I were to reveal the truth.

"Fuck him!" she growls when I remain silent.

"I wish it were that easy," I mumble.

"I'm serious, Summer." Her eyes darken with impending storm clouds. "He can't make you do anything. Just ignore the big jerk."

Everly is new to Hawthorne, so she obviously doesn't understand the social hierarchy that exists here. She doesn't realize the power Kingsley and his family wield. I've had a little taste of it, and it was more than enough to last a lifetime.

Remorse rushes through me. I hate that I've dragged her into a situation she'll likely regret three months down the line. She doesn't understand how formidable these enemies are or how long these people hold on to grudges. This is not a forgive and forget type of crowd.

My gaze drops to my tangled fingers. "I really appreciate you sticking up for me, but you might want to reconsider your loyalty." As difficult as it is, I force out the rest. "People like Sloane and Kingsley, they won't forget whose side you were on when this all went down, and I don't want to see you take the brunt of it. You're new here and still getting the lay of the land. If you want to back off or distance yourself for the time being, I won't hold it against you."

When she remains silent, I glance at her.

Everly pokers up on the bench like someone just rammed a two-by-four up her ass. *"Did you seriously just say that to me?"*

My eyes widen as my mouth tumbles open.

Umm...

"I—"

She cuts me off as her voice rises. "I don't give a damn about these assholes! They can all fuck off!" She leans forward and stabs a finger in my direction. "I thought we were friends."

Stunned by the outburst, I whisper, "We are! That's why I'm doing this."

Doesn't she get that?

Even though it's been less than two weeks, Everly and I have grown close. Each day I was gone, she called or texted to check in with me. She stopped by the house to drop off a casserole and a pretty floral journal to write in. Every bit of kindness she showered upon me touched my heart more than she'll ever realize. Which is precisely why I don't want her getting caught in the crossfire of my bullshit. She deserves a fighting chance at this school, and she certainly won't get that by befriending me.

It takes effort to swallow down the thick lump that has formed in the middle of my throat. "I just wanted to make you aware of the situation." I glance around at the sea of unfriendly faces. "Maybe you haven't noticed, but I'm kind of on the outs right now, and that won't change anytime soon."

"You know what? That first day of school, you were the only one who reached out and introduced themselves to me. None of these people did that. I would rather have one true friend than a bunch of fake ass bitches who don't give a shit about me." Her scornful gaze bounces over my shoulder. "You think I wanna be friends with Sloane?" Disgust fills her face as she shakes her head. "No thanks. I knew plenty of girls like her in New York. I'm not interested in going down that road again. We have less than a year to get through Hawthorne Prep and then we'll be free of this hellhole. We can do it together."

Tears threaten to gather in my eyes, and it takes effort to blink them away. I'm not even sure the friends I had in Chicago would stand by me through all this. It's a sobering realization.

"We've got this, okay?" Everly lays a hand over mine before squeezing it. "So, now that we got that straightened out, how do you want to handle this?"

As I gnaw my lip with indecision, Austin plunks his tray down next to me.

"Hey," he says, unaware of the conversation he's interrupted.

"Hi," I murmur.

Everly gives him a smile before her attention drops to his lunch. "Wow, hungry much?"

"All the damn time." He grins before digging in. Austin has double portions of everything. The overflowing tray of food could feed a small country.

Her brows skyrocket across her forehead. I can't tell if she's disgusted or impressed or if it's a combination of both. "You must have one hell of a metabolism."

"You have no idea," I mutter.

Austin shoves a forkful of meatloaf into his mouth before glancing over his shoulder. "Glad to see we're no longer sitting at asswipe central. I'd rather be banished to no-man's-land than put up with them any day of the week."

I shrug, relieved that Austin wasn't here when Kingsley sent Sloane over to do his bidding. My brother would have lost his proverbial shit. And then it would have all hit the fan. As he and Everly talk about a class they have together, a fresh burst of nausea explodes in my belly before threatening to revolt. When I jump to my feet, their conversation grinds to an abrupt halt.

"I need to use the bathroom," I blurt before adding, "I'll be right back." Not waiting for a response, I hightail it from the cafeteria, down the hall, before pushing through the door to the restroom.

Thankfully, it's empty. Once in front of the sink, I turn on the faucet and splash cold water against my cheeks. The nausea churning in the pit of my gut continues to roil. I'm half afraid I'll vomit. I squeeze my eyes closed and focus on my breathing.

Deep, slow inhalations.

After a few minutes, the nausea gradually recedes. When I glance up, the image in the mirror is almost enough to leave me wincing. Kingsley wasn't wrong this morning when he told me I looked like shit. My eyes are hollowed-out, and my normally sun-kissed complexion has been leeched of all color. And I've lost more weight. It's staggering to realize how much my physical appearance has changed since we were uprooted from Chicago. And the last week has only made the situation worse. Everly is lucky. She can focus on graduation and getting the hell out of Hawthorne, but that's not in the cards for me. Unless Mom discovers a way out of the contract, I'll be tied to Kingsley for the foreseeable future.

And if that's not a depressing thought, I don't know what is.

When the bathroom door swings open, I twist around, expecting to find my new friend. Instead, I'm pinned in place by dark eyes.

2 5

Kingsley flips the lock on the bathroom door. The sound is like a gunshot in the silence of the small tiled space as he leans against the thick slab of wood. My heart jackrabbits painfully under my breast as my mind registers that I'm trapped without an escape route.

"You're not very good at following directions, are you?"

The low menace of his voice sends a fresh wave of nerves scampering across my flesh. Fear pumps through me like a living, breathing entity. Everly may not know the backstory, but she's right about one thing.

"I don't have to follow your orders. I'm not yours. You don't own me."

He smirks as amusement leaps into his eyes. "Is that so?"

I lift my chin, trying to hold on to my bravado. "Yes."

"You're wrong about that. I own every piece of you." He pushes away from the door and saunters toward me. "And I always will."

"*No.*" His words are like a fist wrapped around my heart, squeezing until every bit of life has been forced out of me.

"Oh, yes," he says with a smirk.

Full-fledged panic slams through me as he stalks closer. My feet trip over each other as I scramble backward. When my shoulder blades crash into the wall, I realize there's nowhere left to go. What I've learned about Kingsley is that he's a wild card. He doesn't play by any set of rules. He makes them up as he goes. As attractive as I find that quality, it scares the hell out of me now.

"I love the scent of your fear," he murmurs when he's close enough. "Or is that arousal? I can never tell with you."

I shake my head, wanting to dismiss his words, but on some dark level, I wonder if they're true. Buried beneath the distress is a thin layer of excitement. It makes my blood pound a little faster and my heart race a little harder. His nearness electrifies me, setting me on edge. It sharpens my senses until my body vibrates, functioning on a higher level.

How fucking sick and twisted is that?

A smile curves his lips as arousal leaps to life in his eyes. "As much as you don't want to be turned on, you are. As much as you wish you didn't want me, that doesn't change the fact that you do."

I hate that he's right and recognizes it when I'm only just learning it for myself.

When he's less than a foot away, he stops. I flatten my body against the tile, trying to keep as much physical distance between us as possible. Not that it will do me a damn bit of good. One stroke of his fingers and I'll be lost. Swept away on a tide of sensation.

I realize it, and so does he.

My breath gets wedged in my throat as he reaches out, picking up a stray lock of hair before twisting it idly around his finger.

"Tell me I'm wrong." His knowing gaze flicks to mine, pinning me in place. When I remain silent, he tugs on the thick strands. "I'm still waiting."

"I don't want you." The fib slips almost effortlessly from my lips.

"Liar." His teeth flash as he presses closer. The heat of his body singes mine as his steely strength aligns with my softer curves. He places one hand on each side of my head until I'm caged in. There's no way to escape.

Fear courses through me, but he's right— it's tinged at the edges with arousal. It simmers beneath the surface, desperately trying to break free. Even though he has yet to touch me, my breathing turns shallow.

"What's wrong, Summer?" His voice is full of innocence. He's all too aware of the effect he has on me.

"Nothing."

"I'm beginning to wonder if you're a compulsive liar." His lips feather over mine until the sensation becomes agonizing. "Are you even capable of telling the truth?"

I turn my face away before squeezing my eyes tightly closed. His warm breath drifts across my cheek before he presses a kiss against the corner of my eye.

"Stop."

"Is that really what you want?" he asks softly, stroking his lips across my flesh.

No, it's not. I love the feel of his mouth against me, but it's not real. It's a game he's intent on playing. And the only way he wins is if I get hurt.

"Yes."

"Prove it." Every bit of sunlight disappears between us as his body dwarfs mine, and the thickness of his erection digs into my belly. "Push me away."

My hands rise, flattening on the sinewy lines of his chest.

"Come on," he taunts, continuing to pepper kisses that are as delicate as a butterfly wing against my skin, "you have to do better than that."

His mouth turns insistent, licking and biting between soft caresses. As much as I want to push him away, the urge to drag him closer thrums through me.

What's wrong with me?

How can I feel this way?

My fingernails sink into his shirt, digging into the white cotton fabric and the slab of muscle that lies beneath.

"Are you actually trying to hurt me?" Humor laces his voice as he nips at my ear before sucking the lobe into his mouth.

Carefully, I turn my face until my lips can brush against his. The way his warm breath drifts across me is almost drugging. All I want to do is inhale a giant breath of him. "Maybe."

"Oh, baby girl, you don't have to try so hard. Haven't you realized how much damage you've already inflicted?"

His silky words are like a punch to the gut.

"I never meant for it to happen." My heart clenches until it feels like it's being squeezed by a vise.

"It doesn't matter." His lips twist with bitterness. "I would have given you everything. *Every damn part of me.* And you threw it away."

"I didn't," I whisper brokenly.

"Yeah, you did." One hand drops from the wall to my shoulder before trailing over my collarbone until his wide palm can settle on my breast. When he flexes his fingers, my nipple pebbles in response. "I won't say it again. Push me away or I'll take you right here."

I twist beneath him as he digs into my flesh. We both know that I'm not trying to break free but attempting to get closer.

"Are you really this needy after I fucked you last night?" His palm opens before his thumb and forefinger wrap around the stiff little bud before giving it a vicious pinch.

I whimper as arousal reverberates throughout my entire being before settling in my core like a heavy stone. His hand trails over my rib cage before stopping at my hip.

"Last chance," he threatens.

All I have to do is flatten my hands against him and give one powerful push. Just one to prove that I'm capable of walking away. That I don't still crave him. It shouldn't be difficult. He's an asshole intent on inflicting as much damage as he can. How can I not walk away from that?

Push him away and leave!

As much as I want to, my fingers refuse to straighten. A choked sob falls from my lips as my forehead drops against his chest, and I squeeze my eyes tightly closed to blot out the hard truth of my predicament.

"Are you done fighting me?" he asks, lips hovering at my ear.

"Yes." I don't have the energy to struggle.

"Good girl."

What I want is for him to wrap his arms around me and tug me close. I need the comfort of his unwavering strength. At this moment, I'm strangely fragile and precariously close to splintering apart.

His hand slides from my hip to my core. "This is mine." There's a beat of silence. The only thing that can be heard is the harsh breath that falls from my lips. "Do you understand?"

When his fingers bite into the soft flesh beneath my panties, I groan out my answer. "Yes."

"And you'll give it to me any time I want?" The question is followed by another possessive squeeze.

"Yes," I gasp.

"Was that so difficult?"

When I remain silent, he slaps the tips of his fingers against my pussy. I yelp in surprise as a strange rush of excitement pulses through me.

He smirks. "Why am I not surprised you like that?"

Embarrassment floods my cheeks until it feels like they are on fire.

"If you weren't so deceitful, you would be fucking perfect," he growls. "Take off your panties."

My eyes flare wide as I shake my head. His fingers stroke over the seam of my lips. A strangled moan slips free when he pushes the cotton against my slit. As much as I hate myself for it, my legs widen as I thrust my pelvis toward him, wanting all the pleasure he's willing to give me. When he presses his fingers deep, the cotton slides against my slick lower lips.

"I won't ask twice."

What I've come to realize is that Kingsley doesn't make idle threats. I was an idiot for allowing Everly's words to take root. This boy owns me just like he claimed, and there's nothing I can do to change it.

A whimper of protest falls from my lips when his fingers disappear. His muscled forearm returns to the tile wall beside my head so

I'm once again caged in. My fingers remain twisted in his shirt. It's as if I'm hanging on for dear life.

"Take them off," he threatens, "or I'll do it for you."

I gulp down my rising nerves only to realize that a heady mix of excitement rushes through me. "You need to move."

"Nope."

"Then I can't—"

He presses closer. "Figure it out. And do it quickly. We're running out of time."

I loosen my fingers from the thick white material before allowing my hands to fall to my sides. From behind hooded eyes, he watches as I gather up the plaid fabric before my fingers can slip beneath the hem to rest against my thighs. They skim over bare skin until I reach the elastic band of my panties. I hook my fingers inside the one-inch strip and slowly drag them down until the material no longer covers my core.

When he doesn't step away, I say, "That's as far as they'll go."

"Wiggle out of them."

"What?" He can't be serious.

His irises dilate as they remain focused on my face. "You heard me."

I glance away, wishing he would leave me alone even though I haven't felt this alive in a long time.

"Eyes on me, baby girl." His lips brush over mine. It's a featherlight touch. Barely there before it's gone. "You don't need to think. Just do what I say."

As awkward as it feels with him shoved up against me, I squirm. His cock grows harder as my pussy brushes against him. The thin cotton slips farther down my legs before pooling around my heels.

His lips curve as he presses them against mine. The caress is fleeting, and then he's sliding along my body, dropping into a squat. He reaches for them before tugging at the material. When I shift my feet, he picks up the panties before stuffing them into the pocket of his khakis.

His gaze flicks to mine as his hands settle on the flesh above my knees before spreading them apart. My breath catches as his palms slide upward, brushing over the hem of the skirt before meticulously gathering it into his fingers. Slowly, the tartan material rises until I'm completely bared to his sight.

Kingsley makes a point of dropping his gaze and staring at the V between my thighs. "Are you as wet as you look?"

I pin my lower lip with my teeth, refusing to answer.

Not bothered by my silence, he shrugs. "Guess I'll have to find out for myself, huh?" His thumbs settle on each side of my slit before pulling the flesh apart until my clit is exposed. "Fucking gorgeous," he mutters, swiping his tongue across the tiny bundle of nerves.

Pleasure explodes in my core as he buries his face against me, feasting on my pussy as if he hasn't eaten in days. My muscles tighten. Even though he's barely touched me, I'm moments away from shattering into a million pieces. Chilled air wafts over my wet flesh as the warmth of his mouth disappears.

"Now turn around." Kingsley might be on his knees, but we both know I'm the one at his mercy.

"Hmm?" His words don't immediately penetrate the sexual haze clouding my brain.

He bites out the command for a second time. *"Turn. Around."*

A scream of frustration bubbles up inside me. My body is wound impossibly tight as it throbs with arousal. When I don't spring into action, Kingsley grabs my hips and spins my body until my front is plastered against the wall. The forceful movement has the air evaporating from my lungs.

He snaps out the next order. "Lift your skirt."

What?

My skirt?

Hell no!

"Don't make the situation any worse."

I don't realize he has risen to his feet until the front of his body is pressed against my back, all but crushing me to the unforgiving tile. His voice is nothing more than a low growl at my ear. When the pressure from behind disappears, I turn my head until the side of my face can rest against the wall. I squeeze my eyes tight and drag the hem of my skirt up until it's midway over my cheeks.

"Higher."

"King—"

"Do it!"

My fingers shake as I raise the plaid material until it hovers at my waist. Cool air hits my bare ass as my breath gets trapped in my throat. My face goes up in flames as I imagine Kingsley behind me, eating me up with his eyes. With the silent tick of every second, tension curls like a wisp of smoke in the pit of my belly.

And lower.

So much lower.

My pussy throbs with awareness as arousal crashes dangerously within me. It takes everything I have to stifle the moan building inside when he finally reaches out and trails a finger across one taut curve before doing the same to the other side.

"A perfect heart-shaped ass," he murmurs thickly as his fingers sink inside my soaked heat, carefully stoking those flames all over again. Tension builds as my muscles turn lax, and I use the wall to hold myself up. If I didn't, I would slide down the tile and puddle on the floor. As a sigh falls from my lips, he cracks a wide palm against one cheek and then the other. Two movements in quick succession. The sound of flesh striking flesh rings out in the silence of the room.

My eyes fly open as I yelp, clenching my muscles against the attack.

"Stop," I whimper as he smacks me again. I rise to the tips of my toes as my back arches to avoid the unexpected punishment. Arousal explodes in my belly. The swollen lips of my pussy rub against the fabric of my skirt as I force myself to the wall.

Oh God...this shouldn't be a turn-on.

"Tell me who you belong to."

He's fucking crazy!

When I remain silent, the heat of his palm falls on me.

And then again.

"You!" I yell, breathless with the pleasure building inside me. *"I belong to you!"*

"That's right." His palms soothe the tender flesh as tears of resentment burn the back of my eyes.

"I hate you," I whisper, heart pumping furiously with a heady concoction of excitement and anger.

He continues to massage my aching flesh before his fingers dip between my lower lips, thrusting deep inside my heat.

"Is that why your pussy is practically dripping?" he asks as his body hovers over mine, his thick erection jutting against my ass cheeks. I inhale a shaky breath as he flexes his hips. Images of how he took me last night roll unwantedly through my head, stoking unwanted desire to life.

His fingers slip from me, sliding around my body until they can settle on my clit. He rubs circles, keeping up the firm pressure until my hips are jerking against his hand.

"As much as you want to hate me, you don't," he whispers in my ear before the delicious pressure and the heat of his body disappear.

My teeth sink into my lower lip to stifle the sharp sense of loss that surges through me. It's on the tip of my tongue to beg as my senses riot beneath the surface.

"From now on, when I tell you to do something, you damn well do it."

Fuck off!

Even though I don't give voice to the response, he cracks one cheek and then the other as if he hears it loud and clear. The stinging slap feels somehow sharper on my tender flesh.

"Fine!" I hiss between clenched teeth.

When he disappears, I wilt against the wall, dropping the skirt into place as the door to the bathroom slams shut.

It's only when he's gone that I realize the bastard has my panties.

26

Somehow, I manage to make it through the rest of the afternoon without further incident. Every time I pass Kingsley in the hallway, he smirks, gaze lingering on my skirt as if he has X-ray vision. It only makes me more self-conscious of my pantiless state. In each class, I remind myself to sit with my knees pressed firmly together.

By the time the bell rings at half past two, I'm more than ready to get the hell out of here. As I open my locker to gather up my books, I find my underwear dangling from the silver hook inside. With a quick glance around, I stuff it in my pocket before disappearing into the bathroom.

When I return, Everly is waiting at my locker. I grab my bag, and we leave the building together. She chatters about a couple of boys who have snagged her attention on the ride home. Twenty minutes later, she's pulling into my drive and dropping me off.

For a moment, I stare at the arched windows and stone façade of the sprawling mansion. How ironic is it that this is the only place where I can breathe?

With a shake of my head, I slip through the front door and drop my backpack in the entryway. As I do, an avalanche of emotion crashes over me. Dad's loss is more pronounced here. I can't imagine the pain of his death ever diminishing. I squeeze my eyes tightly shut in an effort to find my bearings. Once under control, I force myself to the staircase to check on Mom. As I reach for the banister, a noise from the kitchen draws my attention and has me swinging around.

What the hell was that?

My heart thumps a painful rhythm as I peek down the hallway toward the back of the house. Other than Mom, no one else should be here. Austin is at football practice. And if he wasn't, I would have seen the G-wagon parked in the drive.

When there's another noise, I realize it wasn't my imagination at all. Someone is definitely in the kitchen. I search the surrounding vicinity for a weapon. The only viable option is a vase filled with colorful blooms that was delivered late last week. I suppose if it becomes necessary, I can always hurtle the crystal container before making a mad dash for the door. I tiptoe to the grand piano and pick up the heavy vase before creeping down the hallway.

As I reach the arched doorway to the kitchen, the refrigerator slams shut.

A hungry thief?

Well, they picked the wrong house. There's not much in the way of food here. With both hands, I hoist the vase over my head, ready to inflict serious damage.

"Ouch!" a female voice hisses.

I step into the sun-drenched space and find Mom near the stove with her thumb shoved between her lips. When she sees me, her brows pinch together, and I realize I still have the vase hoisted over my head.

She pulls her thumb from her mouth before pointing. "What's going on?"

"Oh." I lower the heavy crystal before setting it on the long stretch of granite counter. "I, ah...thought someone might have broken in."

Her lips lift. It's the first smile I've seen from her since Dad died. "And your plan was to bludgeon them to death?"

I shrug, feeling foolish. "I was going for a distraction."

"You would have definitely created one." Mom grabs the teakettle from the stove before pouring the steaming liquid into a floral-colored mug.

With her attention preoccupied, I'm able to study her. She's wearing a sweatshirt and black yoga pants. Her dark hair looks freshly washed and has been pulled up into a smooth ponytail.

Not only is it nice to see the change in her demeanor and appearance but it's also a relief to hear her joke around. It's a small glimpse into the mother she once was and not the woman she morphed into after her husband's death. For the first time in two weeks, the vise that has been gripping my heart loosens. Not by much, but enough to suck in a full breath.

Her eyes widen when she glances at me, and I realize tears are clouding my vision.

"Oh, sweetie," she rasps, emotion thickening her voice as she steps around the island and pulls me into the comforting circle of her arms.

With her body pressed to mine, I realize how fragile she has become. In less than two weeks, she's lost a substantial amount of weight. We cling for what feels like an eternity before reluctantly separating.

Tears stream down her cheeks before she swipes at the wetness. "I'm sorry you've had to go through this."

"It's all right, Mom."

"It's really not." She exhales a shaky breath in an attempt to regain her composure. "I was making a cup of tea. Would you like one?"

"Sure, that sounds good."

She grabs another mug from the cherry wood cabinet and fills it with boiling water before adding an Earl Grey tea bag to steep. Something about the ritual seems to calm her nerves. With her emotions back in check, Mom holds a cup in each hand before moving around the island and settling on a stool.

She clears her throat. "So, how is it over there?"

We both know the place she's alluding to.

Rothchild Mansion.

When I remain silent, her voice dips. "Are you doing all right?"

Nope, not at all. But I can't tell her that. I can't admit to anything that might propel her backward into the quagmire of grief. "It's been fine."

"Has it?" Her eyes narrow as she searches mine for the truth I'm reluctant to share.

"Yeah." Unable to hold her probing gaze, I look away. "Has there been any word from the lawyer?" It's a glimmer of hope in the darkness and, at this point, all I have to cling to.

Kingsley is so intent on punishing me for my betrayal. I'm not sure how much more I can endure without coming unhinged. Every day, he forces me closer to the edge.

Mentally.

Emotionally.

Sexually.

She jerks her head into a tight nod. "I spoke with him this morning. He's still looking into our options." Mom reaches over and grabs my hand before squeezing it. "One way or another, we'll get you out of this. I promise."

"Okay." Even though nothing has changed, her words fill me with optimism. And right now, I need that more than anything.

A rare slice of peace falls over me as we sit at the kitchen island and sip our tea. We've done this a hundred times before, and something about the routine of it is comforting. Yet I can't help but nervously eye the digital clock on the microwave. Every minute that ticks by brings me closer to six o'clock. I dread being in the same house as Kingsley. I dread the way he touches me, breaking down every barrier until I'm nothing more than a mass of quivering hormones to do with what he pleases. There was a time when we were so much more.

"Honey?"

Her voice has me blinking out of those disturbing thoughts. "Yeah?"

"Are you feeling all right?" Her hand drifts to my forehead and then to my cheek. I'm tempted to sink into her comforting touch. It seems like forever since someone has taken care of me. "You look pale."

She doesn't have to tell me that I look like shit because I'm well aware of it.

"It's probably stress," I say offhandedly, not wanting to discuss my appearance.

Her lips sink into a frown. "Do they feed you?"

The protein bar Kingsley forces on me every morning comes to mind. "Yeah, I can have whatever I want."

"Good." There's a pause. "You're thinner than what I'm used to."

The same could be said for her. I guess this is what grief does. It ravages the people left behind until they become unrecognizable.

"I know." I give her a thin smile. "Sometimes I forget to eat. I'll work on that."

Nervous energy careens through me. I busy my hands by lifting my cup and bringing it to my lips. Something about hot tea is intrinsically comforting. The way it coats my throat in warmth, soothing me from the inside out. "Have you thought about the next step?"

"What do you mean?" Her brows knit together as she takes another drink.

I shrug, groping for the right words. "With the company. What will happen to it? What will happen to us?" A month ago, our futures seemed so set. Now, everything is in free fall. It's a disconcerting sensation.

"I don't know." Uncertainty swims in her eyes as her voice softens. "I've been trying to get through this...*loss*. Sometimes it's all I can do to get through each day. There are times when an hour feels like too much to handle."

I nod, unable to imagine how difficult all this must be for her. Mom is only forty-four years old, and now she's a widow. "I'm sorry. Maybe it's too soon to have this conversation."

"No, it's not." She shakes her head as some of the sadness and grief fade. "The only thing I'm certain of is that we can't stay here. I have no idea what will happen with the company. That's something I need to figure out with the lawyer."

Relief pumps through me at the knowledge that we're on the same page. The sooner we get the hell out of Hawthorne, the better off we'll all be.

She releases a measured breath as her voice grows steadier. "The first thing we need to do is figure out what options we have regarding the contract. If this Roland Donahue is worth the money he's being paid, he'll find a way to get rid of the affidavit without Keaton coming after us." Bitterness flashes across her face. "I'd give him the damn company if I could. We've already lost too much." Tears gather in her eyes as she reaches out and takes hold of my hand. "I won't lose you, too."

I swallow down the emotion that swells in my throat. "You're not going to lose me."

She nods before swiping at a stray tear. "I'm sorry for forcing you into this situation."

There's little point in rehashing the past. It won't do us a damn bit of good. "It's okay."

"I really hate that you're over there." Before I can respond, she asks, "They've given you your own room, right?"

"Yup."

"Good." Her shoulders collapse as relief fills every line of tension in her face. The past two weeks have aged her by a decade. Maybe more. "I was afraid you were still sleeping with him."

Guilt rushes through me as I bite my lip and glance away. This isn't a conversation I want to get into with her.

"Summer?" Her voice turns sharp with disbelief. "Please tell me you're not having sex with that boy!"

"Mom," I groan, face flooding with heat, "please, I can't talk about this right now. I really can't."

"*Oh, Summer...*" Shock and dismay settle over her features. It's so reminiscent of the last look Dad gave me that I'm barely able to hold her gaze. I want to melt into the floor and disappear. "*Please, please, please* tell me that you're using condoms."

Last night crashes through my head. I don't know if Kingsley used one. Protection, unfortunately, was the last thing on my mind.

Although I sure as hell won't be admitting that to her. The conversation that would follow is enough to make me spontaneously combust on the spot.

"Yeah," I mumble, "we do."

"I asked you before, but now the situation is different." There's a pause as she examines my eyes, searching them carefully for the truth. "Is he forcing you to have sex?"

My attention gets snagged by the dark liquid at the bottom of my cup. It's so much easier to focus on than meet her probing gaze. "Can we just drop this?"

"Please, I need to know he's not hurting you."

"He's not." I glance up. "Kingsley isn't forcing me to do anything." Images from hours ago tease and taunt me.

Push me away, Summer, or I'll take you right here.

The sound of Mom's voice dispels the memories, and for that, I'm grateful.

"I found an OB-GYN in town. I was going to schedule an appointment before your dad died. I'll call tomorrow. No matter what is happening, it's important that you're protected."

She's right. If the past couple of days have taught me anything, it's that I have no willpower where Kingsley is concerned.

"After I set up the appointment, I'll text you the information, and we'll get this taken care of."

"Thanks." As uncomfortable as this conversation has been, it was necessary. Mom's right. I need to be on the pill. The idea of an unexpected pregnancy is terrifying. If there's anything that could make this situation worse, that would be it.

A topic change seems to be in order. "Did you want help cooking dinner before I leave?"

A smile lifts her lips as the concern pinching her expression gradually fades. She looks more like herself than she has in a while, and it's a relief to see. "Sure, that would be great."

I go to the fridge and open the doors before peering inside. Austin picked up a few groceries last night, but not nearly enough to stock it. She stands beside me as we rifle through the contents.

It's slim pickings.

"Hmm." Her brows furrow. "What would you say to ordering a pizza?"

That sounds like the best idea I've heard in a long time. When my belly growls, I realize I've barely eaten anything all day. And just like that, I'm famished. It feels like I could easily wolf down three pizzas by myself. "Sure, I could get on board with that."

"Perfect. I'll grab my phone and make the call."

A few hours later, I pull the door to our house closed before heading over to the Rothchild Mansion. For the first time in days, I'm hopeful we'll find a way out of this mess. I just have to hang on a bit longer.

27

"Thanks for coming with me," I whisper, filling out a ream of paperwork at the physician's office. Usually, Mom completes all the forms, but I told her I could take care of it myself. It's like they want to document my entire life story. I'm ten minutes away from a carpal tunnel diagnosis.

"No problem," Everly says, scrolling through her Insta. "It's not like I had anything else to do. Maybe you haven't noticed, but I don't exactly have a social life here in Hawthorne."

"Do you miss New York?" I've been so wrapped up in my own shit that I haven't even thought to ask. It wasn't all that long ago I was in her shoes. The town of Hawthorne isn't an easy place to fit in. And the prep school is even less so.

"Kind of." She shrugs, eyes growing distant. "We lived on the Upper East Side, so there was always a ton of stuff going on."

I know what she means because it was the same in Chicago. There were museums, malls, movie theaters, major league sporting events, and concerts. We were constantly on the go. I have no idea what people do in Hawthorne for fun.

Tip cows?

Party in a cornfield?

It remains a mystery.

By the time I sign the last page, my hand is cramping up. I shake it out before taking the clipboard to the front desk.

The receptionist shifts the sliding glass partition and gives the documents a cursory glance before flashing a smile. "Great. They'll call you back shortly."

With a nod, I return to the chair I've been camped out in. After ten minutes of fidgeting, a door opens to the inner sanctum, and a woman in scrubs glances at the chart in her hand before calling out my name.

I pop to my feet, more than ready to get this over with. "Hi."

"Good afternoon, Summer. I'm Colleen, one of the nurses. I'll get you started."

She holds the door open for me before stopping at a scale. "Let's check your weight."

I step on the metal contraption and am surprised to discover that I've lost ten pounds since I moved to Hawthorne. I had suspected it would be a few, but that seems excessive. The nurse jots down the number, and then we're moving through a long narrow hallway dotted with college and medical school diplomas.

"We'll be going to room eight," she says as we pass by a cluster of desks.

Once inside the compact space, she takes my blood pressure and temperature. So far, everything is normal. She settles at a tiny desk with a laptop and types in the information before glancing at me. "So, tell me what brings you in today."

"Um..." My gaze skitters away as embarrassment licks at my cheeks. "I'm interested in birth control. Maybe the pill?"

"All right." She types in a few more things. "The doctor will go over all of your options after the exam."

I jerk my head and blow out a steady breath. I've never been to an OB-GYN. There was never a reason. Now there is. I'm not exactly sure what to expect, and that sends anxiety spiraling through me.

"What was the first day of your last menstruation?"

Good question. I should probably know the answer to that. My brow creases as I mentally trip over the previous month. The days and weeks have blended together to become more of a blur. A prickle of unease grows in the pit of my belly. My periods have always been unpredictable. From what I've read online, the pill can help regulate that.

"Um, I'm not sure."

"Give me your best guess."

I throw out a number that seems plausible. "Maybe five weeks ago."

"Okay. The first thing we'll do is a urinalysis. There's a bathroom across the hall. The sample bottles are already in the room. Use the Sharpie to write your first and last name on the label. After you've collected the sample, set the container in the small door on the wall and lock it." She rises from the stool and pulls open a drawer from the cabinet before grabbing a pale-yellow paper gown. "Then you can change into this. Take off all of your clothing, even your bra and underwear. The flaps of the gown go in front." She pauses for a beat as I process all the information hurtled at me. "Any questions?"

I shake my head, trying to remember each step. Mom had offered to come with me, and I'd turned her down flat. As I sit on the exam table, I kind of wish she were here. I feel alone and a little scared.

"All right," the nurse smiles gently as if she can sense my apprehension, "Dr. Davis will be in shortly."

"Thank you."

She bustles out of the room, leaving the door slightly ajar.

First order of business...the urine sample.

A few years ago, Mom broached the subject of a gynecologist. Since I wasn't sexually active, I'd nixed the idea. Who wants to go to the doctor and have a pelvic exam for shits and giggles?

But now...

It's completely necessary, and I'm kicking myself for not doing it sooner.

Once in the bathroom, I scrawl my name on the plastic container and do my best to collect a sample. Ironically, now that I need to pee, I can't force myself to go. It takes at least five minutes to finish up. As soon as I return to the examination room, I strip off my skirt, shirt, and undergarments before wrapping the gown around my body. Then I grab my phone and settle on the paper-covered table to wait for the doctor.

Ten minutes crawl by before there's a light rap of knuckles on the door. A short, blonde woman in her late forties smiles before glancing at the chart in her hand. She has a kind smile and warm eyes that instantly put me at ease.

"Hello, Summer. I'm Dr. Davis. It's nice to meet you." When she offers a hand to shake, I reach out and take her narrow one. "I understand you're here for an exam and to discuss birth control options."

That would about sum it up. "Yes."

She settles on the swivel stool before laying the chart on the desk and turning to face me. "How long have you been sexually active?"

There's no reason for embarrassment, but still... "Less than two months."

"Okay. Do you have a permanent partner?"

I scrunch my nose. "Like a boyfriend?"

Her lips lift slightly as she nods. "A boyfriend or one partner who you're intimate with."

My gaze skitters away. "Yes." While Kingsley is *definitely* not my boyfriend, I suppose he falls into the *permanent partner* category.

She nods before wheeling the stool closer. "The reason I ask is because we checked your urine sample for hCG —

hCG?

I have no idea what that is.

Why would they check for that?

"And it turns out you're pregnant," she finishes quietly.

Pregnant.

The word reverberates in my head.

No. That's not possible.

The roar of the ocean fills my ears until it drowns out almost everything else. My tongue darts out to moisten parched lips. The saliva filling my mouth disappears, leaving it to feel as dry as the Sahara.

I can barely croak out the question. *"Are you sure?"*

"I'm afraid so. The urinalysis is ninety-nine percent accurate." She rises from the stool. "We'll take blood work when we're finished. Why don't you lie back on the table, and I'll examine you? Afterward, we can talk about your options."

When I walked through the office door thirty minutes ago, I had assumed we would discuss an entirely different set of options. My mind buzzes as I recline on the table. It's like I'm having a strange, out-of-body experience, and this is happening to someone else.

I can't be pregnant.

Tears prick the back of my eyelids.

"I'll start with a breast exam."

Dr. Davis peels back the left side of the paper gown until my breast is exposed and asks me to place my left arm above my head. Barely do I feel her fingers as they move steadily in a circular motion, gently pressing against the soft tissue. Then she moves to the right side and repeats the process.

"I didn't feel anything that would be cause for concern, which is good."

I want to burst out laughing, but somehow manage to keep it contained.

Hello, lady, I'm pregnant!

That alone is cause for concern.

Like...major fucking concern.

Dr. Davis extends the metal stirrups and helps place my feet inside them.

"Would it be correct to assume this pregnancy was unplanned?"

That question opens up the floodgates as a rush of hot tears fills my eyes. I jerk my head into a nod. If I attempt to speak, I'll end up sobbing, and I don't want to do that. Stupid as it sounds, it never occurred to me that I could get pregnant. Kingsley wore condoms. It seemed like we were being careful.

Clearly, that wasn't the case.

"Let's finish up with the pelvic exam, and then we can talk."

The rest of the visit goes by in a blur of information. Turns out I'm six weeks pregnant. My periods have always been irregular, and I've never done a great job of keeping track. If Mom hadn't scheduled an appointment, who knows when I would have realized I was late. Especially considering everything that's happened. For all I know, I got pregnant the first time we had sex. Or maybe in Door County at Kingsley's beach house.

Kingsley.

Oh God...

What *am* I going to tell him?

Am I going to tell him?

I can't believe this is something I have to think about.

Once I'm dressed, I push out through the door to the waiting room. Everly glances at me before jumping to her feet and searching my face. It's as if she can sense that all isn't right. The truth of the matter is that nothing has been right for a while. But it's even more fucked up than I suspected.

"Everything good?" she asks carefully.

"Yup." I nod and glance away, unable to hold her curious stare. "Just ready to get out of here."

"Bet you're glad that's over with." She swipes her purse from the chair before slinging it over her shoulder. "Pelvics...so not fun."

I almost bark out a laugh. Instead, I keep the sound buried deep inside. I'm afraid if I release it into the air, the laughter will quickly turn to tears. As tempted as I am to confide in Everly, I need to keep this to myself until I figure out what I'm going to do.

Each time I think the situation can't get worse, I somehow manage to jackhammer to an all-new low.

28

I'm startled awake when rough hands grip my hips and flip me over before pulling me to my knees. My panties are ripped away, and he's inside me in one smooth stroke, filling me to the brim.

Kingsley.

Even though I'm half asleep, I would recognize his touch anywhere. The feel of him surrounding me, pounding into me, as his hips jerk against mine, fills some deep need inside. I can't explain it. All I know is that there is comfort in his possession. As much as I try to keep the moan locked inside, where he can't revel in my submission, that becomes impossible. The gratification is too much to absorb, and the broken sound slides from my lips, filling the silence between us. No matter how much I want to hate this, I don't.

Unwilling to deny myself the pleasure unfurling like a flower, I squeeze my eyes shut and focus on it. Neither of us wants the connection binding us together, but it's there nonetheless.

The first time Kingsley took me, a tentative link was formed. As a twin, I know exactly what it's like to feel as if you're one-half of a whole. When my body is locked in intimacy with his, that's exactly how it feels. It's totally addictive. I want to hold on to the sensation with both hands and make it last forever.

But it never does. The high I get from our fucking only lasts for a few blissful minutes before disintegrating into nothingness.

Soft grunts fall from his lips as he drives into me. His tempo picks up, becoming more frantic, and I feel myself getting pushed closer to the precipice. Before I'm able to get there, he thrusts against me and comes with a long guttural groan.

For the first time, our bodies are no longer in perfect synchronicity.

The storm swirling madly through me, picking up traction, disperses like a fog into nothingness. The disappointment that rushes in is swiftly followed by sorrow.

As he collapses against my back, his body drapes over mine almost protectively. His harsh breath drifts across my neck as I stare at the wall of windows into the darkness. Even though his cock is softening, there's still a feeling of fullness inside me. It's a fragile connection in the shadows of the room when words escape us.

A heartbeat later, the bond is shattered when Kingsley pulls out of my body before rolling from the bed. Silently, I watch as he grabs his boxers from the floor and hauls them up his hips.

His head turns as his gaze falls on me, pinning me in place. My breath hitches, a tiny bubble of hope expanding in my throat as I wait for him to make the first move. Instead of bridging the yawning distance between us, he stalks to the door, quietly closing it behind him until the lock clicks into place.

I squeeze my eyes tight as tears prick my eyes. Now that Kingsley is gone, I roll onto my side and curl up in a tight ball, feeling more isolated than before. The hard truth is that nothing about our relationship has been normal. It's been fucked up and doomed for failure from the very beginning, and nothing will ever change that.

Not me.

Not Kingsley.

And certainly not the baby growing in my belly.

The only thing true and pure between us was the day we spent on his boat when he didn't know who I was. Other than that, it's all been a game. A web of deceit. I don't trust him, and he doesn't trust me.

How can we possibly bring a baby into this world?

A wave of grief crashes over me as I realize the answer.

29

It takes effort to drag my ass from bed the next morning. As soon as I rise to my feet, a wave of nausea hits, threatening to suck me under. Unlike the previous mornings, I now understand the reason behind it. My hand flutters to my lower abdomen as I press my palm against it, almost as if I can feel the new life flourishing inside. At this point, it's the only thing that makes this pregnancy real.

The heavy weight of this decision presses down on me as I jump in the shower and dress in my school uniform. I add a bit of concealer under my eyes, golden shadow to my lids, and gloss to my lips. I might feel like shit, but I don't want anyone to comment on my appearance or ask questions.

Especially Kingsley.

Until I decide what to do, I'm keeping this new development to myself. Dr. Davis encouraged me to take some time and think about a decision. I've already made a follow-up appointment, and she offered counseling services if I need someone impartial to discuss the situation with.

If the circumstances were different, the outcome would be as well. Kingsley and I don't have a relationship, and if I've realized anything over the past month, there is too much bad blood between our families for us to move past it.

How can I bring a baby into that kind of toxic environment?

Pushing those depressing thoughts from my head, I grab my backpack and purse before walking through the gallery and hustling down the stairs. I've become a master at timing my arrival perfectly, so I make it to the foyer moments before we walk out the door. I don't want to spend any more time alone with Kingsley than I absolutely have to. And I certainly don't want to have an unexpected encounter with Keaton. The last creepy conversation was enough to last a lifetime.

I spot Kingsley at the bottom of the staircase, scrolling through his phone. A deep sadness fills me as images from last night flit through my head. It only solidifies the notion that it's much too late to fix this broken relationship.

The chime of my cell chases those thoughts away, and I pause, unzipping my purse to slide the phone from the dark depths of my bag before glancing at the screen. The message is from Austin.

Mom is making pancakes. Wanna come over?

It might not sound like much, but Mom being out of bed this early is huge. And making pancakes?

It's a little ray of sunshine in the suffocating darkness that has become my life.

I quickly type back that I'm running late but am glad Mom is doing better.

As I slide the phone into my purse, I stumble on the last tread. My bag slips from my shoulder before falling. Everything—makeup, phone, wallet, and a bunch of loose change—spills, clattering across the marble tile. I grab the banister before I face-plant at the bottom of the staircase. Kingsley leaps forward, his phone slipping from his fingers as he reaches for me. The air gets knocked from my lungs as his arms wrap around my body before hauling me close.

"You all right?" His voice is nothing more than a rumble in my ear.

An answering shiver scampers down my spine. Even though I should separate myself from him, all I want to do is burrow into his solid warmth. I'm so tempted to close my eyes and inhale a deep lungful of his rich masculine scent. Instead, I ignore the clamoring demands of my body and step away. My gaze lands on my purse and the contents strewn throughout the foyer. If this is any indication of what's in store, it'll be a shit day.

A huff of breath escapes from my lips as I drop to my knees, grabbing a slim tube of lip gloss and mascara before stuffing it into the empty bag. Kingsley hunkers down beside me. I scoop up my wallet and my phone. Thankfully, the screen isn't damaged. He dumps a few odds and ends into the bag. I'm scanning the area to see if I've missed anything when my gaze falls on the green pamphlet from the doctor.

Oh, shit.

I'd forgotten to take that out of my purse. My heart skips a painful beat as I lunge for it, but he beats me to the punch, snatching the folded paper before glancing at it.

My fingers tremble as I extend my hand. "Can I have that, please?"

It takes everything I have inside not to rip the leaflet from his fingers. If I do, it'll only prove how important it is. And then he'll do the exact opposite just to spite me. I know how his mind works.

His brows jerk together as he stares at the front page. "What is this?"

"It's not important," I mumble.

From his crouched position on the floor, he glances up, skewering me in place with the intensity of his gaze. His voice turns sharp as he holds up the pamphlet. "Where did you get this?"

Unwilling to tell him the truth, I press my lips together and remain silent.

"*Summer?*" His hand snakes out to wrap around my wrist. "*Is this yours?*"

I wince as his fingers bite into my flesh. When I try to jerk away, his hold turns punishing.

"Answer me, dammit!" He drags me across the marble until his face hovers inches from mine and his warm breath can ghost over my lips. "*Are you pregnant?*"

"Yes." The answer slips free before I can think better of it.

Air hisses from his lungs as his grip disappears, and he falls backward onto his ass. His eyes widen as emotion crashes over his features.

Shock.

Anger.

Regret.

"Why do you have this?" He glares at the paper. "Are you planning on getting an abortion?"

"I don't know," I whisper, heart thundering painfully under my breast. "I haven't decided yet."

He drags a hand over his face as if he were expecting a different response. "Were you even going to tell me?"

I pin my lip with my teeth and defiantly hold his gaze. How can he ask me that question when we're barely on speaking terms?

Apparently, my silence is answer enough.

Storm clouds gather in his eyes. If I had thought I'd seen fury from him before, I was wrong. *"You were going to abort my baby without ever mentioning it?"*

I wince as his voice cracks over me like a clap of thunder. My tongue darts out to moisten my lips as tears sting my eyes. "When exactly was I supposed to share the good news? Between you bending me over and fucking me?"

The rage dims as guilt and shame flash across his features. A hot stain of color flags his cheeks. When he remains silent, all the resentment and frustration that have been simmering beneath the surface boil over.

Who the hell is he to judge me?

"We're both eighteen years old! How am I supposed to bring a baby into this world when we hate each other? And that's not something that will ever change."

His expression becomes shuttered as every bit of emotion vanishes as swiftly as it appeared. I couldn't begin to guess at the thoughts crashing around inside his head. He folds the informational pamphlet before shoving it into the pocket of his khakis and rising to his feet.

Before I can move, he extends a hand and helps me to mine. "Come on, we'll be late."

Thrown off by the abrupt shift in his demeanor, I jerk my head into a nod before trailing him to the Mustang parked in the drive. He walks around the vehicle, popping open the door for me. A few minutes later, the engine is revving, and we're speeding away from the subdivision. I sit stiffly next to him, waiting for him to hurtle questions at me. Instead, the ride to school is made in silence. A million thoughts flutter through my head, but none make it past my lips. Kingsley must feel the same because his attention stays focused on the ribbon of road in front of him.

Once parked in the school lot, we exit the vehicle. I have no idea what to expect from him. If there is one thing that has become a constant, it's that his behavior is unpredictable.

From the corner of my eye, I spot Sloane lounging next to her silver BMW. Her gaze is focused on Kingsley. When he doesn't move to join her, the smile fades from her face as her eyes narrow. I can practically feel her penetrating stare boring into me, trying to figure out what has changed. Normally I would give her a one-fingered salute, but I don't have the energy for it today. My concerns are much greater than Sloane.

"Are you ready?"

My attention snaps back to Kingsley, and I'm surprised to find him at my side. "Yup."

Before I can readjust my backpack onto my shoulder, he slips it from my fingers and holds it in his hand.

"I can carry that," I mumble under my breath. There's no reason for him to play the part of the chivalrous knight. We both know it's nothing more than a pretty façade.

"I've got it," he grunts in response.

It might appear as if we're one unit, moving toward the three-story stone building, but nothing could be further from the truth. No longer are we two parts of the same whole. We couldn't be any further apart if we were standing on opposite shores of the same ocean. When sadness mushrooms up, I quickly snuff out the useless emotion.

Our feet slow as we reach my locker, and he silently hands over my backpack.

"Thank you," I force myself to say.

He jerks his head into a nod before taking off down the hall without another word. Confusion swirls through me as I stare after him.

"Hey, girl."

My gaze shifts to Everly, and I hoist my smile, not wanting her to glimpse the turmoil that swirls beneath the surface. "Hi." I lower my voice before adding, "Thanks again for coming with me to the doctor."

"It wasn't a problem." She flashes a grin. "Who knows, maybe at some point, you'll have to return the favor."

I really hope not.

Then I remember that Everly knows nothing about the unexpected pregnancy.

I force a cheerfulness to my voice that feels strangely foreign. I can't remember the last time I felt any genuine happiness. It's like I'm in the middle of a shitstorm with no way out. "Oh? Is there someone you have an eye on?"

"Hardly." She snorts. "I'm destined to be a lone, lonely loner."

A chuckle escapes from my lips. That's doubtful. Everly might be oblivious to the way the boys around here look at her like she's a juicy Big Mac they want to sink their teeth into, but I'm not. The long auburn hair that cascades down her back in a wavy curtain is in perfect contrast to her vibrant blue-green-colored eyes and clear porcelain complexion. Add a curvy body to that list and it's a wonder she isn't fighting the guys off with a stick.

"But that doesn't seem to be the case for you." She steps closer and lowers her voice. "Spill it, sister. What's going on with Kingsley? I noticed you two walk in together."

I shrug. "I'm not sure. It's—"

"Complicated?" she finishes with a good-natured smirk.

"Yeah." A smile tugs at my lips as I nod. "Sorry for being so secretive. Maybe someday, I'll explain everything, but I can't do that right now."

"That's too bad," she says with a pout. "Something tells me it's a good story."

She has no idea. And it's probably better that way.

When I remain silent, Everly reaches over and squeezes my shoulder. "Don't worry about it. I'm just being a nosy bitch."

"You ready for class?" a deep voice interrupts.

Both of our heads whip up.

Kingsley.

My gaze collides with his. It's all too easy to become trapped within his dark depths as the world falls away and I forget to breathe. For a sliver of a moment, he's nothing more than the gorgeous boy I met on the beach. The one who made me laugh. The one I couldn't stop thinking about for months afterward.

If only it were possible for the past to fall away as easily.

30

"Ms. Hawthorne?"

I glance up from the paper I'm drafting on *Wuthering Heights*. "Yes, ma'am?"

Normally, I try to avoid conversing with Ms. Pettijohn as much as possible. It's no secret that the woman scares the crap out of me.

"Would you deliver this packet to Mrs. Baxter in the office?"

"Sure." I rise to my feet and force myself to her desk at the front of the classroom. "Should I leave right now?"

The older teacher glances at the digital clock on the wall. Five minutes are remaining. "Why don't you gather up your belongings and take them along. It's doubtful you'll make it back in time before the bell rings."

Ms. Pettijohn hands over the manila envelope and I collect my books before leaving the room. As I pass by Everly's desk, I whisper, "See you at lunch."

She nods and continues to work on her outline. My attention gets snagged by Duke, who sits directly behind her. The blond boy glares at the back of her head with a narrowed gaze. I don't understand what his problem is. He took an instant dislike to Everly on the first day of school, and nothing since then has swayed his opinion.

Before this, I never paid him much attention. Maybe I was so focused on Kingsley that I never noticed the cruelty in the stern set of his lips. Or how odd it is that he's always surrounded by classmates yet remains separated from them.

It takes a couple of minutes to make my way through the intersecting corridors of Hawthorne Prep to the office. I push open the frosted glass door and find the school secretary sitting behind her desk, typing away at her computer. Thankfully, Mr. Pembroke, the headmaster, isn't here. We didn't get off on the best of terms when he threatened to expel Austin. Like most people at this godforsaken school, I get the distinct impression he doesn't care for us simply because of our lineage.

The moment I step inside the office, the older woman glances up, and a friendly smile breaks out across her face. She's probably the only person at Hawthorne Prep who is genuinely happy we're here.

"Summer!" she exclaims. "I haven't seen you in a while."

Her warmth is infectious, and I find myself returning the easy greeting. "Hi, Mrs. B." I set the packet on the long stretch of counter that separates us. "Ms. Pettijohn asked me to deliver this."

"Wonderful!" She rises from her chair and waddles over to the counter before picking up the envelope. "You've saved me a trip."

"No problem." I point toward the door. "I should probably go before the bell rings. I need to stop at my locker before second hour."

I almost make it to the frosted glass door when her voice halts me in my tracks. "Summer?"

With raised brows, I pivot to face her again.

"I'm sorry about your father." The wattage of her natural cheerfulness dims. "I know there's a long history in this town with the Hawthornes, but your father was never a part of that."

A prick of sadness explodes inside me. I'm barely able to force out a response. "Thank you."

"If there's anything you or your family needs, please don't hesitate to ask. Hawthorne Prep is so much more than a school. We're a tight-knit family."

A gurgle of disbelief rises in my throat, but I keep the sound buried deep inside. Unlike the majority of people here, Mrs. Baxter's senti-ments are genuine, and I know she means well. Perhaps she even sees it that way.

"I appreciate that, Mrs. B. I'll let you know if anything comes up."

She nods. "Have a good day, Summer."

Yeah, that's doubtful. It pretty much tanked the moment I cracked my eyes open this morning.

"Thanks, I will." I give her a slight wave before pushing out of the office and into the empty corridor.

Once the door closes behind me with an audible click, I inhale a deep breath before forcing it out again. There are moments, little slivers of time, when I forget Dad is gone. When I fail to remember that my world has been blown to smithereens and will never be pieced back together again the same way. Then something happens, or someone makes an innocuous comment, and I'm jarred back to the harsh reality of our situation.

I'm startled out of those thoughts when strong fingers wrap around my upper arms and spin me around until I'm flattened against the paneled wall outside the office. A dark presence looms over me and sends my heart racing.

"*Kingsley.*" His name is a gasp on my lips.

Silently, he buries his face against the crook of my neck before inhaling a big breath of me. His mouth drifts across the delicate hollow below my ear. No matter how tense my muscles become, it doesn't take long for my self-control to crumble, and then I'm melting beneath the hard lines of his body. When he's shielding me like this, it's difficult not to feel protected from everything in the world. I'm the first to admit it doesn't make a damn bit of sense. Kingsley is the last person I should feel safe with. He's the one intent on inflicting pain.

But this morning has brought a shift to our relationship. One I'm unsure how to process.

Silence rains down on us as our harsh breathing echoes off the vacant corridors. A million questions explode in my brain and sit perched on the tip of my tongue. Not a single one escapes from my lips. For whatever reason, I'm loath to ruin the fleeting closeness we've managed to discover. If I had my way, I'd stop time and stay in his arms forever.

When the bell rings, the fragile peace shatters. It's there and gone in the blink of an eye, almost as if it were nothing more than a figment of my imagination. He pulls away, disappearing through the hallway before I can think of a way to detain him. Loneliness and despair rush in, threatening to swallow me whole.

And this time, it's so much worse than before.

31

"Need a ride home?" Everly asks, sidling up beside me as I grab a couple of books from my locker.

Homework is piling up, and I need to get my head in the game before I blow my chances of getting into college. "Yeah, that would be—"

"There's no need for a ride," Kingsley cuts in, interrupting our conversation for a second time that day, "but thanks for the offer."

A fresh burst of nerves skitters across my spine. Spending time alone with him requires me to be in a certain mindset with my walls locked firmly in place. After the closeness we shared in the hallway this morning, I haven't had a chance to erect them again. If I'm being completely honest, I haven't been able to stop thinking about the way he touched me.

Did it mean anything?

Or was it just another mind fuck?

That's the question that plagues me most.

"No." I shake my head. "That's all right. I'd rather—"

With a flick of his eyes, he dismisses me before turning to the girl at my side. His tone is firm. He's not asking permission; he's telling us the way it is. "I appreciate you watching out for my girl, but I'll take it from here."

My girl?

Where did that come from?

What I hate most is that the endearment makes me feel all warm and tingly inside.

Everly's brows shoot up across her forehead as if she is just as surprised to hear him refer to me like that as I am. Her gaze bounces from him to me as if to determine my thoughts on the matter. The last thing I want is to put her in the middle of our skirmish. I like the auburn-haired girl way too much to see her make an enemy out of Kingsley.

"It's fine." Much like a magnet, my gaze is drawn to him. "There are things we need to sort out."

"Are you sure?" Her eyes narrow as skepticism colors her voice. Maybe I haven't confessed everything going on with Kingsley, but she's seen enough to draw her own conclusions.

I nod and force a smile to my lips. There doesn't seem to be a way out of the situation. Instead of walking away, she takes a step toward the dark-haired boy, crowding into his personal space. She's a couple of inches shorter than I am, and next to Kingsley's towering figure, she looks like David to his Goliath. My mouth falls open when she rams a finger into his chest.

"Just know that I'm watching you," she warns.

I glance at him with wide eyes, afraid of what his reaction will be.

Instead of getting annoyed, his lips curl into a thin smile. "Noted."

A heavy silence falls over the three of us as she gives him the hairy eyeball before swinging around to face me. "I'll text you later."

Unsure how to respond, I shift from one foot to the other. "Umm, okay."

Was there really a time when I thought Everly was timid?

The idea is almost laughable. The girl has huge balls.

Huge!

With one last narrowed glare at Kingsley, Everly takes off with the strap of her messenger bag slung over her shoulder.

We watch as she disappears down the corridor before he says, "You like her." It's not a question, more like a statement.

What's not to like?

Everly doesn't let anyone push her around, and she gives zero fucks if she offends the popular people at Hawthorne. For those reasons alone, it would be difficult not to like her.

"Yeah, I do." She's turned out to be a good friend. One who is willing to stick by my side through thick and thin. That's not easy to find. Especially in high school.

I clear those thoughts from my head and make a last-ditch effort to escape his dangerous presence. "Don't you have football?"

As much as Kingsley enjoys the sport, his life doesn't revolve around it. In that regard, he and my brother couldn't be more different. Austin lives and breathes the game. It's his sole reason for waking up in the morning. Take that away, and he would be lost.

"Practice was canceled for the afternoon."

"Oh." Well, damn.

"Your brother is staying after to lift with a couple of the guys," he adds.

No surprise there.

Football and lifting have always been a physical outlet for Austin. He used to spend an hour or two a day working out. Now it's more like three or four. His dream is to play in the NFL. In order for that to happen, he needs to keep his grades up and get recruited by a top Division I university. His dyslexia has always made academics a challenge. Being ripped away from his team in Chicago and the starting QB position to move to Hawthorne only made it worse. Layer on Dad's sudden death and me being forced to live with the Rothchilds and you have the perfect recipe for disaster. I've always been the one to make sure that Austin was on track with homework and grades. Without me living at home, it's not as easy to keep tabs on him.

"Ready to go?" he asks, breaking into my thoughts.

Devoid of any other choices, I jerk my head into a nod. As I reach for my backpack, Kingsley snatches it from the locker.

Why does he do this?

Why does he have to be nice?

It only stirs up more confusion, and that's exactly what I don't need. It would be so much easier if he'd be a domineering asshole without a single redeeming quality.

"You don't have to carry it," I snap, frustration bubbling up inside me. "I'm not an invalid."

Hurt flickers across his face before his expression hardens and his jaw tightens. "Did I say that you were?"

As tempting as it is to argue, what would be the point? It's never gotten me anywhere in the past. No matter what, Kingsley always gets his way. The guy could move mountains if he put his mind to it.

I huff out an exasperated breath, knowing it's better to get this over with. The sooner we get out of here, the faster I can flee to the safety of my house.

In silence, we head for the exit before pushing out into the bright sunshine. There's a crispness to the air that feels invigorating. Red and golden-colored leaves carpet the ground and crunch beneath the soles of our shoes as we walk toward the parking lot.

Students have gathered in small clusters and are talking and laughing. Blazers have been shed and collars loosened. A handful of people call out greetings to Kingsley as we pass by. When we're about a hundred feet from the Mustang, he clicks the key fob and opens the passenger side door. I slide onto the black leather as he dumps both bags into the back seat before walking around to the other side.

When he nears the hood, Sloane materializes out of nowhere. I watch from inside the vehicle as she reaches for his arm. Hot licks of jealousy bubble up before I can stop it. My eyes widen when he jerks his arm from her hold. The top of the convertible along with the windows are rolled up, encapsulating me in the confined space. I watch their lips move and hear the light buzz of conversation, but I'm unable to make out what's being said. Hurt and confusion flash across her face, and I realize she's pleading with him. I scrutinize Kingsley's expression only to find it closed off.

The possessiveness that had flared to life moments ago dissolves into something that feels suspiciously like pity. Kingsley pushes past the blonde before jerking open the door and sliding onto the seat beside me. Sloane blinks away a sheen of wetness before turning glaring eyes toward me. The hatred swirling through her blue depths sends a chill of unease slithering down my spine. If she could knife me in the back and get away with it, she would do it in a heartbeat.

When Kingsley turns the key, the engine purrs to life. Instead of disclosing any details from their private conversation, he remains aggravatingly silent. I clamp my mouth shut, refusing to pry.

One second.

I won't ask.

Two seconds.

I don't even want to know.

Three—

"What was that about?"

Dammit.

"Nothing." Irritation wafts from him in heavy waves as he stares straight ahead. "I've told her a dozen times that I'm not interested, but she doesn't get it."

Reluctantly, my gaze fastens on to Sloane as she returns to her friends a few rows over. She tosses another look full of longing at Kingsley as he backs out of the parking spot in front of the gray stone building. She's the last person I should feel sorry for. The girl has been a huge raving bitch to me every chance she gets. But for some reason, pity fills me.

It must be the hormones.

"She likes you," I murmur, almost to myself.

He flicks a surprised glance at me before his expression turns to ice. "That's not my problem, now is it?"

That is such a guy response, it almost sets off my temper. "I don't know, it kind of seems like your problem." I watch him from the corner of my eye. Again, I shouldn't ask...

It's certainly none of my business.

But that doesn't stop the question from popping free. "Did you have sex with her?"

A muscle ticks in his jaw as he stares stoically out the windshield.

When he fails to respond, I snap, "I'll take that as a yes." Deep down, I *knew* he'd slept with her. Sloane's unrelenting possessiveness was the first tip-off.

His lips tighten into a thin line. Just when I wonder if he'll ignore me, the words spray from his mouth like bullets. "Yeah, we did. But it was a year ago. I was clear from the beginning that it was nothing more than sex, and she was fully on board with it."

Seriously?

Are guys *really* that stupid?

Or do they only hear what they want to?

Unable to help myself, I snort and roll my eyes. "You don't know anything about the female sex, do you?"

Heat leaps to life in his dark depths as he pins me in place with the force of them. "I sure as hell know how to bring one to her knees and make her beg for more."

And just like that, the tables have been turned.

Since that's not a statement I'm going to touch with a ten-foot pole, I brush it aside. "Here's a little FYI for future reference, when a girl says she's cool with *just sex*, she's not. Most of the time, she wants more."

"Again, not my problem. The girls I've been with always know the score up front. It's one of the conditions to me laying hands on them. If I make it clear from the beginning that it's nothing more than fucking, then they should do us both a favor and heed the warning instead of trying to make it into something it'll never be."

That little speech makes me want to vomit.

Did I know the score up front?

His words leave me cringing with a need to fold in on myself. Maybe that's all I ever was. Another stupid female to add to an already lengthy list.

"Is that all it was between us?" It takes effort to swallow down my rising nausea. *"Just sex?"* I don't understand why I'm so intent on inflicting more damage on to myself. It's not like it matters.

Yet, for some inexplicable reason, it does. More than I want to admit.

His fingers tighten around the steering wheel as we careen down the country road, picking up speed. The engine revs and the scenery flies by the passenger side window in a blur of gold and green. "Is that what you think, Summer?"

I shrug and remain silent.

"You know damn well it wasn't," he bites out, anger vibrating throughout his tone.

Do I?

How am I supposed to know that?

Red barns dot the landscape along with small herds of black and white spotted cows. There's something peaceful about the vast openness, yet it does nothing to settle the turbulent emotions attempting to break loose.

"You were never just a fuck. It always meant more," he admits in halting tones.

I glance at him, startled by the admission. Something reluctantly loosens in my chest before thawing. The need to guard myself against him thrums through me. Kingsley has the power to inflict untold amounts of damage. Kind of like Godzilla wreaking havoc on a small Japanese fishing village. I'm nowhere near ready to allow that to happen.

When we zoom past the turnoff for our subdivision, panic fills me. "Where are we going?"

"You'll see."

Being trapped alone with Kingsley is a double-edged sword. How is it possible to love and hate something in equal measure at the same time?

Ten minutes later, he swings into the gravel parking lot of the Dairy Barn, an ice cream stand in the middle of Hawthorne. Memories of the first time we came here rush through me. As promising as the outing had begun, it had ended in disaster. I'm not looking for a repeat performance.

He cuts the engine before shifting his body toward mine. My breath stalls when he lifts a hand to cup the side of my face. Instead of ducking away, I sit rooted to the leather, unable to escape the contact.

His touch shouldn't feel so good. And it certainly shouldn't create a sense of rightness in me. If I were smart, I would knock his hand away. Instead, I close my eyes and relax into his palm as he cradles my cheek. If I didn't understand it before, I do now. I'm a glutton for punishment with masochistic tendencies.

"You realize we're going to have to talk about this, right? I won't let you push me away."

Deep down, I've always known that. It's why I didn't want to tell him until I had a better handle on the situation.

My eyelashes flutter open, only to find his gaze piercing mine. "I know."

He draws closer, the scent of his aftershave scrambling my senses. All I want to do is strain toward him. How am I supposed to fight not only him but myself as well?

"Have you given it any more thought?"

My teeth sink into my lower lip as I shake my head and glance away. "I need time."

Gentle fingers guide my face back to his. There is no running or hiding from him. He won't allow it. "Do I get a say in the matter?"

"Do you really want one?" I fire back, already knowing what the answer will be.

Anger flashes across his face as tension crackles in the air between us. "How can you ask that?"

"How can I not? You've made your feelings crystal clear." There's a beat of silence before I add, "You hate me."

The fury filling his voice drains away. "That's not true," he mumbles as his hand falls from my face, coming to rest on his thigh. "I know things have been rough between us—"

Ha!

A gurgle of laughter explodes from my lips. *Is he joking?* "That's the understatement of the decade. Maybe even the century."

He releases a measured breath before conceding, "You're right, okay? But this is a decision we should make together. It doesn't just affect you. It involves me, too."

I chew my lower lip and stare sightlessly out the windshield. As much as I hate to admit it, he's not wrong. This baby is his as much as it's mine. Maybe he should have equal say in the matter.

Air gets trapped in my throat when he carefully places his hand over my flat belly. The palm is so wide, the fingers tapered, the nails short and blunt. The heat of his touch burns a hole through the white shirt and waistband of my tartan skirt down to my skin. If I thought the connection between us had been severed, I was wrong. It's there, humming dangerously beneath the surface.

"How pregnant are you?"

There is nothing amusing about this situation, but that doesn't stop the snort from escaping. "Very."

He huffs out a laugh as some of the tension loosens from his rigidly held muscles. "That didn't come out the way I intended."

Instead of waiting for him to reframe the question, I blurt, "Six weeks. We have time to..."

"Make a decision?" His lips sink into a grim line.

I'm barely able to push out a response. "Yeah."

His hand tightens over my belly, the fingers curling into my pelvic bone. There shouldn't be anything comforting about his touch. And I certainly shouldn't feel less alone because he's here, wanting to be a part of this decision.

All he's doing is confusing matters.

And that's the last thing I need.

That night I wake to Kingsley slipping into my bed and stripping off my T-shirt and panties. Silently, I wait for him to flip me over and take me from behind. Instead, he gathers me into his arms until every hard line of his body is pressed against my softer ones.

His lips ghost over mine without ever quite touching them. The warmth of his breath is drugging. I want to inhale giant gulps of him. If I didn't know better, I'd almost think he was asking for consent, but that can't be the case. Kingsley doesn't ask permission. Whether by gentle means or brute force, he takes what he wants.

When I lift my mouth to his, seeking his touch, his lips settle over mine. A groan rumbles up from deep in his throat as the velvety softness of his tongue sweeps across the seam of my lips. As soon as I open under the firm pressure, he plunders the inside of my mouth, ravaging me with an aching sweetness that blots out everything but the physical pleasure he's intent on doling out. The kiss becomes so deep that I don't know where he ends, and I begin. It dredges up feelings of how it once was between us before life imploded, obliterating everything in its wake.

His arms tighten as he rolls onto his back, taking me with him until I'm settled on top, my thighs spread to straddle his narrow waist. The lips of my bare pussy are splayed wide against his taut abdominals. As he draws in a breath, I feel the shift of toned muscle beneath me. I sit up, finding purchase by bracing my palms against the solid width of his chest. When he flexes, his thick erection glides over my delicate flesh, setting off a shower of fireworks in my core.

Once.

Twice.

Three times.

The friction we create is staggering. My eyelids threaten to close as my head lolls back. Sensation ricochets through me, echoing in my fingertips and toes. His hands bite into my hips, anchoring me in place as he rocks against me.

"Open your eyes," he rasps.

It takes a herculean effort on my part to lift my head and crack open my eyes. And then he's snagging my gaze, holding it captive with his own. Sparks explode deep in my core. He's not even inside me, and there is already so much pleasure.

"Look at where we're connected." There's a pause as my gaze drops to my spread thighs. The movement of his hips becomes more pronounced. His thick length slides against my lower lips before the crown of his cock peeks from between my folds, bumping my clit.

It's erotic as hell.

My pussy is drenched, making it easy for him to slide against me.

We've never had sex in this position. Watching him move adds a whole new dynamic, heightening all of my awareness. I find myself unable to look away from the sight. As amazing as this feels, I need more. It's like being taunted over and over but never quite reaching the pinnacle. Frustration spirals through me, and my movements become desperate.

He must realize what I need because he jerks his hips and gently slides inside my wet heat before filling me to the brim. A moan falls from my lips at the sensation of him stretching me wide. I feel every inch of him buried deep inside. And this time, there is no condom to come between us.

"Look at the way you ride my cock."

At his urging, my gaze once again drifts to where our bodies are truly connected. Not only do I feel him pulsing inside me, but I see it. I can watch the way he rolls his hips, pulling out only to thrust in with more force. When he's buried in me like this, there is no better feeling, and the bond between us is undeniable.

"I've never fucked without a condom," he grits between clenched teeth as if it takes all of his willpower to hold on. "It feels so damn good."

He's right.

It *does* feel good.

I wouldn't have thought it possible, but there's something about his bare cock surging rhythmically that makes the pleasure a thousand times greater. He flexes his muscles, pulling out before sliding home.

When a whimper escapes from my mouth, his movements still.

"Am I hurting you?" His voice turns rough with fear.

I shake my head and bite my lip. His concern melts something deep inside that I'd rather not acknowledge.

"Are you sure?" His fingers tighten around my hips, stilling my movements.

"It doesn't hurt," I pause before adding, "it feels really good."

His thrusts become slower. Gentler. His hands drift from my hips over my rib cage before settling on my breasts, palming the soft weight.

Need pools in my core as his body rocks against mine. There has never been this element of tenderness to our sex. I'm almost afraid to read into what it means. The way his fingers stroke over me is more worshipful than anything else. And I realize that I like this just as much as when he gathers the length of my hair in his fist, nips at me with sharp teeth, or pinches my nipples with rough fingertips.

Our bodies move in perfect harmony. Every thrust of his hips makes me soar higher until it feels possible to reach out and touch the stars that crowd the night sky. It doesn't take long for my world to splinter apart. His name is a fervent cry on my lips. He holds back, never quickening the pace or driving too deep. The rhythm remains constant.

His gaze stays pinned to mine as he groans out his own release. Waves of pleasure crash over his features, and I find myself unable to look away. There's something beautiful about watching this strong boy fall apart and knowing that I'm the one who made it happen.

Instead of crashing back to earth with a painful thud, I drift like a feather on a gentle breeze. Gradually, my breathing evens out and my rigidly held muscles loosen, turning lax. My mind clicks back on as I anxiously wait to see how this will play out. This is usually the part when he pulls his softening cock from my body and rolls from the bed, leaving the room as quietly as he appeared.

The thought of that happening after the intimacy we shared has sorrow pushing in at the edges, threatening to swallow me whole. It's brutal to feel so intensely connected to Kingsley, only to have him callously sever the link.

Our gazes stay locked as his hands slip from my breasts, trailing over my rib cage, before sliding around to my spine. He drags me to his chest, pressing me close. The breath escapes from my lungs in a rush as a tempered bubble of happiness explodes.

I squeeze my eyes tight and allow the steady thumping of his heart to fill my ears. For the first time since Dad died, I can truly breathe again, and within a matter of moments, I'm drifting off to sleep wrapped up in Kingsley's embrace.

"Ready for lunch?" Everly asks as I slam my locker door closed. "I'm freaking famished."

"Yup." With my brown paper bag in hand, we walk through the crowded corridor to the cafeteria. Everly chatters about an upcoming party that we've heard whispers about, but I'm only listening with half an ear.

My gaze gets snagged by Kingsley, who lounges against his locker as a group of football players surrounds him. When he catches sight of me, he straightens, pushing away from the blue metal and clearing a path through a sea of guys until he stands in the middle of the hall.

"I'm not going to lie," Everly whispers from the side of her mouth, "you two give me whiplash."

My gaze never deviates from the dark-haired boy. She's not wrong. Unfortunately, that's a perfect way to describe our relationship.

Whiplash.

It's as exhausting as it is exhilarating. The constant push and pull between us feels as if it will never dissipate. It's like a fire burning out of control. Even now, I'm not sure if containment is possible.

"Hey," he says when we're close enough.

"Hi." Heat slams into my cheeks as images from last night flash through my brain like a slow-motion picture show. Once again, our relationship has changed, morphing into something new. There is a fragile peace that has sprung up between us.

A truce of sorts.

During the day, he hovers protectively over me, but there is still a distance between us. We aren't the same as we once were. Under the cover of darkness, though, it's an entirely different story. He doesn't allow me the same freedom. I'm exposed and vulnerable. He worships my body, forcing me to orgasm over and over again until I want to die with the pleasure he is capable of giving. It's as if he's trying to convey all the pent-up emotions that scratch and claw beneath the surface of our relationship. Afterward, I fall into an exhausted sleep against his chest. When I wake in the morning, his arms are wrapped protectively around me.

Kingsley falls in line beside me as Everly flanks my other side. The throng of rowdy football players trail us, talking and jostling one another. A sheath of long blond hair catches the corner of my eye, and I turn, gaze colliding with a heated blue one.

Sloane.

Unconcealed hatred wafts from her in hot, suffocating waves. She crosses her arms against her chest and stares daggers at me.

Once we reach the cafeteria, Everly and I split off from the guys as they head to the hot lunch line while we make a beeline for our usual table.

Her feet falter as she grumbles, "I liked it better when we sat by ourselves."

I glance at her and then to the table in the center of the room. Jasper, Delilah, Austin, Duke, and a couple of other boys are already digging into their lunches.

My guess is that her reluctance has everything to do with Duke. They've fallen into a strange pattern. Everly does her best to ignore him while the blond boy goes out of his way to needle her. He's constantly poking and prodding. I don't understand what his problem is. Before she started at Hawthorne Prep, Duke mostly kept to himself and didn't bother anyone. It's like she brings out the worst in him.

"I don't mind if we sit somewhere else." Over the past several weeks, Everly has become a really good friend. If she's not comfortable eating lunch at our usual table, then we'll move. Kingsley won't be happy about it, but he can deal.

Indecision flickers across her face.

"Look," I say, "I know you're not crazy about Duke—"

She snorts before muttering, "How did you guess?"

"Did something happen between you two?" Maybe there's more going on than I'm aware of.

"No," she grumbles stubbornly, eyes narrowing, "I just don't like him. It's nothing more than that."

Hmm.

Why do I have the strange feeling she's holding back? There are definite undercurrents simmering beneath the surface between them, but I'm just not sure what they mean. And let's face it, I've had my own crap going on and haven't been paying as much attention as I should.

And that's on me for being a shitty friend.

My gaze flickers to the table again, and I'm surprised to realize that Duke has straightened on the bench and is watching us. Well, not *us* exactly.

More like Everly.

Yup, his focus is *definitely* locked on Everly.

From what I can tell, he doesn't give a damn if she notices his blatant interest. If I was uncertain about something going on between them, those questions have been laid to rest. Now I just have to figure out what it is.

I clear my throat to recapture her distracted attention since she's full-on glaring at the blond boy. If looks could kill, he'd be dead on arrival. "Maybe it would be better if we sit somewhere else for today."

Her shoulders jerk back as she straightens to her full height. "You know what? Forget it, we'll sit at our normal table. If that asshole thinks he can intimidate me, he's got another thing coming."

Well, she's right about that. Everly has turned out to be the type of girl who isn't easily cowed. By anyone. And that includes Duke.

Maybe I should say—*Especially Duke.*

Sparks are already flying, and we haven't even reached the table yet. The two of them in such close contact seem like a disaster waiting to happen. "Are you sure? I really don't mind if we move."

Everly presses her lips together as determination settles over her face. She looks ready to do battle, and I won't lie, it's a little frightening. "Nope, it's all good."

Sure, she says that now, but I'm worried about what will happen in ten minutes. The table could explode into a war zone.

"Clearly, you two have a problem, and I don't want to make it worse."

"It's a little late for that," she huffs.

I glance at Duke, unsure what to make of the bizarre situation. There's always been a remoteness to his demeanor as if an invisible shield separated him from everyone else at Hawthorne Prep. Everly, however, snaps him right out of his indifference. He gets this look in his eyes when she's around. A strange mixture of anger and irritation.

Maybe even lust.

Then again, I could be reading into things that aren't necessarily there.

"Is it possible for you guys to sit down and clear the air?"

"If clearing the air involves Duke Carmichael kissing my ass, then sure," she mutters as we weave our way toward the table, "I'm all for it."

Her snappy retort has the corners of my lips twitching.

As we reach the long stretch of polished wood, Everly takes the seat as far from Duke as she can possibly get and remain in the same zip code. His lips curl into a feral smile, as if he understands her motivations for strategically positioning herself where she has. It's like they're playing an intense game of chess.

A few minutes later, Kingsley settles next to me with his tray. The way his muscular thigh brushes against mine sends a thousand little tingles cascading down my spine. Without realizing it, my body has become highly attuned to his. I used to wonder if anyone else could make me feel this way. Deep down, I already know the answer.

When Everly pulls out the sandwich from her brown paper bag, I do the same, nibbling at the PB and J Mrs. Fieber packed this morning. On the way out the door, she handed over a homemade protein bar and fresh-squeezed orange juice in a travel mug along with my lunch.

After a couple of minutes, Kingsley grumbles in my ear, "You need to eat."

"I don't have much of an appetite." Too much is ricocheting around in my brain. Too many decisions need to be made. Too much hangs precariously in the balance. And all of it weighs heavily on me.

When I don't immediately dig into my meal, he picks up a fry from his plate and holds it to my lips. Embarrassed by the attention, I keep them pressed stubbornly together. Instead of withdrawing, he arches a brow and stares me down. Since we both know I won't win in a battle of wills, I open my mouth a fraction. It's carefully that he presses the thin cut of potato between my lips.

All too easily, I become trapped in his mahogany-colored gaze. And just like that, everyone around us fades into nothingness.

After the fry disappears, his fingers brush against my lips.

As I chew and swallow, Kingsley closes the distance between us so that only I am privy to his whispered words. "Good girl."

The low sound of his voice scrapes something deep inside me, sparking arousal in my core. I can only liken it to the strike of a matchstick that ignites an inferno in my panties.

For the next ten minutes, he patiently feeds me until I finally say, "Enough." It only makes me realize how little I've been consuming for my belly to fill so easily.

"Damn girl, that was smoking hot," Everly murmurs in my ear, knocking me out of the sexual haze that had slyly wrapped its way around me. This boy is completely dangerous.

"Hi, Kingsley."

My belly sinks at the sound of Sloane's flirty voice. One flick of my eyes tells me that the blonde has sidled up to the table with her minions in tow. His gaze stays fastened on me as he grunts out an unintelligible response.

When Kingsley says nothing more, she glances at the other boys crowded onto the benches. "Hey."

There's a chorus of greetings and a few chin lifts in return. The corners of my lips twitch as Everly rolls her eyes with abandon.

"Just in case you haven't heard, Aubrey's parents are out of town for the weekend, and she's having people over Saturday night." Sloane flips her long blond hair over her shoulder before cocking a hip. "I hope you'll be there."

She glances at everyone before her attention settles on Kingsley. It's painfully obvious that Sloane has feelings for him. It's also equally apparent that he doesn't return them. And if there's anyone that she blames for that, it's me.

"Nah, probably not," he says offhandedly, "but thanks for the invite."

Before she can convince him otherwise, one of the football players pipes up. "Hey, what about me? Am I invited?"

"Doubtful." She smirks at the guy, giving him a coy look from beneath the thick fringe of her lashes. "But maybe I'll let you convince me otherwise." Her gaze flickers back and forth between the now grinning guy and the boy sitting next to me.

"Go for it, Axel," Kingsley interjects. "She needs to find someone else to obsess over."

A punch of color stains Sloane's cheeks.

"Kingsley," I mutter with an elbow to his ribs. He grumbles in response but says nothing more.

"Hey, I got an idea. We can tag team her!" an obnoxious voice shouts from somewhere down the table. "I heard you're into that, Carmichael!"

Everly's eyes widen at that bit of news.

I'm surprised when Duke rises from the bench and glares at the guys who are joking around at Sloane's expense. "Shut the fuck up and leave her alone, dickhead."

Most girls would be in tears, but not Sloane. Instead, a wicked smile curves her lips. "Maybe I am, but you sure as hell won't be finding out."

Um, wow.

With a flounce, the blonde swings away from the table as her cronies fall in line behind her. As the guys go back to their conversations, I give Duke a considering look. Why would he stick up for Sloane? I didn't realize they were friends. I've never seen them speak two words to each other. Everly's brows pinch together as if she's trying to figure out the same thing.

"Carmichael," another guy cracks, "you don't mind if I bone your cousin, do you? She's one hot piece of ass."

Duke jerks his broad shoulders as he resettles on the bench. "I don't give a fuck what you do. Although my advice is to be careful. That girl is like a praying mantis. She'll fuck you and then bite your head right off."

Cousin?

Well, I certainly didn't see that one coming. I never realized they shared the same surname.

It's almost a relief when the bell rings, signaling the end of lunch and the beginning of a five-minute passing period before the start of fifth hour. I dump my uneaten food into the garbage can before falling in line with Everly. Kingsley stays behind to talk with a couple of the guys.

"Do you have any plans after school?" Everly asks as we head out of the spacious dining hall and into the corridor. "If you're not busy, we could get started on the AP psych project."

"Sure, that sounds good." Maybe we can work at my house. It might be a nice distraction for Mom.

Every day that passes by, Mom seems more and more like her old self. She's still adjusting to our new normal, but each morning, she gets out of bed and dressed, putters around the house, and takes care of the bills that were piling up.

As we turn into the hallway where our lockers are located, someone rams me between the shoulder blades. With a yelp, I stumble. My arms pinwheel in an attempt to regain my balance in the sea of students who surround us. The force is enough to send me pitching forward.

"Summer!" Everly gasps, reaching out to grab me, but it's too late. There's nowhere to go but down.

I trip over my feet as the floor rises to meet me. Or maybe it's the other way around. A hand flattens against the top of my shoulder, pressing me down instead of assisting me up. My hands and knees take the brunt of the fall as I slam into the unforgiving marble before rolling to my side with a grunt.

Everly drops down as a pointy shoe connects with my abdomen. A scream tears from my lips as I curl into a tight ball, attempting to protect myself from the attack. The one thought that fills my brain is the tiny embryo growing in my belly.

My harsh breath fills my ears as my arms wrap around my head. People surround me, pressing in. Panic floods through me at being trapped on the floor. The moment seems to stretch forever until firm hands wrap around my body, scooping me off the cold tile as Kingsley gathers me into his arms.

"Are you all right?" His concerned gaze searches me for obvious signs of injury. "What happened?"

Tears prick my eyes as I blink them back, unwilling to let them fall in front of everyone who now crowds around us. "I don't know." It takes effort to keep the wobble from my voice. "I was shoved from behind and tripped."

He growls, searching the crowd of blue blazers with suspicion. I do the same, looking for one in particular, but don't see her gloating face in the vicinity. Still...I know who's responsible, and there's no way it was an accident.

34

I twist onto my side as a lightning strike of pain shoots through my lower abdomen, jolting me from a sound sleep. A moan slips free as a vicious cramp grips me.

"Summer?" Kingsley's groggy voice penetrates the cloud of agony that surrounds me as he lays a hand on my shoulder. "What's wrong?"

It's only when I try to pry my eyelids open that I realize they're screwed tightly shut. It takes a moment to find my bearings and separate my dreams from the reality unfolding around me. The bedroom is swathed in darkness. Through the unadorned window, I'm able to make out splashes of pink and purple color as the sun peeks over the horizon.

"I'm not sure," I whisper as another spasm twists my insides. "My stomach hurts."

Those words have him jackknifing in the bed. Almost tentatively, his hand settles on my belly. "Do you think something is wrong with the baby?"

Fear slices through me, right down to the marrow in my bones. "I don't know." I can barely force out the response. Releasing it into the eerie silence of the room is frightening.

My belly seizes again, and I fold in on myself as pain ricochets through my womb. This feels like the cramps I get with my period. What I don't know is if this normal or something to be concerned about.

"Where's the number for the doctor?" Kingsley throws off the sheets before exploding into motion.

"There's a card in my purse." I point at the dresser, a grimace twisting my expression as a moan falls from my lips.

Kingsley clicks on the lamp next to the bed before shooting across the room. He rifles through the contents of my leather bag before pulling out an appointment card. His brows pinch together as he grabs his cell phone and punches in the number. With the fullness of his lower lip tucked between his teeth, he waits for someone on the other end to answer.

When I pull myself to a seated position, scooting closer to the edge of the bed, he barks, *"What are you doing?"*

"I need to use the bathroom." My fingers shake as they curl into the sheets.

He blows out a steady breath, his nostrils flaring as he tempers his tone. "Stay put until I talk to the doctor and we figure out what's going on."

"I need to go." When he remains silent, I add, "It can't wait."

From the way his lips thin, it's obvious he wants to argue. As I slip from the mattress and rise unsteadily to my feet, a sticky warmth fills my panties. Kingsley's eyes widen as he stares at my bare thighs before the phone drops from his fingers, clattering to the floor. Before I can register what's going on, he sweeps me off my feet and into his arms.

"I'm taking you to the hospital." Fear threads its way through his snapped words.

An answering sob gathers in my lungs as I burrow against the strength of his chest. "What's happening?"

"I don't know."

He sets me carefully on the bed before rushing to the dresser and yanking open a drawer, grabbing the first thing his fingers come in contact with. A purple Northwestern hoodie and a pair of leggings. I stare sightlessly at the ceiling as my mind cartwheels. Even as I lie on the bed, blood seeps from between my thighs. The hot stickiness of it makes me queasy.

I draw in a shaky breath before gradually expelling it from my lungs, trying to calm myself from the inside out. At any moment, I'll spin out of control. When Kingsley returns, there's a deep frown tugging at the corners of his lips as he pulls the hoodie over my head and assists me into the black stretchy pants.

I focus on his face, and it grounds me in the here and now. When I attempt to sit up, he slips his arms around my body and lifts me against him. I press my face into his chest as he strides from the bedroom. Beneath his T-shirt, his heart jackhammers a steady beat.

Thump.

Thump.

Thump.

Kingsley stalks through the second-floor gallery before descending the curving staircase. His grip tightens, pressing me closer. Once at the bottom, an inaudible hum of words is exchanged before we're out the door. He hits the locks of the Mustang before gently setting me inside and reclining the seat so I'm able to lie flat. With barely a blink, he's sliding in beside me, revving the engine and shooting from the driveway.

As we turn out of the subdivision, Kingsley glances at me, concern brimming in his dark depths. Our gazes lock and hold as he reaches over, entwining our fingers before giving them a comforting squeeze. "Everything will be okay."

His words reverberate throughout my head as the scenery whizzes by the passenger side window.

How can he be so sure?

At this moment, as pain spirals through me, nothing feels like it will ever be all right again.

35

Soft morning light filters into the room as I curl onto my side and stare sightlessly at the wall of windows. The tears refuse to stop. It's as if a faucet has been turned on as they leak insistently from the corners of my eyes.

By the time we arrived at the hospital, it was too late, and I had miscarried. The little being filling my belly is no longer a possibility.

A decision that has yet to be made.

And I have no idea how to feel about that. I can barely admit there is relief in the knowledge that the choice has been taken out of my hands. As soon as that thought creeps into my brain, guilt rushes in, nearly swallowing me whole.

How can I be relieved about losing my baby?

Kingsley's baby.

A pervasive feeling of sorrow blankets everything, eclipsing all other emotions that try to take root. Even though I was confused, I'm brokenhearted that my body rejected the pregnancy.

The emergency room physician was very matter of-fact about the situation. Miscarriages are not uncommon. They can happen before a woman even suspects she's pregnant. In a way, I suppose it makes sense. If I hadn't gone to the doctor and taken a test, I might not have realized it either. I would have chalked up the cramping to a bad period that was late. The doctor reassured me that this doesn't mean it'll happen again or that I'll have a difficult time getting pregnant in the future.

At eighteen, that's not something I had ever considered.

Until now...

Now the possibility is there, circling in the back of my mind like a hungry shark.

The entire time we were in the emergency room, Kingsley was at my side, holding my hand, asking questions, making sure I was being properly cared for. We weren't there for long. In the end, nothing could be done. I was given a pelvic exam and an ultrasound to confirm the miscarriage. Then I was discharged and sent on my way. The ride home was made in deafening silence, neither of us attempting to fill it. There didn't seem to be any words that could do justice to the moment.

Kingsley has remained subdued in the twenty-four hours since. His dark eyes have become inscrutable, his thoughts a mystery. All I know is that from the moment he found out about the pregnancy, he wanted me to keep it. He tried to take care of me. I'm the one who was filled with doubts and uncertainty regarding whether I could bring a baby into this world at such a young age and into a future marriage based on nearly eighty years of bad blood between our families.

Once we pulled into the circular drive, Kingsley helped me into the house before carrying me up the sweeping staircase. I wrapped my arms around his neck and clung to him, craving the closeness. After that, he tucked me into bed, told me to rest, and disappeared from sight. I haven't seen him since. Every couple of hours, Mrs. Fieber knocks on the door, setting a tray of food on the nightstand.

7-Up and buttered toast.

As if I have the flu, and it will pass in a day or so. She's remained stoic, but her expression is less severe as if she's been apprised of the circumstances. That only makes the tears fall harder.

Gingerly, as if my entire body is riddled with pain, I unfurl from my huddled position before rolling onto my back and sitting up.

There is a hollowed-out hole that fills my chest cavity and a heaviness that weighs me down. I can't imagine not carrying this pain with me for the rest of my life.

As I glance around, a gasp slides from my lips when I find Kingsley sitting in a wingback chair situated across the room, silently watching me.

When he says nothing, I clear my throat. It feels scratchy and raw as if I haven't used it in years. "What are you doing here?"

He jerks his shoulders as his face remains expressionless. "Watching you sleep."

The deep scrape of his voice sends a shiver careening through me.

When another heavy silence blankets us, I force myself to ask, "For how long?"

It's strange to think of Kingsley sitting in the corner, staring at me while I've been oblivious to his presence. As more light floods into the room, his facial features take shape, and I'm able to see the deep purple bruises that decorate the delicate skin beneath his eyes.

"All night."

The admittance comes as something of a surprise. "You slept in the chair?"

He shakes his head and drags a hand down his face. "No, I didn't sleep."

I swallow down the guilt as my gaze fastens on to the window that stretches from the floor to the ceiling and the trees that dot the background beyond it. "I'm sorry about the baby."

The apology is bitter and tastes like ashes on my tongue. Before I can say anything more, Kingsley hurtles out of the chair and lands on the bed. He drags me into his arms, crushing me against the steely strength of his chest until every molecule of air has been wrung from my body and there is nothing left inside.

No emotion.

No life.

Just an empty carcass in place of the person I once was.

Wetness treks down my cheeks as I bury my face in the hollow of his neck and breathe him in. The familiar scent of his woodsy cologne wraps around me, filling me with solace. One by one, my muscles loosen as I melt into him. We cling like two survivors of a storm that will never stop raging.

"You have nothing to apologize for." His lips brush over the top of my head. "It wasn't your fault."

"How do you know? Maybe it happened because I wasn't sure if I wanted to keep this baby." Grief and guilt stab at my heart. It's like a thousand tiny slashes that leave anguish behind in its place.

His grip tightens as his voice turns gruff. "You heard what the doctor said. The pregnancy was in its early stages. Most women don't realize they're expecting at that point." There's a beat of silence before he adds softly, "We both know it's not possible to will away a pregnancy."

Somewhere in the back of my brain, I acknowledge the truth of what he's saying, but it still feels as if my indecision set this ugly chain of events into motion. As if the choice was ripped away from me because of my confusion.

Kingsley untangles himself from me until he's able to meet my gaze. I'm struck by the realization that the somber boy now staring at me does not resemble the lighthearted one I met at the beach in June. It's like they aren't even the same person. Then again, maybe I'm not the same girl he met either. It's as if we have crammed years of living into a few brief months. And we're both exhausted by it.

When Kingsley clears his throat, I shove those depressing thoughts to the back of my mind. "I had a conversation with my father last night."

The air gets wedged in my throat as I steel myself for the inevitable bomb he's about to drop.

"I convinced him to void the contract between our families."

My brows jerk together. "What does that mean?"

Any emotion that had seeped into his voice disappears. "You'll no longer be forced into marriage, and your family will keep ownership of Hawthorne Industries."

"*Why?*" The idea of Keaton performing a complete one-eighty makes little sense. The revenge he sought against my family has been all-consuming, and now, for some unknown reason, he's willing to drop it and move on?

Kingsley stares out the window before jerking his shoulders. "I think we can all agree that there's been enough pain and loss to last a lifetime. Several of them. I don't think any of us can stomach more."

Sorrow rushes in, flooding every cell in my body. The price that has been extracted is higher than any of us could have ever imagined.

"Dad's lawyers have drawn up new documents for your mother to sign that will split Hawthorne Industries evenly between our families."

"What about everything that was stolen from your ancestors? Your father is willing to let eighty years of lost profits and interest go unpaid?" I may not know Keaton well, but from everything I've witnessed, this seems completely out of character.

Kingsley swipes his tongue across his front teeth as if carefully considering how to answer the question. "I won't lie, it took convincing on my part." I glimpse a flatness in his eyes that I've never seen before. Exhaustion and defeat creep in at the edges. "I can't do this anymore. It needs to be over so we can move on."

His words are like a punch to the gut, and I find myself unable to suck fresh oxygen into my lungs. My heart constricts as if his fist has tightened around it, wringing the very life from me. Maybe he has chosen not to give voice to his thoughts, but I hear them loud and clear.

The loss of our baby is my fault. No matter what I do or where I go, it's a guilt I will always carry around with me.

Before I can offer another apology, he continues, voice devoid of emotion. "Mrs. Fieber packed up your belongings. As soon as you're ready, I'll take you home."

My mouth turns cottony as my heart beats a painful staccato. In the silence of the room, my thickly whispered voice is deafening. "That's it then?"

"Yeah." Emotion flickers across his face before it's snuffed out. It's there and gone before I can figure out what it meant.

I glance away, blinking back the wetness that pricks the back of my eyelids. Grief and sorrow fill me, which doesn't make a damn bit of sense. Why am I upset by this? It's exactly what I wanted. Even though I had feelings for Kingsley, I didn't want to be forced into a relationship or marriage. I fought for the right to choose.

And now I have it. I've been magically released from the shackles of this contract.

From the suffocating hold Keaton had on me.

This is amazing news.

So...why doesn't it feel like it?

3 6

With my suitcase in tow, I stand in front of the entrance to the house that once belonged to my grandmother. As I reach for the handle, it's ripped open, and my mother hovers impatiently on the other side of the threshold with tears shining in her eyes. Her hand snakes out before yanking me into her arms, crushing me against her thin form. If I've lost weight gradually over the past couple of months, her loss has been more dramatic in a matter of weeks.

My arms slip around her slender frame and squeeze her tight as if I'll never let go. As confused as I am about how life has unfolded in the past twenty-four hours, it's a relief to be with her. Ironically, this place didn't feel like home even a couple of short weeks ago, and now...

I can't imagine being anywhere else.

"Oh, Summer!" she whispers, thick emotion overpowering her voice, making it wobbly. "Why didn't you tell me about the pregnancy?"

My body wilts against hers. It's as if all the oxygen has been sucked from the atmosphere, making it impossible to breathe. Humiliation licks at my cheeks. I hate that she knows about this. It feels like a shameful secret that needs to be forced into the shadows.

"I couldn't." I'm embarrassed that I didn't do a better job of protecting myself. That I was stupid to assume condoms would be sufficient.

She pulls away enough to search my eyes. "There's nothing you can't tell me." She pauses before adding, *"Ever!"*

"I'm sorry," I whisper.

"There's nothing to apologize for. I'm the one who's sorry! I was so consumed by my grief that I wasn't there for you when you needed me most. I don't know if I'll ever be able to forgive myself for letting you down."

"It wasn't your fault." I draw in a deep breath, attempting to steady all the emotions that riot painfully in my chest. Once it's all locked down tight, I release it back into the world. "It happened, and I dealt with the situation the best I could."

Her teeth sink into her lower lip as a tear treks down her face. She pulls me back into her arms for another bone-crushing embrace. "It's a relief to have you home where you belong. Thank God this night-mare is finally over."

"Is it?" I ask, disbelief tinging my voice. "Is it over?"

Since we first received word about Grandma Rose's death, our lives have been turned upside down and inside out. Every time I assumed it couldn't get worse, somehow it did. It was like a Greek tragedy being acted out. And now...

Now it's really over?

The curse that had fallen over our family has finally been lifted?

"Early this morning, Keaton delivered copies of the voided contracts along with new ones that divide Hawthorne Industries evenly between our families. I took a cursory glance at the paperwork, and he's agreed not to go after restitution for what his family was cheated out of decades ago. I'm sending the documents to our lawyers to go over, but everything seems to be in order."

Her verification of the information feels like an enormous weight lifted from my shoulders. For the first time in weeks, I can inhale a full breath. No longer am I being crushed to the ground by expectation and forced demands.

It's almost too much to take in and process. "What happens now?"

Even when she takes a step in retreat, her arm stays wrapped around my waist as if she can't bear the thought of releasing me. "I'm not sure yet, but I was thinking we could go back to Chicago." She glances away before blinking the moisture out of her eyes. "With your father gone, there's nothing left to keep us here. I don't want anything to do with that miserable company. Keaton offered to take over the day-to-day operations. And I'm considering it."

Did I hear her correctly?

"Do you trust him?" Because I sure as hell don't.

"What does it matter?" Her eyes grow distant as if swamped by memories. "The whole point of this move was to make a new life together, a better one for our family."

A thick lump settles in the middle of my throat, making it impossible to swallow. None of us could have predicted this outcome. The very fabric of our family has unraveled. Dad is gone, and the three of us have been left behind to pick up the tattered pieces.

As if that's even possible.

"I emailed my old boss, Terry, and asked if I could get my job back. We have a telephone conference set up for tomorrow to discuss the possibilities."

My mind spins as I try to absorb all the changes. When we moved here in August, what I wanted most was to return to my old life.

And now it's over. We can finally leave this hellhole behind.

So why aren't I jumping up and down, screaming at the top of my lungs like I just won the lottery?

Instead, I feel numb inside. There's a giant void where my emotions should be.

Mom strokes her fingers through my hair, drawing my attention back to her. "What do you think about that?"

I hoist my lips into a weak smile, tamping down the confusion that churns through me. "It sounds good."

"Putting everything behind us and starting fresh is exactly what the three of us need."

When I nod, she draws me to her again before pressing a kiss against the side of my face. "I'm glad you're home."

"Me, too."

That, at the very least, is the unvarnished truth.

Everything else?

I'm not so sure about. And somehow, that realization is just as disconcerting.

3 7

The light rap of knuckles against my door has me springing to attention. For a fleeting moment, my heart trips at the possibility that Kingsley stands on the other side of the thick wood. I haven't seen or spoken to him since I was ushered out of Rothchild Mansion two days ago. It never occurred to me that I could miss him so fiercely. It's almost as if a piece of me is missing. The air stalls in my lungs as the door swings open.

"Hey." Austin pokes his head around the corner, hovering over the threshold as if he's a vampire in need of an invitation. When I fail to respond, he asks, "You doing okay?"

Stupid as it is, disappointment rushes in from every corner until I could drown in it. I hoist my smile, unwilling to cause him any more distress. "Yup, I'm fine. No need for concern."

He shrugs, carefully inching his way into the room as if my grief is contagious. "Can't help it. I'm worried about you."

"Don't be," I say, brushing off his discomfort. "I'm fine. Couldn't be better."

That's a lie, but nothing my brother can say or do will change it, so the truth is better left unsaid. I need to work through this on my own.

237

No one can help me with it. As difficult as it is for them, they can only sit by and watch me flounder.

"You haven't left your room in days." Anxiety flickers in his eyes as they search over me, looking for obvious wounds. Luckily—or maybe unluckily—they're all on the inside, away from prying eyes.

The only emotion my brother knows how to emit is anger. He's never been the touchy-feely type. So him being here, checking on me, speaks volumes.

"Did Mom tell you that we might move back?" he asks, sidling closer to the bed before gingerly settling at the end. As he does, the mattress sinks beneath his heavy weight.

"She mentioned it the other day."

"Guess she had the phone conference, and her boss said the position is hers if she wants it." He tilts his head, carefully assessing my reaction. "What do you think about that?"

It's bizarre he even has to ask. Stranger still, there isn't a ready answer tripping off my tongue. The decision to leave Hawthorne should be a no-brainer. Our bags should be packed and our return to Chicago imminent. Yet here I am, conflicted about the decision. The thought of walking away from Kingsley sends a hot rush of pain flooding through my entire being. The sensation of not being able to breathe takes hold as if I'm being choked from the inside out.

"I'm not sure," I force myself to admit. I'm almost afraid of Austin's response. He's been gunning to leave Hawthorne since day one.

It's a surprise when he confesses the same. "Me, neither." His broad shoulders collapse as uncertainty flickers across his expression. "Is it weird that I can't remember what life was like a couple of months ago?"

A mirthless chuckle escapes from my lips. "Not really. In a strange way, it's like we've lived here forever."

"And most of it has sucked ass." One side of his mouth hitches with reluctant humor.

"Yup," I agree, "it has." No other period of my life has been riddled with so many traumatic experiences. I should want to put them behind me and move forward.

His brows furrow as if my answer is just as startling. "You're not sure you want to leave?"

I shake my head as a slight smile lifts my lips. "That's totally messed up, right?"

He plows a hand through his hair. "Probably."

"I thought you would be ecstatic to get the hell out of here."

"I know." He shifts his body toward me, looking as perplexed by the revelation as I am. "Have you ever heard the old saying—you can't go home again?"

I jerk my head into a tight nod as my belly prickles with unease. "Yeah."

"In a weird way, it feels similar." Sadness and bewilderment flicker across his face as he stares at his entwined fingers. "Too much has happened, and it feels like no matter how much we try, nothing will ever be the same again."

As painful as the admittance is, he might be right. Returning to Chicago won't bring our father back. It won't wipe away the grief and sadness that make up my entire being. And it won't erase my feelings for Kingsley.

But is staying in Hawthorne the answer?

It's a complicated question without a solution.

3 8

—————

*L*ater that evening, I lie in bed and stare sightlessly at the ceiling. No matter how hard I try, sleep evades me. I toss and turn, my mind filled with chaos. Questions that don't have obvious answers. Grief that has no immediate outlet.

Unable to stand another moment, I throw off the covers and jump from the bed. I pull on a sweatshirt and leggings before grabbing the afghan that has been tossed over the back of the chair in the corner and make a beeline for the patio door.

I'm going to the only place that has any chance of soothing my soul.

As soon as my bare feet hit the deck, the crisp breeze slaps at my cheeks, instantly cooling them. The scent of fresh pine and dried leaves that carpet the ground drifts on the air. For a moment, I shutter my eyes and inhale deeply, allowing the scent to work its way through my body. Once it's released back into the world, I close the door, ready to escape the stifling confines of the house. From the corner of my eye, a sleek black object catches my attention, and I ground to a halt. My gaze falls on the telescope that had been set up on the Rothchild balcony near my bedroom. Drawn to the expensive piece of equipment, I reach out, trailing my fingers over the smooth metal of the scope. My chest tightens as thick emotion clogs it. At every turn, Kingsley throws me off-kilter. He's an enigma I can't wrap my brain around.

Why would he do this?

Unwilling to read too much into the gesture, my hand drops to my side as I back away and rush down the staircase. Does he realize that his generosity only sends me spiraling into further mental chaos?

Once at the concrete patio, I skirt around the edge of the pool until my toes sink into the plush carpet of grass. Halfway across the lawn, a noise breaks the stillness of the night, and I freeze like a deer in the harsh glare of headlights.

After about ten seconds, another whapping sound breaks the silence. Unlike the first time I heard the noise, I recognize it immediately. Kingsley is in his yard, throwing a ball at the bounce back with his lacrosse stick.

My heartbeat picks up its tempo before crashing against my chest. It's agonizing to realize he's only a dozen yards away on the other side of the thick foliage that separates our property. As close as he feels, he's light-years away. Even if I wanted to cross the gaping chasm that separates us, I have no idea how to go about it.

Too much damage has been inflicted on both sides.

At this point, it feels irreparable.

Even as those thoughts crash around inside my head, I take a tentative step in his direction. A need so strong bubbles up, propelling me forward. It's as if there is a delicate thread connecting us to one another. Nothing has severed it.

Deep down, I don't think anything ever will.

My feet shuffle forward cautiously as my heart pounds faster, harsher until it fills my ears. The sound of the ball hitting the trampoline-like woven material becomes more insistent.

Is he able to sense my presence?

Does he realize I'm on the other side of the bushes? That I want to find a way to blot out the past and start anew?

But how could we move forward?

My father is dead.

I've lost our baby.

And eighty years of bad blood sits between us.

The fresh wave of grief that crashes over me is so powerful that my knees nearly buckle with the force of it. His name swells in my throat before I slap a hand over my mouth to keep the sound buried deep inside. With the afghan clutched to my chest, I force myself to retreat. The sound of the rubber ricocheting off the bounce back intensifies until it reaches a frenzy.

I stumble back a step.

Then another.

And a third before forcing myself to swing away. Whatever fragile possibility had been swirling through the air vanishes as I rush to the little parcel of land I've claimed for myself in the far corner of the yard. My fingers tremble as they arrange the blanket on the lawn with painstaking precision. My heart thumps a painful rhythm as I block out the boy next door.

It's easier said than done.

Once I've stretched out and found a comfortable position, only then do I realize the repetitive sound of the ball has disappeared. Other than the wind rustling through the treetops, the night has grown eerily silent.

I focus my attention on the sky stretched out overhead. There must be a million stars crowded against the velvety blackness. Even though we've been here for two months, the brilliance and clarity never cease to steal my breath away. Fresh amazement spirals through me.

When my mind is full of angst, a routine has always helped settle it. In need of that now more than ever, I begin the hunt for familiar constellations. Automatically, my gaze fastens on the North Star or, as it's otherwise known, Polaris. This is the point at which the entire northern sky turns. The axis of the Earth is nearly pointed at it, so it remains fixed in place while other stars circle it.

After that, I move on to the Big Dipper. The big ladle in the sky is one of the first arrangements I could identify. Next, there's Pegasus, a white-winged horse flying through the galaxy. I shift my gaze, knowing I'll find both Andromeda and Pisces. One by one, my muscles relax, losing their rigidity as I sink further into the earth.

If we end up moving, stargazing in the backyard is what I'll miss most. In a dark night sky, it's possible to see up to forty-five hundred stars. With the light pollution in Chicago, only thirty-five are visible to the naked eye.

And just like that, my mind returns to the dilemma that drove me outdoors.

Deep down, I realize there's nothing here for us.

Or, more accurately, *me*.

At the very least, leaving this town behind in our rearview mirror will be cathartic. The closing of one chapter and the beginning of another. Hawthorne has been filled with untold amounts of pain. A forced engagement, Dad's sudden death, and an unexpected pregnancy. In Chicago, I can begin healing and, in time, forget about everything that happened here.

Even though nothing will ever dull the pain of Dad's demise, there will be a certain amount of comfort to be found in returning to a place where our family made so many good memories. Where life seemed almost idyllic compared to this.

As those thoughts coalesce, forcing me toward a decision, the sound of Kingsley's ball ricocheting off the bounce back punctures the stillness, destroying the sliver of peace I had found. No matter how much I want to drive him to the outer recesses of my mind and heart, it's not possible.

He will always be there, pushing at the edges, demanding entrance.

39

My gaze slants toward my brother as we drive to school in silence. It feels like we've come full circle in the two and a half months we've been in Hawthorne. My life is once again my own, and we are pariahs at the exclusive prep school.

Since my return home, Austin has grown solemn. I would be more concerned with the change in his behavior if so much hadn't taken place in such a brief period. My gut tells me this has everything to do with the decision we have yet to make. Neither of us has broached the subject since the other night. By unspoken agreement, we're avoiding it for the time being.

Whether he meant it to, his words about not being able to go home again have been echoing through my head. What if we uproot our lives for the second time in a matter of months and nothing in Chicago is the same?

It's a scary prospect.

My brother hits the blinker, signaling our turn onto school property. The elaborate stone and wrought-iron gate looms before us as we roll forward before passing through it. Not so long ago, driving onto the picturesque campus would have unleashed a horde of nerves, making me sick to my stomach. All of these snotty kids with their

244

fancy cars, entitlement issues, and wealth scared the hell out of me. For whatever reason, that's no longer the case.

My twin parks the car near the front of the building. There is a sea of navy blazers in the parking lot as students stand around in small clusters, laughing and talking. A few watch us from the safety of their groups. We might be Hawthornes, our great-great-grandfather founding this godforsaken town, but that doesn't matter. We didn't grow up here and, therefore, will be considered newcomers until we die. This is the kind of place that takes generations to be absorbed into the fabric of society.

When we moved here, the plan had been to keep my head down and draw the least amount of attention to myself. All I wanted was to get through my last year of high school before spring-boarding to college.

And now?

I no longer care if I make waves or if these people have a problem with me. The seismic shift in my thought process has set me free, and it's liberating. These kids don't matter. None of this bullshit does.

"You ready to do this?" Austin mutters, drawing my attention back to the present.

"Yup." More than ready.

As far as I'm concerned, I own this damn school.

It's *my* name on the building and *my* ancestor who founded it. If these people don't like it or want to resent me for every past transgression my family made, they can kiss my ass. These past months have done their best to break me, but somehow, I've managed to survive. I'm stronger than I realized, and there's something to be said for that.

I straighten to my full height and sling one strap of the backpack over my shoulder. From the corner of my eye, I catch a glimpse of Sloane, along with her wannabes. I've gone out of my way to avoid a confrontation with her, but that doesn't seem to be enough.

Even though I don't have any concrete proof, instinct tells me that she's the one who knocked me to the floor and kicked me. I'll always wonder if the fall had something to do with losing the baby or if it was nothing more than a coincidence. Her lips curve into a nasty smirk as if she's privy to the thoughts running rampant through my head.

"That girl is one hell of a bitch," Austin bites out.

"Yup, she is." Where Sloane is concerned, I'm tired of taking the high road and allowing her to push me around. Anger bubbles up, threatening to erupt.

I don't take more than a few steps when her gaze narrows, and she stalks toward us.

Me.

I'm the one she's gunning for. I can see it in her eyes. We're like two high-speed vehicles destined for a head-on collision. Her friends follow suit, falling in line behind her like some kind of prep school mafia outfitted in matching tartan skirts and blazers. Do they realize how ridiculous they look?

I wait for my heart rate to speed up and my palms to perspire with an explosion of pent-up nerves, but it never materializes. I'm calm, cool, and strangely collected. Sloane Carmichael no longer holds power over me.

"What's wrong, Hawthorne?" Her smug expression morphs into one of malicious delight as she steps closer, invading my personal space. "Has Kingsley finally come to his senses and dumped your pathetic ass? It's about damn time."

Austin crowds behind me. He's more than ready to leap to my defense should I need him. We've always been protective of each other. He's not about to let Sloane get away with disparaging me. He would never get physical with a female, but he sure as hell would verbally cut her to pieces with his tongue.

My mouth snaps open, ready to set her straight. It's been a long time coming. Instead, a deep voice cuts in, stealing my thunder.

"Not that it's any of your business, but Summer is the one who dumped me."

What?

My head jerks as my wide gaze lands on Kingsley, who now stands beside me. He's so close that if I reached out, I could wrap my arms around him. But the physical proximity is deceiving. We both know there's no way to breach the yawning distance that separates us. As tempting as it is to reach out, I tighten my fingers into a fist, so I don't do exactly that.

Sloane's arrogant expression falters briefly before she snorts out her skepticism. "Please, as if she's good enough for you. That girl is a Hawthorne! She's not fit to lick the mud from the bottom of my shoes." Her gaze darts around the growing crowd before she raises her voice. "Everyone here hates the Hawthornes, and we always will!"

"No, not everyone." The words might be quietly spoken, but they ring out clearly for all to hear. "And you're wrong about her not being good enough. When it comes down to it, Summer Hawthorne is way too good for me, and you know what else?" His throat constricts. "She's too fucking good for *you!*" His gaze narrows before coasting over the sea of curious onlookers who have gathered around us. *"Or any of you."*

Kingsley falls silent. His hands tighten and bunch at his sides as he scans the packed parking lot, waiting for someone to step out of line. A muffled cough or two is the only sound that can be heard. It's almost as if everyone is holding their collective breaths.

Thick emotion swells in my chest until I have to blink it out of my eyes.

Even though his voice remains calm, there's a steely strength buried beneath it. "If anyone touches one damn hair on Summer Hawthorne's head or even looks at her the wrong way, they'll fucking answer to me."

His gaze crawls over the thick crush of students before coming to rest on Sloane. Her face drains of all color beneath the heavy weight of his stare. Her friends, who had been quick to flank her, shrink away, visibly distancing themselves.

When he finally skewers me with his somber gaze, it's as if the world falls away, and it's just the two of us. Emotion rushes through me, threatening to swallow me whole. Before I can gather my thoughts or even thank him for coming to my defense, he takes off, striding toward the stone building without so much as a goodbye. I can only stare after him in stunned silence, my gaze trained on his broad back.

Now that the show is over, the thick tension permeating the air dissipates, and the crowd scatters like rats from a sinking ship. Some escape to the safety of the school while others congregate in tiny clusters with their heads bent together. A wave of whispers ripples around us. People stare at me before glancing at Sloane, who stands rooted in place, looking shellshocked by Kingsley's public rebuke.

It's almost enough to make me feel sorry for her.

Almost, but not quite.

"It pains me to say this, but maybe he's not such a dickhead after all," Austin grumbles.

A gurgle of laughter escapes from my lips. Leave it to Austin to sum up the moment succinctly.

"Holy shit, did that seriously happen?" Everly pipes up from beside me.

"Sure did," my brother responds.

"Damn." Almost speculatively, she stares toward the school. "I just fell a little bit in love."

My gaze tracks Kingsley's movements before he disappears inside the stone building.

Yeah, me too.

4 O

My teeth sink into my lower lip as I stare at the phone lying in the middle of my bed like it's a venomous snake seconds away from striking.

Should I do this?

Is it really a good idea?

Or am I opening myself up to a world of hurt?

Ten minutes later, I'm still trying to figure out the answer. Almost hesitantly, I reach for the phone and stare at the blank screen. Even the thought of composing a text makes me nauseous.

What would I say?

How can I convey what's been circling through my head for days?

I exhale a shaky breath before typing out a sentence. Then I read it over a million times before deleting it and taking a stab at a second attempt.

Ugh.

Why does this feel like a matter of life or death?

With a furrowed brow, I glare at the text. It seems so inadequate. A quick succession of finger taps makes it disappear. Then I retype a simple sentence, read through it at least a dozen times before losing my patience and hitting the send button. As soon as the message is fired off, a groan slides from my lips as a bubble of anxiety wells in my chest. If it were possible to snatch it from the air, I would do it in a heartbeat.

My mind grows fuzzy as I hyperventilate before giving myself a quick mental slap.

For fuck's sake, girl, pull it together! For better or worse, it's over with. There's no going back.

As terrified as I am, I'll always regret it if I don't see this through to the bitter end.

Decision made, I straighten my shoulders and grab the afghan from the armchair before heading to the tiny balcony. Anxiety churns in my gut as I rush down the steps and cross the concrete patio that skirts the pool until my bare feet can sink into the cool blades of grass.

I stop and prick my ears, attempting to pick up the slightest noise. Crickets chirp, a few birds call from where they are nesting in surrounding trees, and the engine from a car grows faint before eventually disappearing. My teeth sink into my lower lip before sucking the fullness into my mouth as doubt flourishes.

Why did I think this was a good idea?

Maybe I should save myself the humiliation and return to the house. There's no reason for me to sit out here and wait for a guy who won't show up. I hug the blanket to my chest, knowing deep down I can't escape the inevitable. I have to make one last-ditch effort before throwing in the towel.

It's not a conscious decision to stumble forward. All I know is that each step brings me closer to the little corner at the back of the yard that borders the golf course. Trembles wrack my body as I arrange the blanket on the ground before stretching out and settling in for the duration. It feels like I'm playing a game of Russian roulette with my heart, and that's the riskiest decision I've ever made.

With every agonizing second that ticks by, the nausea in the pit of my belly grows until I want to curl up into a tight ball and rail at myself for being foolish enough to think this would end well.

Breathe.

I focus on the sky before rattling off the names of familiar constellations, but it's not enough to distract me. After five torturous minutes slide by, any hope that we could put the past behind us and start fresh dies a slow, agonizing death. What has become glaringly obvious is that I read too much into Kingsley's gestures. The telescope. Him sticking up for me with Sloane. They didn't mean as much as I suspected. The finality of this moment has tears pricking the back of my eyes as an ache rushes in to fill the gaping hole in my chest.

Emotion churns beneath my skin, attempting to claw its way out. I release a measured breath and refocus on the pinpricks of light painted across the velvety darkness. I take in the sheer beauty and the amazement I feel each time I stare at the solar system. How can you not marvel at the impossibility of it all? Usually, that's enough to put my problems into perspective, but tonight, it does nothing to ease the sorrow that fills me.

"Hey."

Startled by the deep voice, I shift my gaze until it lands on Kingsley. His lower half is encased in black sweatpants, the top in a gray hoodie. The air gets sucked from my lungs as I find him staring down at me with an inscrutable expression. My heart flutters in response to his proximity. It's become such a familiar sensation, one I've experienced dozens of times since spotting him on the beach. And nothing that has happened between us has changed that.

When I remain silent, completely tongue-tied by his presence, he asks, "Is there room down there for me?"

I blink to awareness before scooting over. As I do, he drops beside me before stretching out. I'm ridiculously cognizant of our points of contact. Shoulders. Elbows. Hips. Through the thick cotton hoodie, my skin buzzes with awareness.

Over the past couple of hours, I've manufactured a thousand little speeches in my head. Everything I wanted him to know. And now that he's here...

My brain goes silent.

Not only do the crickets chirp around us, but they also chirp inside my head.

Awkwardness descends as I clear my throat. It feels dry and scratchy as I lift my arm and point at the sky.

If all else fails, talk about astronomy.

"Do you see the bright star directly overhead?"

He follows the line of my hand. "Yup."

"That's Deneb." I move my finger up and then to the right. "Now look above it and over a smidge. That's Vega." I give him a moment to locate the pinprick of light. "Straight down from there, you'll see another one. That's Altair."

He shifts his head, and it gently bumps mine. "Hmm." His brows slide together as he continues to stare. "It looks like a triangle."

"That's exactly what it is," I admit with a slight smile as some of my nervousness melts away. "Those three points are known as the Summer Triangle. It's an asterism." It's so much easier to gaze at the sky and point out stars than to reveal my feelings and wait for him to accept or reject them.

"An asterism?" he repeats.

"Yup. It's not a constellation but a noticeable pattern of stars in the sky."

"Huh," he says with a nod, "that's pretty cool."

"It really is." Since I can't bring myself to open up just yet, I instruct, "Now go back and find the first star I pointed out."

"Deneb?"

"That's the one," I say in surprise.

Kingsley lifts his hand and gently places it over mine so that our fingers touch. He squints and moves them until he's able to aim at the brightest light. The contact has electricity zipping through my fingertips and shooting down my arm.

His head swivels until his gaze can pierce mine. "Now what?"

Huh?

Air leaks from my lungs as I mentally jostle myself back to awareness.

Right...

I move our hands a fraction so he's able to find the approximate location. "Straight down from Deneb is a line of three stars. Do you see them?"

"Yup." He moves our hands as if tracing the pinpricks of light.

"Okay. Now go back to the second star, and you'll notice that there are two flanking it on each side, giving it the appearance of a cross." I pause as he squints. "Do you see what I'm talking about?"

"Mm-hmm." As he tilts his head to get a better look, I catch a whiff of his cologne, and my insides contract in response.

"That's known as the Northern Cross. It's the backbone of the Milky Way."

When he remains silent, I turn toward him. With his attention focused elsewhere, I'm able to look my fill. Kingsley is probably the most handsome boy I've ever seen, but staring at him now makes my heart spasm. From the thick slashes of his eyebrows to the slant of high cheekbones and a perfect cupid's bow of a mouth, he's absolute perfection. A furious rush of emotion fills me.

Sadness.

Regret.

Longing.

We were doomed for failure from the very beginning. Maybe we really are like Romeo and Juliet, just like Everly claimed.

Minus the suicides.

"There are a lot of little stars clustered around there," he murmurs.

I clear my throat along with those distracting thoughts and refocus on the canvas of the night sky. "Yup, it looks like a haze or a river of stars running through the Northern Cross. It's pretty, isn't it?"

"Kind of magical. I can see why you like astronomy so much." Kingsley lowers our hands until they can rest between our bodies, but he doesn't untangle our fingers. They remain connected.

We remain connected.

I draw my lower lip between my teeth, realizing I need to force out my feelings before the moment can pass us by. For all I know, it's already too late. A fresh burst of fear blooms in my belly. If I don't take the risk, I'll never know what could have been. No matter how daunting it is, I can't walk away from Kingsley until I've exhausted every avenue. If he doesn't return the sentiment, then yeah...it'll suck, but I would rather lay it all on the line than walk away with my pride intact.

It's those thoughts that spur me into action and have me rolling on top of his prone body. My knees slide around his waist until I'm able to sit astride him. Kingsley's eyes go wide as I shackle each wrist with my fingers before dragging his arms overhead and pinning them to the ground.

When he opens his mouth, I shake my head and lower my face until my lips can sweep over his. I'm afraid of what he will say.

"Just let me get this out," I plead.

His mouth snaps shut. It's a heady sensation to have him at my mercy with my hands locked around his wrists and my body pinning him to the earth. From the time we've been together, it's become obvious that Kingsley enjoys being in control. *Especially sexually*. If he wanted, he could easily change the dynamic and flip me over so that I'm the one at his mercy. Or he could tell me to fuck off and walk away. The hands that bind him are nothing more than symbolic. We both know who holds the real power.

The moment is bittersweet. For all I know, this could be the last time I kiss or touch him. If that turns out to be the case, I'm not sure how I'll move forward. It's possible that I could mourn the loss of him for the rest of my life. It's a disconcerting realization and only makes me hyperaware of how important it is to tell him everything that's in my heart.

Unable to help myself, I nip at his lower lip before tugging the plump flesh into my mouth. I suck on it once. Twice. And then again before releasing it.

"I've missed you, Kingsley."

Other than the groan that escapes from deep in his chest, he remains silent.

The need to kiss him pounds through me, but I can't delay the inevitable any longer.

"Do you remember the morning my mom walked in on us?"

The sexual haze clears from his eyes as he jerks his head into a tight nod.

"Until that point, she hadn't realized we were sleeping together. I asked why it mattered, and that's when she admitted they were looking for ways to break the contract. Even though I hadn't mentioned anything to them since the day I was told about it, neither wanted me to be forced into marriage."

Emotion flickers in his eyes as he draws in a deep breath before releasing it. His chest rises and falls with the gradual movement.

"If I could go back and do it again, I'd tell her that as much as I didn't like the idea of being coerced into some kind of archaic arrangement, I was happy with you. That I wanted *you*. Instead of admitting the truth, I remained silent. Maybe if I had been honest, everything that happened could have been avoided." I shrug as grief fills me, threatening to suck me under. "Maybe then Dad would still be alive." It's a painful acknowledgment to make. "It kills me that I broke your trust. I made you doubt me and my intentions. That's the last thing I wanted to do."

A heavy silence falls over us as a fresh wave of nerves surges through me. I don't know if what I've admitted has made a difference. The stillness of his body leads me to believe that it hasn't. I inhale a shaky breath, ready to slink home and lick my wounds in private. I laid it all on the line, and it wasn't enough.

"Are you finished?"

"No," I whisper urgently. There has to be something else I can say to sway him. A burst of adrenaline shoots through me as I rack my brain. All I know is that it can't end like this.

When I remain silent, he hikes a brow.

Everything inside me deflates like a balloon with a pinprick. "Yeah, I guess." My face heats with embarrassment. This will probably be the portion of the evening where he tells me to fuck off.

And who can blame him?

"Good." With one swift motion that takes me by surprise, he rolls us over and pins me against the afghan. Even though my hands are still clasped around his wrists, they're now pressed to the ground as he props himself up on his elbows. "Is it finally my turn to talk?"

I nod as my teeth sink into my lower lip before mentally steeling myself for the worst.

"You might not realize it, but the day we spent on the boat was the best damn one of my life. It only took a couple of hours to fall for you, Summer. More than anything, I wish our relationship could have been normal. I hate that all this family bullshit had to get in the way of everything and fuck it up."

A tiny bubble of hope fills me as the air gets lodged at the back of my throat.

"But that's exactly what happened, and we can't change it. We can't go back in time and rewrite history. It is what it is."

And just like that, any optimism budding to life inside me plummets back to earth before crashing and bursting into a raging inferno.

"It's no secret that I was pissed off when I overheard what your parents were up to. It made me feel like everything between us had been a game."

Unable to keep quiet, I blurt, "It wasn't—"

He silences me with a kiss. When he finally pulls away, his mouth twitches at the corners. "I know," he murmurs. "Deep down, I realized the contract bothered you and that you didn't want our relationship tied to the company. I had a hard time separating the two. Stupid as it sounds, my pride was bruised. It felt like a rejection."

"I'm sorry," I repeat, unable to say it enough. "It was never my intention to hurt you."

"I realize that, too." This time, when he presses his lips to mine, it's long and slow. Liquid heat pools in my core as my toes curl with need.

I've missed *this* and *him* so much. More than I ever thought possible. Whatever it takes for him to forgive me, I'll do it.

"I don't want us to be over," I murmur.

His lips lift into an arrogant smirk, one that makes my heart flip over painfully in my chest. "Oh, baby girl, we will *never* be over. All I was doing was biding my time and giving you a bit of space."

A relieved smile breaks out across my face as all the nervous energy careening through my body melts away.

Not wanting him to have any lingering doubts, I say, "I choose *you*, Kingsley Rothchild. I choose *you* because I want to, not because I have to or have been forced into it. In the end, that's all I wanted. The freedom to choose."

Gently, his lips stroke over mine. "From the first moment I saw your perky ass in the air on that beach, I chose you."

A gurgle of laughter erupts from me as my mind tumbles back to that moment. "You are so damn romantic," I sigh teasingly.

With a grin, he nips at my mouth. "I'll show you romantic later."

My heart bursts with all the happiness that fills it, and the words slip free. "I love you, Kingsley."

His body stills as he pulls back enough to search my eyes. I don't give a damn if he returns the sentiment. It's important that he knows exactly how I feel.

"I love you, too."

As soon as his lips slant over mine, I open so his tongue can delve inside and tangle with my own, transporting me to a place only he's capable of. After a few minutes, he groans, rolling us over until he's once again on his back and I'm draped over him, head resting against his chest. His arms stay wrapped around me, anchoring me in place.

Anchoring me to him.

And I wouldn't have it any other way.

This is where I belong.

Where I have *always* belonged.

With Kingsley.

EPILOGUE

KINGSLEY

I STAND at the controls and cut the engine before dropping the anchor into the water. We're about thirty minutes from the marina, and not another boat is in sight. It's almost as if we're alone in the middle of nowhere.

Summer is already spreading out her towel on the bunny pad at the front end of the boat. With one smooth movement, she strips off her cover-up and drops it to the side. Her long dark hair has been plaited into two thick braids that slide down the slender line of her back. The microscopic black bikini she's wearing leaves little to the imagination.

If I had my way, she wouldn't be wearing a damn stitch of clothing. Give me twenty minutes and that's exactly how she'll be. Buck naked, writhing beneath me, moaning out my name as I thrust deep inside her body.

That image is enough to have me standing at attention as I grab my towel and head to the front before dropping beside her. A smile spreads across her gorgeous face when I close the distance between us and smack a kiss against her lips.

"I'm so glad we could spend the week here," she sighs.

Here just so happens to be the Rothchild family beach house in Door County, Wisconsin. This place holds special meaning for us. It's where we met five years ago and where she ran to when she thought it was possible to hide from me.

Like that was ever going to happen.

Not fucking likely.

She could go to the ends of the earth, and I would still find her.

"Me, too," I agree, trailing my fingers over the bare flesh of her belly before tracing a path along the elastic band of her bikini bottoms.

It's been a big year for us. A couple of weeks ago, we graduated from Northwestern University. Summer is the proud owner of a bachelor's degree in astronomy, and I have one in business. We applied for graduate programs at the same school. Two months ago, we found out that we were accepted, and we'll start back in the fall. The plan is to continue living in Chicago for the foreseeable future. During sophomore year, Summer secured a volunteer position at the Adler Planetarium and recently parlayed it into becoming a full-time staff member.

That's my girl, always going after what she wants.

I've been working at a small consulting firm downtown to gain experience. And we have a kick-ass apartment with amazing views of the lake that's within walking distance. So yeah, I won't lie, life is pretty damn sweet right now.

And it will only get better.

At some point, I'll be expected to return to the small town I grew up in and take over Hawthorne Industries. We've talked about what the future looks like.

Marriage.

A couple of rug rats.

A house.

The whole shebang.

I glance at Summer's left hand and the gigantic rock that sparkles in the bright sunlight. It's enough to straight-up blind you.

Hey, what can I say?

I like to mark my territory.

And Summer is definitely mine.

Just like I'm hers.

And that, my friends, will never change no matter what life throws at us.

The End

HEARTLESS

SKYE

"Yay! The bitches are back together again, and tonight we ride!" Lanie wraps her arms around me and squeezes tight. "It's been too long, girl! *Way too long!*"

A reluctant smile curves my lips. "I know. It's good to be back." The circumstances surrounding my return are less than ideal, but I'm happy to see Lanie again. She's been my best friend since middle school, and I've missed her. FaceTime and texting are nice, but it's not the same as talking in person. She links her arm through mine as we walk across the open field.

I glance at the cute cowboy boots that adorn her feet. When she told me that we were going to a field in the middle of nowhere, I didn't believe her.

That was my first mistake.

Second mistake?

Not going with sturdier footwear.

Instead, I'm wearing a pair of flimsy sandals. They're cute as hell, but that's not going to do me a whole lot of good across this terrain.

Lanie insisted we celebrate my return by dragging me to a bonfire in a farmer's field. Already, the place is crawling with drunk-off-their-asses, barely legal adults. Shouting and raucous laughter fill the balmy night air.

Even though I know it won't do me any good, my gaze coasts anxiously over the ever-swelling crowd. Nerves dance across my spine as I silently pray Hunter will be absent from the revelry. Or, if he is here, we'll somehow be able to avoid one another.

If I know Lanie—and I do—she'll be up my ass to cut loose and have fun. How can I do that when Hunter and I now attend the same college? At any given moment, I could turn a corner and smack right into him.

The thought of that happening makes me nauseous.

As much as I want to play it cool and act like my ex-boyfriend doesn't matter, the words slip from my mouth before I can stop them. "You don't think he'll be here, do you?" I shoot her a look that's rife with concern.

Lanie doesn't bother to ask who I'm referring to. She doesn't have to. She's all too aware of my past. She had a front row seat to our relationship and its demise.

"I don't know." She pauses and pops her shoulders into a careless shrug. "Maybe."

"*What?*" My feet grind to a halt as my mouth dries, turning cottony. I'm barely aware of the blades of straw poking my feet through the leather sandals. "But you said—"

Her expression hardens, transforming into one of impatience. "Even if he *is* here, the chances of you running into him are slim." She waves an arm toward the massive group of students who have gathered to mourn the end of summer by drinking themselves into a stupor. "Look around. Half the university is here. There's no way you're going to see him, Skye, so stop worrying about it and live a little."

My teeth sink into my lower lip before I suck the fullness into my mouth. No matter what Lanie says, I'm going to worry.

When I remain silent, my best friend plants her hands on her hips and glares. Here comes Lanie's version of tough love.

"Would you rather sit home by yourself on a Saturday night

because you're too chickenshit to show your face? Afraid that you *might* run into Hunter Price?"

I'm sorry, is that really a question?

From the annoyed expression that flickers across Lanie's face, I decide to keep those thoughts to myself.

"Skye Elizabeth Sinclair!"

I wince as my full name cracks through the air. It brings an unpleasant image of my mother to mind. This is what I get for living with someone who isn't afraid to call me out on my bullshit. Maybe I should have taken Dad up on the offer to live with him.

I decide to go with something close to the truth. "I was hoping to avoid him for a while," I mutter. "That's all."

And when I say a while, *what I really mean is forever.*

Is that really too much to ask?

Lanie sighs as her expression softens. Marginally. "I know, but you're going to run into him on campus or at a party eventually. It's inevitable. Accept it and move on."

I snort.

Easy for her to say. Lanie doesn't have any ghosts from her past that are ready to jump out and scare her.

I have a carefully constructed plan in place for the year. It involves lying low and flying under the radar, so Hunter doesn't even know I'm here. "Yeah, I guess…"

Unwilling to let me backslide, Lanie loops her arm through mine and pulls me toward the growing group of partiers. "It'll be fine. I promise."

Unfortunately, my bestie isn't in a position to guarantee me anything, and we both know it.

The closer we get to the party, the more my anxiety ratchets up. At least night has fallen. The only light emanates from the bonfire that flickers in the distance and the stars that twinkle across the dark velvety sky.

For the time being, I'll remain vigilant. There's really nothing more I can do.

I inhale a deep breath before carefully blowing it out.

Maybe Lanie's right, and I'm making a big deal out of nothing. It's been three years since we've seen each other, and a lot has happened since then. We've both moved on with our lives. I'm sure he's forgotten all about me. As those thoughts circle through my head, my shoulders loosen from around my ears, and my heart stops thumping a painful beat.

The moment we reach the outer ring of people, Lanie is swept off her booted feet and spun around in a tight circle like a rag doll. Her short floral dress flies around her thighs. Laughter rings throughout the air as her arms slip around her boyfriend's neck.

Jaxon Conway has a typical football player's physique. He's a mountain of a man—tall, broad in the shoulders, and muscular. He looks like he could easily bench press Lanie's VW Bug. I would be intimidated by him, but he's quick to laugh and has warm brown eyes. He's like a teddy bear—big and gruff on the outside but tender and mushy on the inside.

"Missed you, babe," he growls.

"It's only been a couple of hours since we saw each other!"

"Doesn't matter," Jax complains. "I still missed the hell out of you."

"Aww." Lanie's voice softens, becoming dreamy. "I love you so much."

"I love you more," he responds with enough heat to melt the panties off Lanie's body.

Ugh.

Make it stop.

These two are so sickeningly sweet that I get a toothache every time I'm around them. Although, if anyone deserves a good guy, it's Lanie. Like most girls in their early twenties, she's dated her fair share of assholes. Jaxon is almost too good to be true. Kind of like a mythical unicorn that sprang to life. He's an athlete who isn't interested in screwing as many girls as he can get his hands on.

Ever since I rolled into town a few days ago, Jaxon and Lanie have been glued together at the hip. I get the feeling he'll be our unofficial third roommate for the year.

Know what's been getting a lot of use?

My noise-canceling headphones.

Most nights, those two sound like they're auditioning for a porno. Let's hope it calms down soon.

Jaxon and Lanie coo at each other before their mouths fuse, and they start going at it like a pair of cats in heat. I clear my throat and glance everywhere but at them. If we were hanging out at the town-house, this would be my cue to exit stage left. But we're not at home; we're in the middle of a field a few miles from town. There's nowhere for me to go, and no one for me to talk to.

Awkwardness descends as I flick a piece of straw from my shirt.

Maybe I should take this opportunity to grab a beer. There must be a keg around here somewhere. You can't have this many college kids congregating in one spot and not have alcohol. That would be considered sacrilegious, right?

With any luck, by the time I return, Jaxon and Lanie will have stopped mauling each other long enough for us to move on with our evening. It's not like he's being shipped off to war tomorrow and they'll never see each other again.

Sheesh.

My gaze meanders to them in hopes that they've gotten their fill of each other.

Nope. The face sucking has become even more intense. Any moment, clothing is going to spontaneously combust from their bodies.

I don't really want to be around when that happens.

So...a beer it is.

Not that either of them is paying me the least bit of attention, but I point toward the mass of bodies that have multiplied in the fifteen minutes since we've arrived. "I'm going to grab a drink." When my words are met with kissy noises, I say, "Try not to miss me too much while I'm gone."

Lanie waves a hand absently in my direction as they continue to get it on.

"Okay then," I mumble before reluctantly taking off on my own.

The number of people gathered here is a little overwhelming.

Lanie's right; half the university must have shown up. Everyone is talking, laughing, and drinking. In other words, they're having a great time.

Me, not so much.

It takes a good ten minutes to find the keg. Or maybe I should say *kegs* since there are six of them next to the back end of a midnight black pickup truck blasting music from massive speakers. I can barely hear myself think over the thumping bass. Then again, maybe that's for the best. It's a relief to get out of my head, even for a few minutes.

I locate the line for the beer and take my place at the end of it. I'm not much of a drinker, but I need something to smooth out all of the rough edges so I can relax and enjoy myself.

My flesh prickles with awareness, and I run my hands over my arms to banish the disconcerting sensation. I glance around, scouring the crowd for one face in particular but don't see him anywhere. That alone should alleviate my anxiety, but it doesn't.

My parting with Hunter wasn't what one would call amicable. I don't blame him for being hurt and angry. Whether Hunter understands it or not, I did what needed to be done. As painful as it was, I'd do it all over again. I loved Hunter more than life itself.

A part of me still does.

Probably always will.

If everything I've read online is true, then my sacrifices have been well worth it. Hunter will get snapped up in the NFL draft before graduating this spring. Ever since I can remember, that's been his goal. If one person deserves for all his dreams to come true, it's Hunter Price. Unwilling to dwell on my ex, I shove him from my mind and take in the scene before me.

People are gathered together in groups, greeting one another as if they're long-lost friends who haven't seen each other in decades. It's surreal to be surrounded by so many people yet feel so removed from it all. As if I'm more of an observer than a participant. Other than Lanie and Jaxon, I don't know anyone else. I'm sure people from high school attend CU, but I lost touch with most of them after I moved away.

By the time I make it to the front of the line, I'm antsy and ready to head back to my friends. Even if they're still going at it. Which is really saying something. I'd much rather stand around as a third wheel than be an island onto myself. I dig through my front pocket and hand over a couple of bucks in exchange for a blue plastic cup before it's filled to the rim with golden liquid.

The cute guy manning the keg flashes me an easy grin as his eyes drift over my body. When he's finished with his perusal, his gaze once again settles on my face. Kudos to this guy for not gawking at my boobs like he's never seen a pair of D cups before.

"Here you go, beautiful," he says, handing over the cup with a gallant flourish.

This little bit of silliness lightens my mood. "Thanks."

Our fingers brush as I take the Solo cup from him.

"Next time, cut to the front of the line." He gives me a flirty wink. "I got you covered."

I flash him a grateful smile. Maybe tonight won't be so bad after all.

With my drink in hand, I'm ready to make my way back to Jaxon and Lanie. Only now does it occur to me that they could have moved from the spot where I'd left them.

Who's to say I'll even be able to find my way back?

A knot of unease settles at the bottom of my belly. My fingers go to the purse slung across my chest. It's big enough to hold my phone, but that's about it. I could always shoot Lanie a text, but who knows if she'd hear it. And I have no idea how to navigate my way back to our apartment. The unsettled feeling that had taken up residence in my gut turns into full-on nausea.

Only now do I realize that walking away was a bad idea. I should have stuck to Lanie and Jax like glue. But standing around and watching them make out felt pervy.

And not in a good way.

With those thoughts swirling through my brain, I spin around and slam into a wall of impenetrable muscle. The impact knocks me off-balance, and I stumble back a step. Before I can fall, strong hands reach out and grab my shoulders, yanking me forward. My breath catches, and my heart pounds at the narrowly avoided tumble.

I shake my head to clear it as beer sloshes over the rim of my plastic cup and spills onto the ground at my feet. I'm lucky it didn't end up down the front of my top or the shirt of the unsuspecting person I plowed into.

How humiliating would that have been?

Ugh…I don't even want to think about it.

"I'm so—"

My voice falls off as I glance up, my gaze colliding with narrowed blue eyes. Hunter quickly sets me free as if his fingers have been burned. Neither of us breaks eye contact. All of the raucous noise of the bonfire dies away until it's just the two of us standing alone in the middle of a dark field.

This is the moment I've been dreading.

My eyes roam over his face, cataloging the myriad of changes that time has wrought. When I walked away, Hunter had still been a boy, his lean muscles beginning to thicken. Now the transformation has been complete, and he's a full-grown man. Hunter has always had size on his side, but somehow, he's managed to grow both taller and broader. He must be somewhere in the vicinity of six three or four. I have to crane my neck to hold his gaze. The graphic T-shirt he's wearing stretches tautly across the wide expanse of his chest and hugs the chiseled strength of his biceps. It's enough to make my mouth dry and my knees soft.

If I have one weakness, it's for thickly corded arms. All that tightly harnessed power waiting to break free…

A shiver of desire scampers down my spine before I stomp it out.

Unaware of the effect he's having on me, Hunter's deep voice cuts through my thoughts.

"What are you doing here, Skye?"

It's the harshness of his tone that has my gaze snapping back to his as heat floods my cheeks. I can't stop myself from staring. The little bit of cyberstalking I've done over the years has in no way prepared me for coming face-to-face with my ex-boyfriend. He's grown into his dark looks, becoming even more of a heartbreaker than he was in high school.

My tongue darts out to smudge my parched lips as nerves dance along my skin. I search Hunter's eyes, looking for any hint of softening, but there's none to be found. His gaze is as frigid and detached as I imagined it would be. The tiny kernel of hope that our time apart would be enough to heal our past wounds shrivels and dies inside me.

There is no forgiveness in his heart.

But then again, did I really expect there would be?

Maybe. It would have made coexisting on campus for the next year so much easier.

It's obvious from his terse behavior that Hunter would prefer to pretend I never existed in the first place. As much as I would love to give him that, I can't. Unforeseen circumstances have forced me home.

I straighten my shoulders and attempt to keep my voice level. I don't want him to hear the slight tremble that is working its way through my body. "I transferred to Claremont for my senior year."

His shadowed jaw ticks as he clenches his teeth. *"Why?"*

The way he bites out that one word leaves me wincing.

I take a quick step back and lift my chin, not wanting him to see how much power he still holds over me. Time has done nothing to diminish it. "That's none of your business."

Whether Hunter realizes it or not, he still owns a piece of my heart. It's better for both of us if he never suspects the depth of my feelings.

His hands tighten into fists as he closes the little bit of distance that I've managed to put between us. Instead of scrambling back the way every instinct is clamoring for me to do, I hold my ground until we're standing toe-to-toe. My heart pounds a painful staccato against my breast as his harsh breath feathers across my parted lips.

There was a time when I couldn't get close enough to Hunter.

Now I can't get far enough away.

Sorrow floods through every fiber of my body that it has to be this way between us. Next to Lanie, Hunter was my best friend. He was my first everything.

Date.

Kiss.

Love.

Heartbreak.

Everything we once shared has been blown to pieces, and we're nothing more than strangers. Actually, what we are is much worse. His animosity is palpable. It radiates from him in suffocating waves that threaten to choke the life out of me.

"You shouldn't have come back," he growls. "You don't belong here anymore."

That may be true, but there's nothing I can do about it. I'm here. And I'm not going anywhere.

I shift my weight and force myself to say, "Claremont is big enough for the two of us."

"No, it's not. Stay the fuck out of my way, Skye." His eyes flash with barely suppressed hostility. "You won't like the consequences if you don't."

Before I can summon up a retort, he stalks away. Rooted in place, I track his movements until he fades into the crowd. Not once does he turn around and acknowledge my presence. I've been dismissed. Relegated to the black hole that is our past.

Once he disappears from sight, my knees weaken as the pent-up breath rushes from my aching lungs.

I haven't been on campus for a full seventy-two hours, and in Hunter's eyes, I'm public enemy number one.

Want to read more of Skye & Hunter's story? You can do it here -)
Heartless

CAMPUS PLAYER

DEMI

"Morning, Demi!" Gary, one of the stadium custodians, calls out with an easy smile and wave as he saunters toward me. "Up and at 'em bright and early this morning, I see."

My heart jackhammers beneath my ribcage from the twenty-minute run as I flash him a grin. "Always!"

"You have a good one! I'll see you tomorrow!"

Since I've already moved past him, I holler over my shoulder, "Same place, same time!"

Even with *The Killers* pumping through my earbuds, I almost hear the deep chuckle that slides from his lips. Our morning greetings are a ritual three years in the making. I've been running through the wide corridor that leads to the stadium football field since I stepped foot on campus freshman year. This will be something I miss when I graduate in the spring. Five days a week, I'm up at six, logging in a four-mile run before returning home, jumping in the shower, and heading off to class.

At this time of the day, the stadium is still relatively quiet, with only a few people wandering the hallways. There's something both serene and eerie about it. I've been here on game days when there are thirty thousand fans packed shoulder to shoulder, rooting on the

Western Wildcats football team. Three-fourths of the stadium filled with black and orange is an amazing sight to behold. Football is a religion at Western. Unfortunately, the same can't be said for the women's soccer team. We're lucky if there are a couple of hundred spectators in the stands.

I've come to terms with it.

Sort of.

I keep my gaze trained on the light at the end of the tunnel and push myself faster. As soon as I burst out of the darkness, bright sunlight pours down on me, stroking over the bare skin of my arms and shoulders. It's late August, and summer is still in full swing. A whistle cuts through the silence of the stadium, and my gaze slices to the field. Nick Richards has been head coach of the Wildcats for the last decade. He also happens to be my father.

Two days a week, the guys are up at six in the morning for yoga. Dad is a big believer in flexibility. Even though I'm winded, a smirk lifts the corners of my lips. Watching two-hundred-and-eighty-pound linebackers contort their bodies into Downward-Facing Dog, the Warrior II Pose, and the Cobra is enough to bring a chuckle to my lips. Some of the guys actually like it, but most grumble when they think Dad isn't paying attention. Little do they know that he sees and hears everything.

My father catches sight of me and flashes a quick smile along with a wave in my direction. He has a black ball cap pulled low and aviators covering his eyes. There's a clipboard in one hand as he paces behind the instructor.

When I point to the field, he shakes his head. He might make the guys do yoga, but he refuses to participate. Something about old dogs and new tricks. Every once in a while, I'll tell him that he needs to get out there and set a good example for the team. He usually shoots me a glare in return.

Every Wednesday night, Dad and I get together. Our weekly dinners became a thing when I moved out of the house and into the dorms freshman year. He's busy coaching football, and my schedule is packed tight with school and soccer. Getting together once a week is the best way for us to stay connected. It doesn't matter if we're in the middle of our seasons; we always make time for each other. Especially since Mom lives in sunny California. After eighteen years of marriage, she got fed up with being a distant second to the Western University football program. She packed up her bags and walked out. I hate to say it, but Dad didn't notice her absence for a couple of days. Which only proved her point. Now she's remarried, learning to surf, and is a vegan. I visit for a couple of weeks during the summer before soccer training camp starts up at the end of June.

Even though it's only the two of us, our weekly dinners are set for three people.

I tell myself to stare straight ahead and not glance in his direction.

Don't do it!

Don't you dare do it!

Damn.

My gaze reluctantly zeros in on him like a heat-seeking missile. Long blond hair, bright blue eyes, sun-kissed skin, and muscles for miles. And he's tall, somewhere around six foot three.

I'm describing none other than Rowan Michaels.

Otherwise known as the bane of my existence.

My dad discovered the talented quarterback the summer before we entered high school and took him under his wing. Which has been...aggravating. In the seven years since, Rowan has become an irritatingly permanent fixture in my life. He's the brother I never wanted or asked for. He's the gift I wish I could give back. He's the son my father never had but secretly longed for.

On a campus with over thirty thousand students, one would think that avoidance would be easy to accomplish. That hasn't turned out to be the case. Somehow, we ended up in the same major—Exercise Science. I get stuck in at least one class with the guy each semester. This time it's statistics, which is a requirement. Three times a week, I'm forced to see him. And then there are the weekly dinners at Dad's house.

Every Wednesday, Rowan shows up without fail.

It's so annoying.

No, *he's* annoying!

Our gazes collide, and electricity sizzles through my veins before I immediately snuff it out and pretend it never happened.

I am not attracted to Rowan Michaels.

I am not attracted to Rowan Michaels.

I am not attracted to Rowan Michaels.

Maybe if I repeat the mantra enough times, it'll be true. That's the hope I cling to. I've made it through the last seven years trying to convince myself of this. I only have to get through our final year together, and then we'll go our separate ways—me to graduate school or maybe to the Women's National Soccer League, and Rowan to the NFL. He's one of the most talented quarterbacks in the conference. Hell, probably the country. There is little doubt in my mind that he'll be a first-round draft pick come next spring.

Trust me when I say that Rowan Michaels fever is alive and well at Western University. His fanbase is legendary. The guy is a major player.

Both on and off the field.

Girls fall all over themselves to be with him. They fill the stands at football practice, show up at parties he's rumored to be at, and basically stalk him around campus.

It's a little nauseating. Don't these girls have any self-respect when it comes to a hot guy?

I wince at that unchecked thought.

Fine…I'll begrudgingly admit it; he's good-looking.

I shake my head as if that will banish the insidious thoughts currently invading my brain. Enough about Rowan. It's time to focus on the reason I'm at the stadium at this ungodly hour. I rip my gaze from him as I hit the cement staircase. After half a flight, all thoughts of the blond quarterback vanish from my mind. How could they not when my quads, glutes, and calves are on fire, screaming for mercy as I force myself to the nosebleed section. By the time I finish, my legs are Jell-O, and I still have a two-mile run back to the apartment I share with my best friend off-campus.

I give Dad a half-hearted wave before leaving. It's the most I can muster. His lips quirk at the corners as he shakes his head. He thinks I'm crazy. At the moment, I can't argue with his assessment of the situation. Although, it's the extra training I put in that helps me run circles around the other team in the second half of the game.

The jog home feels like it will last forever. By the time I unlock the apartment door, I'm ready to collapse. I beeline for the shower and jump in before it's fully warm. My skin prickles with goose flesh, but it feels so damn good. Twenty minutes later, I'm dressed and ready to take on the day. My hair has been thrown up in a messy bun, and I'm making a protein smoothie that will fuel me for my morning classes.

Just before taking off, I poke my head into Sydney's room. I know exactly how I'll find her, and that's buried beneath a small mountain of blankets. She doesn't disappoint. We met the summer before freshman year in training camp and have been besties ever since. She's the yin to my yang. The peanut butter to my jelly. The Thelma to my Louise. Where I'm more introverted and cautious, she's loud and boisterous. She's been known to leap without necessarily looking at what she's jumping into. Every so often, it gets us into trouble. Sydney and I have lived together since sophomore year. I gave up trying to cajole her ass out of bed for a six o'clock run after the first week of us cohabitating when she nearly took my head off with an alarm clock.

"It's that time again," I sing-song obnoxiously, "rise and shine."

There's a grunt and then some shifting from under the blankets that tells me she's alive.

When I chant her name repeatedly, each time escalating in volume, she growls, "Get the fuck out!"

"Awww," I mock, "that's so sweet. I love you, too."

Sydney snorts before a hand snakes out from beneath the blankets to give me a one-fingered salute. Then she grabs a pillow and tosses it in my general vicinity. It falls about five feet short of its mark.

I stare at the dismal attempt. "If you're trying to cause bodily harm, you'll have to do better than that."

"Piss off."

"All right then." I shrug. "See you after class." With that, I close the door behind me.

My farewell is met with another indecipherable mouthful. If this weren't something we went through on the daily, I'd worry she was in the midst of a stroke. Sydney is definitely not a morning person. She's more of an early afternoon person. Another thing I've learned over the years? The action of waking up to a brand-new day is a gradual process. She's like a bear rousing prematurely from hibernation. It's not a pretty sight. She's lucky I don't take her insults personally.

I grab my backpack from the small table crammed into the breakfast nook area along with a coffee before heading out the door. The apartment I share with Sydney is located three blocks from campus, which is highly sought out real estate. We're fortunate Dad is friends with the guy who manages the building. It's probably one of the only perks of having a father who is a head coach of a college football team.

You'd think there would be more, but you'd be wrong. Honestly, being Nick Richard's daughter is more of a hindrance than anything else. People assume you receive special treatment on campus, from professors, or that you have an in with all the football players.

Or worse...

Much worse.

After a bunch of ugly—not to mention untrue—rumors circulated freshman year, I've done my best to distance myself from the Wildcats football team. They're a great bunch of guys, but I don't need all the ugly gossip and speculation that comes along with being friends with them.

As I reach Corbin Hall, the mathematics building for my stats class, my gaze is drawn to a clump of students standing around outside the three-story, red-brick building. In the center of that crowd is Rowan. I don't have to see him physically to know that he's close. The muscles in my belly contract with awareness. It's like a sixth sense. One I wish would go away. He's the last person I want to be cognizant of.

As I jog up the wide stone stairs to the entrance, my gaze fastens on him. A smirk twists the edges of his lips, and my eyes narrow before I drag them away and yank open the door to the building.

Relief rushes through me as I step inside the air conditioning and disappear from sight.

"Hey, Demi, wait up!"

I turn at the sound of my name before slowing my step. The dark-haired guy jogging to catch up smiles before falling in line with me.

Justin Fischer.

He's a baseball player and teammates with Sydney's boyfriend, Ethan. We've been seeing each other for about a month. It's still casual at this point. With school and soccer, I don't have a ton of time to invest in a relationship. He seems to understand that and isn't pushing to be more serious.

When he leans in for a kiss, I angle my head. At the last moment, he tilts in the opposite direction, and we end up bumping teeth instead of locking lips. With a grunt, I pull away and chuckle. My fingers fly to my mouth to make sure I haven't chipped a tooth.

Maybe I've been reluctant to admit it to myself, but that kiss sums up our relationship perfectly.

Awkward and a step out of sync with each other.

"Sorry," he murmurs with a slight smile. I search his face and wait for any telltale sign of sexual chemistry to ping inside me. Unfortunately, my insides remain completely unfazed, which is disappointing but not altogether unexpected. I had a sneaking suspicion when we first got together that it might turn out this way.

"No problem," I say, hoisting my smile and brushing aside those thoughts.

"I haven't seen you for a couple of days," he remarks as we turn a corner and continue walking.

"It's been busy." Which isn't a lie. School might have recently started, but the academics at Western are rigorous. And being a Division I athlete is more like a job. If you're not ready to put in the work, don't bother showing up. There's no half-assing it around this place.

"When's your next game?" he asks.

"Tomorrow at six." My gaze flickers in his direction. Not that I expect him to come, but...

Fine, so maybe I do. If he wants to be my boyfriend, then he needs to show a little support.

His dark brows draw together. "That sucks. I've got a mandatory study hour I have to attend."

I shrug off the disappointment. It's another nail in the coffin of this relationship as far as I'm concerned. "That's cool. It's not a big deal."

"But I'll see you tonight?"

Oh. Right.

Tonight.

Well, damn. In a moment of weakness, I threw out an invitation to join our Wednesday evening dinner. It's one I now regret. If only there were a gracious way to rescind the offer.

"If you're busy, I totally understand—"

"Are you kidding? No way." With a grin, he shakes his head. "I wouldn't miss it for the world. I'm looking forward to meeting Coach Richards."

Great. So this is more about my father than me? Exactly what every girl wants to hear.

I force a brittle smile. "Awesome. He's excited, too."

That might be something of an overstatement.

Justin nods toward the end of the corridor. "I better get moving. Professor Andrews is a real stickler for punctuality."

"Yup. See you later."

This time, when he leans in, our lips align perfectly. The kiss is nothing more than a fleeting caress. There and gone before I can sink into it.

And I'm left feeling...absolutely nothing.

I bury the disappointment where I can't inspect it too closely before giving him a wave as he takes off. For a moment, I stand rooted in the hallway and watch as he disappears through the crowd. There's nothing to distinguish Justin from the thousands of guys who look exactly like him on campus. He's of average height and build with dark hair and espresso-colored eyes. He's nice enough. Although, if I'm completely honest, he's a little self-absorbed. He talks about baseball all the time. If Ethan hadn't introduced us, he's not someone I would have looked twice at. We don't have a ton in common.

As much as I hate to admit it, this relationship has probably reached its expiration date.

Now it's a matter of pulling the plug.

Ugh. I hate breakups. Although, it's doubtful this will end up destroying him. I'll have to make it through tonight and figure out the rest.

With a sigh of resignation, I head to the classroom and find a seat tucked away in the far corner of the small lecture hall. A lanky guy I recognize from a few of my other classes settles beside me. He flashes a dimpled smile as we empty our backpacks.

The tiny hair at the nape of my neck rises seconds before Rowan enters the room. It's like my body knows when he's within a thirty-foot radius. I glance at him from beneath the thick fringe of my lashes before shifting away. Air becomes wedged in my lungs as I wait for him to take a seat. And it won't be next to me because I'm—

"Hey man, would you mind moving?"

Surrounded on both sides.

Damnit. I'm hoping the cutie next to me will tell Rowan to go take a flying leap.

What? It could happen. Not everyone at this university is enamored of the football-playing god. Although I realize the odds aren't stacked in my favor. Rowan is the most recognized athlete on campus. People fall all over themselves to accommodate him.

It's a little sickening.

Okay, maybe more than a little.

"Sure, no problem, Michaels." The guy next to me hastily packs up his books before vacating the desk. Unable to ignore him any longer, I glare as Rowan slides onto the seat next to me.

"Did you really think you could evade me that easily?" Laughter brims in his deep voice. A voice, I might add, that does funny things to my insides.

"One can always hope, right?"

"Oh, answering a question with a question." He leans closer, eating up some of the much-needed distance between us. "I like it."

I roll my eyes as his lips stretch into a satisfied grin. Irritation bubbles up inside me when sexual tension blooms at the bottom of my belly. Or maybe that tension has settled a little lower.

It's definitely lower.

I'm tempted to swear like a sailor. How is it possible that I feel nothing for the guy I'm actually dating, and yet my pulse skitters out of control for someone I don't even like? It's so freaking ironic. It's been this way since we met, and nothing I do stomps it out. I can try to fool myself into believing it's not there, but that doesn't make it any less true.

It's a relief when Professor Peters takes his place at the podium and clears his throat. Once he's captured everyone's attention, he delves headfirst into the probability of dependent and independent events.

Grateful for the excuse to ignore Rowan for the next fifty minutes, I open my textbook and concentrate on the lesson. Just as the blond boy fades into the background, his bare knee bumps into mine. Electricity ricochets through my entire being. I glance at him to see if he's noticed the strange energy we always seem to generate and find his ocean-colored gaze fastened to mine.

My guess is that he does.

Damnation.

WANT TO READ MORE? You can buy Campus Player here -) https://books2read.com/u/mYAxqV

ABOUT THE AUTHOR

Jennifer Sucevic is a USA Today bestselling author who has published twenty-two New Adult and bully novels. Her work has been translated into German, Dutch, and Italian. Jen has a bachelor's degree in History and a master's degree in Educational Psychology. Both are from the University of Wisconsin-Milwaukee. She started out her career as a high school counselor, which she loved. She lives in the Midwest with her husband, four kids, and a menagerie of animals.

If you would like to receive regular updates regarding new releases, please subscribe to her newsletter here- Jennifer Sucevic Newsletter (subscribepage.com)

Or contact Jen through email, at her website, or on Facebook.
sucevicjennifer@gmail.com

Want to join her reader group? Do it here -)
J Sucevic's Book Boyfriends | Facebook

Social media links-
www.jennifersucevic.com
https://www.instagram.com/jennifersucevicauthor
https://www.facebook.com/jennifer.sucevic
Amazon.com: Jennifer Sucevic: Books, Biography, Blog, Audiobooks, Kindle
Jennifer Sucevic Books - BookBub